Praise for the Greek to Me Mysteries

"[A] hilarious main character . . . an excellent new mystery."
—Fresh Fiction

"I am hooked . . . If you are looking for a cozy mystery that will knock your socks off, then please do yourself a favor and do not skip this one."   —Girl Lost in a Book

"It was impossible to put this book down . . . I stayed up late to finish the whole thing . . . The characters are richly written and continue to grow . . . A wonderful cozy mystery."   —Escape with Dollycas into a Good Book

"Many books get your attention in the first chapter, but this book literally grabs you with the very first sentence . . . This is a great debut of a very promising series. The author is a talented writer . . . able to paint a picture and set the mood with her wonderful descriptions."   —Smitten by Books

"If you enjoy a book that keeps you entertained throughout the entire story, a book with plenty of surprises, some twists, and a shocking ending . . . then you need to read this book. You will be a fan for life!!!"
—Cozy Mystery Book Reviews

D0179445

A Killer Kebab

Susannah Hardy

BERKLEY PRIME CRIME
New York

BERKLEY PRIME CRIME
Published by Berkley
An imprint of Penguin Random House LLC
375 Hudson Street, New York, New York 10014

ISBN: 9780425271674

First edition / November 2016

Printed in the United States of America
1 3 5 7 9 10 8 6 4 2

Cover illustration by Bill Bruning
Cover design by Danielle Mazzella di Bosco
Book design by Kelly Lipovich

To Patricia Riccio Haertel,
who taught us all how to live

ACKNOWLEDGMENTS

I might be the one putting words on the page, but no book gets written or launched into the world without a heapin' helpin' of support, both personal and professional, from others. Huge thanks to:

My writing posse, the MTBs also known as the Plot Goddesses: Jamie Beck, Jamie Schmidt, Jamie Pope, Katy Lee, Regina Kyle, Linda Avellar, Tracy Costa, Jenna Lynge, Megan Ryder, and Gail Chianese. Special thanks to Jamie Beck for allowing us to use her beautiful vacation home for our nefarious purposes. Casey Wyatt, we'll get you there eventually.

The Wicked Cozy Authors, who know quite a little something about writing mysteries and a whole lot about friendship: Edith Maxwell, Julie Hennrikus, Sherry Harris, Barbara Ross, Liz Mugavero, Sheila Connolly, Jessica Estevao, and Kimberly Gray.

Acknowledgments

Mike and Will, and the rest of my family, who are my always-and-forever loves.

And, as always, the world's best agent, John Talbot, and the world's best editor, Michelle Vega, her able assistant Bethany Blair, and the rest of the amazing team at Berkley Prime Crime. Not sure how I got so lucky, but I feel like I won the literary lottery.

From the deepest desires often come the deadliest hate.

—SOCRATES, ANCIENT GREEK PHILOSOPHER, 469 B.C.–399 B.C.

◆ ONE ◆

Ever wonder if you're a magnet for disaster? In my case, I was beginning to wonder if I was a magnet for death.

I held up a paint swatch to the wall of the ladies' room of the Bonaparte House, the restaurant I manage for my mother-in-law. I felt a frown wrinkle my forehead as I studied the card, which was lit up by the late November sun shining through the wavy glass of the antique window. Nope. Definitely not *Oh-Oh Orchid*. I fanned through the stack to try another.

In the twenty-plus years I'd called Bonaparte Bay, New York, home, there hadn't been a single murder within a radius of ten or fifteen miles. But in the last few months there'd been three. Three people who would never marvel at another sunrise over the sparkling blue waters of the St. Lawrence River. Three people who would never again enjoy a meal of pan fish caught fresh that morning. Three people who would never again hold a loved one in their arms.

And all three of those deaths were connected to me.

Don't get me wrong. I didn't kill anybody. But for a woman who had always thought she had no extended family, it had come as something of a shock to find that I did, in fact, have cousins. But before I'd had a chance to explore those relationships, two of my cousins were murdered, along with an acquaintance who had gotten too close to some surprising truths. My mother and another cousin, who just happened to be my best friend, were still very much alive, though. Thank goodness the threat was over. There were some kinks to be worked out, but I was cautiously optimistic that we who were left could learn how to be a family.

The kitchen door banged shut with a sharp report, causing me to start. I took one last look at *Buttered Up*. That one was definitely pretty, a pale yellow that looked lovely with the original early nineteenth-century woodwork. I put the card on top of the deck and set the samples down on the hideous flamingo pink and black tile counter. If the carpenters would let me, I'd enjoy taking a sledgehammer to that surface myself.

And speaking of the carpenters, that's who was probably in my restaurant kitchen right now.

I hustled through one of the dining rooms, slowing only a little to nod to the old oil painting of a haughty Napoleon that hung over the (nonworking) fireplace mantel. This house had been built two hundred years ago as a place for him to hide out and plot his return to power. Unfortunately for the Little Corporal, his supporters were never able to spring him from Elba or St. Helena. Fortunately for me, this beautiful old stone house survived into the twenty-first century. I lived upstairs, and worked downstairs, and I wouldn't have it any other way.

But it isn't really yours, a voice inside my head said.

Shut up, I told it, not for the first time, as I stepped inside the big commercial kitchen that had been added onto the back of the house half a century ago.

"Hey, Georgie," Steve Murdoch said, not looking up. His soft chambray shirt was embroidered with "Murdoch Kustom Kontracting" over one of the pockets. He held a tablet computer in one hand and tapped something into it with a stylus in the other. I was impressed. I would have expected a simple clipboard and plastic pen from a guy who worked with his hands. Was that tech-ist of me?

"Hi, Steve." I glanced at the clock on the wall. "How've you been? You're right on time."

He looked up at me, his face, still tanned though summer was long over, clouding over then clearing as if with conscious effort. "Eh, I'm all right. One day at a time. And speaking of time, I don't like to waste mine or anybody else's." He nodded toward the small counter and stools over by the walk-in fridge. "Shall we sit down and talk about the project?"

"Coffee and a snack?" I offered. I considered asking what was wrong, but it was none of my business. Advice I should pay attention to as over the last few months I seemed to have developed a hitherto unknown penchant for nosiness. "I've got spice cake with cream cheese frosting." Normally I didn't keep desserts in the house after the restaurant closed for the season. If I wanted something decadent I'd go to the Express-o Bean, the coffee shop a block away. But we'd celebrated my cook's birthday yesterday and I'd saved a couple of pieces.

"Sounds great," he said, and parked his well-fitting Levi's on one of the stools.

A few minutes later, I joined Steve at the counter, setting a plate of cake, a fork, and a carafe of coffee in front of him. I poured him a cup and offered the cream and sugar, which he accepted.

I poured a glug of cream into my own cup and gave a stir. "So," I said. "I want to thank you for your help with getting Sophie on board with this renovation." My mother-in-law—despite having pots and pots of money, and being about to come into a whole lot more once a valuable antique I'd found upstairs was sold next spring—was not a spender. Nor had she seen any reason to update the restrooms, which she'd decorated herself during the Eisenhower years.

Steve forked a hunk of cake into his mouth. He wiped the corner of his mouth with the cloth napkin I'd given him and grinned. "Yeah, sorry about that 'leak' I found. These old pipes can go anytime, you know."

I grinned back. "Wouldn't it be awful if it happened when we had a full dining room? We could be shut down for a week." I only felt a teeny, tiny bit guilty about bending the truth with Sophie. The pipes really were ancient. They really could go anytime. And she really did have more money than she could ever possibly spend. So why not spruce this place up?

"You know I've been itching to work on your rest-rooms," Steve said as he scraped some frosting up off the thick white china plate. "Every time I come in for lunch they taunt me." Steve was a creature of habit, never to my knowledge ever ordering anything other than a Coke and two gyros, extra tomatoes, light on the sauce.

I laughed. "The men's room is even uglier than the women's." I set my coffee cup down in its matching saucer, where the meeting of the two solid white china surfaces gave a pleasant little clink. "So did you bring me some samples to look at?"

"Sure did." He scooted his empty plate across the counter, and replaced it with a number of tile samples that he set down on the stainless steel. I moved them around, feeling the cool, smooth surface of each beneath my fingertips. I settled on a creamy white square with a pearly luster. I closed my eyes and pictured it with the paint I'd chosen earlier. Lovely. Elegant but not fussy. And Sophie would love it, since yellow was her favorite color. It might just soften the blow when she got Steve's bill. My mind was made up quickly. "This is the one. We'll use it for both restrooms, and paint the men's room walls that café au lait color you suggested."

Steve nodded. "Good choice. This tile looks great, wears well, and it's not too expensive." He pulled the stylus out of his shirt pocket. He tapped the rubber tip on the tablet, then turned the screen toward me. "Here's a drawing of what the finished reno will look like."

A 3-D graphic drawing in full color appeared. I gave a low whistle. "Beautiful. Maybe too beautiful. What if my customers come for the bathrooms instead of the food? No public restrooms, you know."

Steve chuckled. "I don't think there's any danger of that. But I'm happy you like the rendering. My son, Ewan, is home on vacation from Rensselaer Polytechnic and he's insisting on bringing Murdoch Kontracting up to date with technology." He drained his coffee cup. "He'll have his master's degree next spring." Steve's pride was evident.

"It must be great to have him home for a while. My Callista will be home from Greece in a few days and I can't wait." My heart gave a little tug. *Just a few more days, Georgie, and you can give your girl a hug.*

Steve tapped the screen again and passed it back to me. "This is the estimate."

The figure was large, but reasonable. Gutting and rebuilding were not cheap. And Steve was doing me a favor by squeezing me in before the holidays. And, well, it wasn't my money. "Where do I sign?"

He handed me the stylus and indicated the spot. My signature looked wobbly on the screen but I supposed it would do. "We'll e-mail you a copy of the signed contract. Since it's supposed to rain, I thought I'd send the demo crew over this afternoon to get started. I can't have them working outdoors today."

"So soon? Not that I'm complaining, mind you. That sounds perfect. Can I have the accountant drop off the deposit check? Not sure if it'll be today or tomorrow."

"Sure, and much appreciated. As is the coffee and cake." Steve rose, shoving his tablet into a briefcase and stuffing his rather beefy arms into the sleeves of his expensive down jacket. "See you this afternoon."

I walked him to the back door. "See you then."

As Steve's truck left the parking lot, a ball of orange fur rose up and came toward me. "Hello, Hortense," I said. "You want some lunch?" The lean marmalade cat seemed to have taken up residence somewhere in the neighborhood because she came by daily now. That might have been because I fed her, outside the restaurant kitchen, of course. She was friendly enough, occasionally rubbing up against my legs and giving a vigorous purr. One of these days I was going to borrow a pet carrier and see if I could get her to the vet for a checkup and some shots, and to find out if she'd been spayed. Or neutered. Honestly, I wasn't at all sure whether she was a Hortense or a Horace.

I went back inside and brought out a can of cat food, which I opened and dumped onto a paper plate and set by the picnic table. A shiver ran through me. It had gotten very cold all of a sudden, and it was still a few weeks before Thanksgiving. Soon the North Country of New York State would be in a deep freeze until next April. Poor Hortense. She couldn't live in the house this winter—pets and restaurant kitchens were mutually exclusive, even if the restaurant was technically closed. Maybe while the carpenters were here, they could rig up a shelter of some kind out back. Or maybe I could find her a real home somewhere, assuming she didn't already have one.

And speaking of the carpenters, I wondered if I should make them some lunch. No, they weren't coming until this afternoon, which meant they would have already eaten. And since they were getting paid hourly, it would be cheaper to have them working rather than eating. Just drinks, then, and a plate of cookies. And I knew just the recipe I wanted to try.

Dishes deposited in the deep stainless sink, I wiped my hands on a paper towel, and headed down the hall to my office.

The heavy oak door was partly open and I nudged it with the heel of my hand. The hinges gave a creak that set my fillings vibrating. Another item for the carpenters to address. I sat down behind the desk and reached for a shoe box that rested to my right.

"Thom McAn" was printed on the sides and ends. The lid was turned upside down and was currently reinforcing the bottom. Which was a good thing because the box was crammed full of pieces of yellowed notebook paper and index cards, some of which had cute designs and some of which were plain white, and old newspaper clippings that looked brittle and about to crumble.

The box belonged to Gladys Montgomery, a lovely older woman who lived in Florida for the winter. During the summer she came north to her cottage a couple of miles south of Bonaparte Bay on the St. Lawrence River. The "cottage" was a three-thousand-square-foot Victorian, one of the elaborate summer homes built around the turn of the twentieth century on the islands and along the shores of the St. Lawrence. My boyfriend, Jack Conway, was caretaking the house for her for the winter. Well, not currently. He was off on some kind of assignment with the Coast Guard, something he wouldn't—or couldn't—tell me about. And I wasn't sure how I felt about that.

Gladys had given me the box before she left and told me to copy what I wanted. That might very well be everything. But it was hard to tell, the contents of the box were so disorganized. Hopefully Gladys wouldn't mind if I did some rearranging. I flipped through the fragile paper gently until I found the one I'd seen a few days ago. Maple Walnut Sandies. Perfect for a cold November day. I placed the recipe on the flatbed of my copier and pressed the print button.

Twenty minutes later the simple dough was mixed and the aroma of warm maple syrup and toasted walnuts wafted through the restaurant kitchen. While the first tray of cookies baked, I laid out a few of the recipes from Gladys's shoe box on the clean prep counter and began to sort. Desserts and sweets went into one pile. Main dishes, side dishes, breads, and vegetables all got their own spot. This project wouldn't be finished today, that was for sure. But I had nothing but time between now and next May when the restaurant opened back up.

I was just popping a ball of raw cookie dough—which was of course a no-no since it contained raw eggs, but, well, I liked to live dangerously—into my mouth and taking the first tray out of the oven when the back door gave its characteristic screech and slam. Two men entered, brandishing sledgehammers. My jaw dropped when I realized the identity of one of the men. My cook's son and my former employee, Russ Riley.

◈ TWO ◈

"Hey, Georgie," Russ said. His unshaven chin was thrust out and he looked me in the eye, as if daring me to question his presence on my premises.

Huh. After I'd fired him a few months ago, his mother, Dolly, had told me that he'd gone to Florida to look for work. Wrestling alligators or maybe operating the rides at some off-Disney park—those would be career opportunities open to him. He was on probation, so leaving the state was not allowed, but I certainly wasn't going to rat him out. The farther away he stayed, the better, after the role he'd played in the mess my almost-ex-husband Spiro had gotten himself into a few months ago.

I wondered, briefly, if I should be afraid. He was holding a sledgehammer. The lump of cookie dough slid down my throat in a buttery blob and I reached for the glass of ice water sitting on the counter. And reviewed where the closest chef's knife was located.

"What are you doing here, Russ?"

His companion, a stocky guy with a butch haircut that screamed former military, seemed to be following the conversation closely. His lips were twisted into the merest hint of a smile.

Russ set down the hammer, removed his Metallica ball cap, and smoothed his thick dark mullet with the fingers of one tattooed hand. He replaced the cap and smiled at me, revealing a couple of missing teeth. "It's hunting season," he said simply, as if that explained everything. Which, if you were Russ Riley, it more or less did.

Funny Dolly hadn't mentioned he was back. I'd seen her only yesterday.

The other guy, still apparently quite amused by the exchange, doffed his cap to me. "Zach Brundage, ma'am." His voice held a slight twang, not quite Southern. Pennsylvania or Delaware perhaps. "Steve said to tell you that he'd be here in a few minutes. He's making phone calls in the truck."

Good. I wouldn't have to worry about Russ with Steve around. Most likely. As long as I could keep him out of the walk-in freezer, which he'd often used as his personal supermarket when he worked here. Not that there was much in there now. Most of the inventory that was left when we closed for the season had gone to the Bay's food pantry.

"Those cookies smell good," Zach said.

"Oh, yeah, Georgie's a great cook," Russ said.

I wanted to smack him. Instead, I told them, like a couple of children, that they'd have to wait until the cookies cooled down.

"We can get to work, then," Zach said. "Come on, Russ."

"I'll lead the way," Russ said. "I know this place like the back of my hand." He glanced over his shoulder at me as they left the kitchen. "And I can't wait to smash something."

Great. My disgruntled former dishwasher was now walking down my hallway with a sledgehammer. I was just about to call Steve and make sure he was on his way when the man in question came in through the back door. A sigh of relief escaped my lips.

Steve glanced over at me. "Sorry," he said. "I should have realized it would be uncomfortable for you to have Russ here."

"Well, a little, maybe." More than a little, but less than a lot. I was probably being paranoid.

"One of the guys on my crew is out with a hernia, so I brought Russ on at the last minute. I'll keep an eye on him. It'll only be a few days and he'll be out of your hair."

"I'd appreciate that." The second tray of cookies went into the oven as Steve went down the hall. I followed him, pulling my cell phone out of my pocket. The guys were standing outside the ladies' room, and Steve gestured inside, already giving orders.

"Excuse me," I said, and pushed past Russ and Zach. "'Before' pictures."

"Good idea," Russ drawled as I snapped a few photos. "You bringing in a TV crew to film us?"

Before I could respond, Steve cut in. "Shut up and get to work, Russ. Didn't you say your truck needed a new tranny? Winter jobs in Bonaparte Bay are hard to come by."

Russ glared, but picked up his sledgehammer and entered the ladies' room, a place I was willing to bet he'd never been while he worked here. At least I hoped not.

"I'll have him out of here as soon as I can," Steve said.

I shrugged. "If he gets out of line, best thing to do is call Dolly."

Steve nodded. "Best damn cook around. It's a long time till spring when I can get another piece of her apple pie."

The timer dinged from the kitchen. I headed back to my domain and pulled the tray from the oven. While the cookies cooled, I set up a platter and loaded the dishwasher, then started a fresh pot of coffee. The unmistakable sounds of smashing tile came from the other side of the house. Every blow caused me to flinch. Destruction, even though it paved the way for something new, was uncomfortable. I set the platter by the coffeemaker and wrote out a quick note that I was going out for a while and that Steve and the crew should help themselves. Would I be held liable if Russ choked on his? It might be worth a lawsuit.

Bundled up in a warm parka, scarf, hat, mittens and boots, I set out.

Theresa Street, the main drag of Bonaparte Bay, was

closed up tight, and had been for a month now. The tourist season ends on Columbus Day, and begins again on Victoria Day, which is the weekend before Memorial Day. Canadians celebrate Queen Victoria's birthday as a holiday—and some of them cross the St. Lawrence River to celebrate it in Bonaparte Bay. But right now, the tour boats were gone, the ticket booth was shuttered, and almost every business in the Bay, from Roger's Jewelry Shoppe to the T-Shirt Emporium run by my friend Midge, were closed for the winter. A couple of businesses stayed open—the Express-o Bean coffee shop and Kinney's drugstore.

I turned up Vincent Street, wiggling my gloved fingers and blowing out a frosty breath. The weather had turned frigid all of a sudden. I'm not sure why that surprised me every year, but it always seemed to come as something of a shock. I stepped up onto the front porch of a house sheathed in white clapboards. A sign hung next to the door: "Peter and Kimberlee Galbraith, Certified Public Accountants." Under that was another sign: "Hair-Brains." I'd be making a stop at both businesses.

Kim peered at me over a stack of files when I entered. She smiled and rose to greet me. Just five feet tall, she could barely see over the pile, even on her feet. Kim and her husband, Pete, both accountants, were still a couple after more than a decade of working and living together. They'd done quite a bit better than Spiro and I had. But that was water under the international bridge and I was optimistic about the direction my life was taking. Spiro was as happy as I'd ever seen him, now that he'd found love with Inky, the guy who ran the tattoo shop in town.

"Hi, Kim." I pulled off my knit cap and gloves and shoved them into my pockets, then smoothed my flyaway hair with my hand.

"Georgie! Seems like ages since I've seen you." Kim came around the desk and sat down in one of the visitors' chairs, motioning me to sit in the other. "Sorry about the mess." She glanced around. "We only have an assistant at tax time and things get a little out of control the rest of the year."

"Looks like a successful business to me, with all the work you can handle." I unzipped my coat. "And Bonaparte Bay needs those. I'm having some work done at the restaurant—"

Kim cut me off. "You're not changing the menu, are you?" Her eyes took on a worried look. "Because a life without Sophie's baklava or Dolly's pies just isn't worth living."

I laughed. I felt the same way. "No, no. Just updating the restrooms. Can you cut a check to Steve Murdoch? He's already started work and I want to get him the first installment." I gave her the figure.

Kim's face clouded over. "Sure. Do you want to wait while I write it out? It'll only take a minute." She went over to the printer, rummaged around in a drawer underneath it, and pulled out a box of checks marked "Bonaparte House." She loaded a check into the printer, then returned to her seat behind her desk.

"Poor Steve." Keys clacked as she worked.

"What about Steve?" I hoped he wasn't sick.

The printer whirred and a sheet of paper shot out the top. "Well," Kim said. "I don't know all the details, but it's going around town that Jennifer's having an affair."

My heart sank. "Poor Steve" was right. Jennifer was nuts. Steve was a decent, good-looking guy with a success- ful business. He did well enough that she didn't have to work outside the home if she didn't want to—which was apparently the case—and she was always dressed to the nines, even just to go to the Dollarsmasher supermarket or the bank.

"I hope this doesn't send him back to the booze," Kim continued. Steve never made any secret that he was a recovering alcoholic. I'd seen him pull out his sober chip more than once at the restaurant and run his fingers around the edge. And I'd heard he was sponsor to a couple of other Bay residents, though I didn't know who.

"That would be a shame." I hoped Steve and Jennifer could work it out. But I was living proof that no matter how amicable or necessary the breakup, there could still be a lot of emotions to sort through. "So who's she having the affair with?" I felt a little guilty about gossiping, but not quite enough to make me want to give it up. Bonaparte Bay could be dead boring in the off-season. Gossip was one way to pass the time during the long winter.

Kim put the check into an envelope and handed it to me. "I heard it was Jim MacNamara."

My lawyer. What a jerk. At least he was single, his

wife having left him years ago. And his son, Ben, was a grown man who now worked with his father. But that didn't excuse him for sleeping with a married woman. Once my divorce was final, maybe I'd look around for another attorney. Right now, well, I wanted the paperwork finished.

"Thanks," I said, deciding to deliver the check to Steve myself and zipping it inside my purse. "See you around at the Bean."

"Gotta keep that place in business." She grinned. "The better they do, the more accounting work for me."

I stood up, throwing my coat over my arm. Kim showed me to the door. "Stay warm."

"You too." I went across the hallway and opened the door to Hair-Brains.

I'd only intended to go in and make an appointment to get my hair done. But Lesley had had a cancelation so an hour and a half later, I found myself walking back to the Bonaparte House with a fresh new haircut, blond highlights and some darker lowlights, and even a manicure in *Pale Petal Pink*. The wind had picked up and I considered stopping in to warm up at Spinky's, the restaurant Spiro and Inky were opening. They'd hoped to have it running by now and to keep it open year-round, but they'd experienced a number of delays and were now planning on a spring opening. Maybe, just a little, I wanted to show off my new look, even though it was hat-flat already. Inky would appreciate it, even if Spiro might not. But it was cold, and dark comes early in November.

As good as I looked, I wanted nothing more than to heat up a couple of frozen tiropita—flaky golden phyllo pastry wrapped around a cheesy filling—for dinner, then to curl up on the couch upstairs and read my new Raphaela Ridgeway romance novel and wait for Jack's call at nine o'clock.

When I got back to the Bonaparte House, the parking lot was empty. The kitchen door was locked and a note was taped on the window.

> GEORGIE. WE FINISHED FOR THE DAY. DEMO'S
> DONE AND WE'LL START CONSTRUCTION
> TOMORROW. YOU DIDN'T ANSWER YOUR CELL
> SO I WENT AHEAD AND LOCKED THE DOOR.
> HOPE YOU BROUGHT A KEY. IF NOT, CALL
> ME. —STEVE.

Fortunately, I did have my key, which I turned in the lock. The place was blissfully silent. No banging, hammering, or snotty criminal ex-employees.

I pulled out my cell phone. There was a missed call from Steve, which had probably come in about the time I was getting blow-dried. I hung up my coat at the back door, dropped my purse inside my office, and headed for the restrooms to document the progress.

"Progress" was a relative term. I snapped a few photos of the men's room first. A pile of debris lay in one corner. The toilets and urinals had been disconnected and were lined up against one wall, destined, I assumed, for the great porcelain graveyard, wherever that was. They were decades old, so I didn't think they had any salvage value, but if some enterprising soul wanted them, they were welcome to them. A fine layer of light-colored dust lay over everything, probably from the old plaster. I was grateful to Steve for putting up a plastic sheet on the doorway to contain the mess.

Across the narrow hall, a similar plastic sheet had been hung in the door to the ladies' room. I drew back the curtain and stepped inside. The same fine white dust coated the disemboweled space. The hideous pink and black tile? Completely gone. It was amazing what three guys and some sledgehammers could do in a few hours. The disconnected toilets here too lined one wall.

I spun slowly, snapping pictures around the room. And froze. A bubble of nausea rose from my stomach and up my esophagus and my eyes closed involuntarily. When the threatened eruption didn't happen, I opened my eyes and stared. I hadn't been wrong. Oh, how I wish I had.

I dialed my cell phone.

"Nine-one-one, what's your emergency?" Damn. Cindy Dumont again.

I swallowed. "Cindy, send Rick or Tim to the Bonaparte House. Tell them to use the back door. Call an ambulance. And don't you dare make a snarky comment or I'll ban you from my restaurant permanently."

❖ THREE ❖

Across the room, partially hidden by the old stall walls that had been removed and stacked along the perimeter, a body lay motionless, sprawled in an ocean of blood that appeared to be seeping into the exposed subfloor of my ladies' room. It was facedown, but unless I had a cross-dresser I could see the body was a man. He wore a dark suit, stained darker by the blood that soaked it. A shiny metal stick about two and a half feet long and the diameter of a dime stuck up like a flagpole from the man's back.

The breath caught in my throat as I stared at the threaded end of that metal stick. I knew what that was. I'd been slicing meat off it in the restaurant kitchen for years. It was the spit that formed part of the vertical rotisserie on which we cooked our gyro meat.

I backed out of the room, getting myself tangled up in

the plastic door and almost falling in my haste to get out. My feet carried me, with no conscious effort of my own, to the kitchen. The rotisserie stood in one corner, cleaned and disassembled for the winter. My hand reached for the knob of the cabinet next to the machine. The spare parts, including the spit, should be inside there. But I pulled back, as though the handle radiated heat. There could be fingerprints on there, ones I shouldn't smudge. Because if that was my spit, somebody must have opened this cabinet and removed it. I'd placed the apparatus there myself, along with the other loose parts, more than a month ago.

But the suspense was killing me. Who was the man lying dead in my restaurant? And was it, in fact, a piece of my equipment that had skewered him? I tore myself away. I couldn't help the man. It wasn't like I could move him without doing more damage than he'd already suffered. And what if the attacker was still here? I threw on my coat and raced outside.

The wail of sirens grew louder. One of Bonaparte Bay's two cruisers pulled into the parking lot, light bar flashing, tires spraying up gravel as the vehicle came to an abrupt stop. Deputy Tim Arquette got out of the vehicle and came toward me, his hand on the butt of his gun. "What's going on, Georgie?"

I pointed to the kitchen door. "Inside. There's a body in one of the restrooms. I came home from getting my hair done and he was there."

Tim gave me the once-over. "Looks nice," he said. "Stay out here. I'll go in and make sure the perp is gone."

I nodded and sat down at the picnic table. My eyes were glued to the back of the restaurant, waiting for Tim to come back.

"Hey," said a voice. I nearly jumped out of my skin.

A few deep breaths of air that frosted my lungs and I was back under control. "Hi, Brenda."

She sat down next to me, tossing her big shoulder bag onto the table. The sky was streaked with the last purple rays of the setting sun. A shiver ran through me.

"Who's dead?" Brenda asked. Bonaparte Bay's Dumpster Diva never minced words. "I heard it on the police scanner," she explained. Brenda Jones had a fairly lucrative business, keeping the Bay's streets and alleys free of returnable cans and bottles. She was also a valuable source of information.

"All I know is that he's wearing a suit."

Brenda frowned. "When I was making my rounds this afternoon, I saw . . ."

At that moment, Tim strode out the door and across the parking lot toward us. He jabbed his finger at his phone screen then put the device to his ear. Brenda and I both leaned a little closer, hoping to hear what he had to say. It wasn't necessary. He spoke loud enough. "Cindy, is that ambulance en route? They're only coming from three blocks away, for God's sake. Not that it matters, he's dead." He paused, presumably while Cindy spoke on the other end. "You heard me right. It's Jim MacNamara."

I sat up straight. Brenda turned her head toward me. "That's what I was just about to say. I saw him walking this way earlier today."

"What time?"

She paused, as if thinking. "Must have been about three o'clock. I left my apartment right after the rerun of last week's ''Squatch Caller' show. That's the one where they sit around and make gizmos that sound like a Bigfoot? Anyway, he was headed this direction, not that I saw him go into the restaurant or anything."

Something niggled at the back of my mind. "What was he wearing?"

Brenda didn't hesitate. "Long black coat, the kind Clive the funeral guy wears? Black fedora on his head, and carrying a briefcase."

The body lying on my floor had not been wearing a topcoat. Nor had I seen one hanging at the kitchen door when I hung up my own coat. And I hadn't seen a briefcase. Not that I'd searched the whole restaurant, but it seemed odd.

Tim walked up to the ambulance that rolled to a stop in the parking lot. He pointed the attendants inside then turned toward us, sitting at the picnic table in the growing dark. "Georgie, you probably heard that. It's Jim Mac-Namara. Any idea why he'd be here?"

I shook my head. "Not unless it was about my divorce. But Spiro and I have everything worked out. We're just waiting for the time to expire before we can get the decree. So no, I can't think of any reason he'd come to see me in person, rather than just calling. Or having his secretary, Lydia, call."

Tim looked thoughtful. "Well, you won't be able to stay here tonight, of course, or tomorrow either probably while the crime scene techs are processing the site."

Deep down I'd known that, but it was still disconcerting. Where was I going to sleep tonight? I had a key to Spiro and Inky's restaurant, and I'm sure they wouldn't mind me crashing upstairs. But they were spending most of their time at Inky's house near his tattoo shop near Fort Drum. And I did not relish the thought of being alone in that big place with another killer on the loose.

There was Midge, my friend who ran the T-Shirt Emporium, but she and Roger from the jewelry shop were on a trip to California to visit her son. And of course my best friend and newfound cousin, Liza Grant, would take me in. My mother, with whom I'd recently reunited, was staying there, at least until Liza closed up her exclusive spa at Thanksgiving. But the castle that housed her and her business was situated on one of the islands that dotted the St. Lawrence—and it was getting dark, and it was November, and it was about twenty-five degrees out right now. Definitely not safe to take a boat ride. One tiny problem and I'd be bobbing like a Georgie ice cube in a St. Lawrence River cocktail. Liza had access to a helicopter for her guests, but this hardly qualified as an emergency big enough for that. So the Camelot hotel, it was.

Brenda adjusted the hand-knit cap that covered her bright red curls. "Uh, you can stay with me if you want. I've got a pull-out couch and I just got groceries."

My heart warmed. "I don't know what to say. That's so nice of you. But I don't want to put you out. I'm sure there'll be a room for me at the Camelot."

Brenda nodded. "Just as well. I've got to do my books tonight."

"But why don't we go grab a bite to eat, my treat?" I was rattled by the murder, and I wasn't quite ready to be alone. "The pizza shop is open."

"Sounds good. I didn't find much on my returnable route, not that I expected to. It'll all still be here tomorrow." She stood. "Let's go. It's cold out."

The back door of the restaurant opened, and two EMTs and a gurney rolled out and across the frozen ground toward the ambulance. The body was covered with a blanket but the shape was unmistakable. My gyro spit, if it was my gyro spit, and I just knew it was, had not been removed. A lump formed in my throat. When would the death and the killing end?

Tim came toward me. "You know the drill, Georgie. Don't leave town, and you'll be needed for questioning."

I sighed. Yes, I knew the drill.

"I'll be down at the pizza shop, then over at the Camelot. Can I go get my purse? It's in my office."

"Better let me bring it out to you," he said.

The interior of the Casa di Pizza was dimly lit and in need of an update, but it was warm and it smelled like heaven. A delicious yeasty aroma wafted out toward us as we sat ourselves at a blue vinyl booth well away from the door so we wouldn't be blasted by cold air every time a customer came in.

The lone server on duty came toward us with menus. I didn't recognize her, which was unusual in a village the size of the Bay, this time of the year. She filled water glasses and set them in front of each of us. "Let's get an appetizer and some salad before the pizza," I said to Brenda, who nodded. "What do you like?"

"How about the sampler platter? Wings, potato skins, mozzarella sticks?"

She was playing my comfort-food song. I'd pay for it tomorrow but it sounded wonderful tonight. I nodded to the server. "Sampler platter, a pitcher of Molson's, and two house salads. And a pizza with everything?" I looked to Brenda for confirmation and she nodded.

The server took down the order, though I would have thought she'd have been able to remember it since we seemed to be the only people in the place. "What kind of dressing for the salads?" she asked.

"Thousand Island," Brenda and I said in unison.

"Jinx, buy me a Coke," Brenda said, emitting a laugh that rattled in her throat. I knew she'd given up smoking a few months ago but it was clear she was still suffering the effects of her years of puffery.

"You want a Coke too?" The server looked perplexed.

"Just an expression," I assured her. "The pitcher of beer will be fine."

I leaned back in the booth. It had been a while since I'd been in here, probably since last fall. The place hadn't changed much. Built somewhere around the turn of the last century, as was most of downtown with the exception of the Bonaparte House, which was quite a bit older, it had exposed brick walls and a high ceiling covered in embossed, white-painted tin squares. Booths flanked the walls, and a number of tables marched down the center of the room. At the back was a chest-high counter where our server was now placing our order, and beyond that was the kitchen. There were apartments upstairs for the college-age seasonal help. In fact, I'd lived here with three other girls crammed into a two-bedroom, one-bath unit the summer I took my first job at the Bonaparte House. Which seemed like a glacial epoch or two ago.

Brenda and I tucked into the appetizers when our slightly clueless server set the plate in front of us. I dipped a mozzarella stick into the cup of marinara and took a bite. Perfect. Crispy on the outside, gooey on the inside, and topped with a spicy tomato sauce. "So," I said. "How's business?"

Brenda wiped her fingers on her paper napkin, then took a sip of beer. "It was a good year. I made enough to cover my winter expenses, and there's enough extra to buy a second boat. I'm getting an intern next summer."

"An intern? Is there enough, uh, business for that?" I put a potato skin on my plate and added a dollop of sour cream.

"There is if you place collection units on the islands and empty them every few days." She broke into a self-satisfied smile.

Wow. That was brilliant. Islands were, well, islands. Trash had to go somewhere, as did recyclables. "What a great idea. Let me know if you need capital." I had some money put away, money I hoped would someday be enough to buy the Bonaparte House from my mother-in-law. But Brenda seemed like a good investment.

"Thanks," she said. "I'm good for now and I like to keep my overhead low. That way I can put more into my IRA."

There was so much more to this woman than met the eye. She continued to surprise me.

Our salads arrived. But they weren't delivered by our server extraordinaire. Franco Riccardi, the owner of the Casa, set two salads down before us. Each was covered in the pinkish dressing named for the Thousand Islands.

"Mind if I join you lovely ladies for a moment?" Franco asked.

I scooched over on the vinyl booth. "Not at all," I said.

"Brenda." He nodded in her direction. Everybody knew Brenda.

"Is it true that Jim MacNamara's dead?" His big brown eyes searched my face.

I sighed. "I think so. I found him at the restaurant, lying on the floor." Probably best not to give out too much information, not that it wouldn't get out from other sources.

"Damn. He was a good customer. Though I use a lawyer in Watertown for most things."

"He's handling my divorce. I suppose his son will take charge of the law firm now. But he's only been out of law school a couple of years."

Franco's lips turned down at the corners. "Not impressed with that kid. His father made him get a job one summer to build his character and he picked here. Refused to wash dishes or bus tables, but agreed to make deliveries. I would have fired him but I was doing his old man a favor."

I forked up some salad. The dressing was creamy, tangy, and textured with bits of sweet pickle and finely chopped hard-boiled egg. It was tangier than the version we served at the Bonaparte House. Of course, every restaurant in the Thousand Islands had its own version, all claiming to be the original.

Franco looked at me expectantly. "Well? What do you think?"

"It's good. Lemony. Is it a new recipe?"

Franco leaned forward. His excitement was almost palpable. "Actually," he said, looking around. "It's a new *old* recipe. I was cleaning out some junk in one of the third-floor rooms and I came across it in a box of old cookbooks. It was a handwritten recipe dated 1907."

I thought of Gladys's recipe box, the contents of which were now strewn all over my prep counter. I hoped the crime scene techs would leave everything alone. I'd feel awful if something happened to one of her mother's recipes.

"You think it's an original?"

"Well, that would be the Holy Grail of salad dressings, wouldn't it?" Franco grinned. "Who knows? It's the earliest one I've heard of. And guess what?" His dark eyes sparkled.

"What?" Brenda seemed interested. I never would have figured her for a food history buff, but Thousand Islanders are proud of their namesake condiment.

"It isn't even called Thousand Island dressing," Franco announced. "Of course, you can tell by the ingredients—it can't be anything else—but it's called 'Sophias Sauce.' No apostrophe."

"Sophia? I'd always heard it was invented by Oscar of the Waldorf. The guy who invented the Waldorf salad and Veal Oscar?"

Brenda piped up. "That's what they say on the *Lady Liberty* boat. The tour guides say that Oscar was making dinner for George Boldt and ran out of dressing, so he used the ingredients he had and whipped up Thousand Island dressing."

I nodded. "That's the story I've heard too."

Franco grinned. "Those tour guides also tell you that if you look down into the St. Lawrence at a certain spot, you can see the international border between the U.S. and Canada."

I nodded. Not that I'd been on a tour boat in years, but my customers at the Bonaparte House were always asking if some of the things they'd heard were true. "So what makes you think this is the one?" I ate another bite of salad. "It's tasty. What is that? Worcestershire sauce? It has a deeper flavor and it's not as sweet as what we serve at the Bonaparte House."

"That's right," Franco said. "I'll make a copy of the recipe for you and have somebody bring it over to the restaurant."

Brenda frowned, ever so slightly. "You're not going to try to copyright it or trademark it or anything? That woman at the River Rock Resort says she's got the original recipe and I heard she's trying to get it declared legally hers."

Franco scoffed. "Angela Wainwright? She mixes mayonnaise and ketchup, slaps it on some zebra mussels, and calls it fine cuisine."

I had to laugh. The River Rock was located on some prime riverfront property but it was not known for its food. It would have been a blessing if those invasive zebra mussels were edible, actually. Maybe we could get rid of them. "You sure you want to give it away?"

"The way I see it, this recipe belongs to Bonaparte Bay and the other towns of the Thousand Islands." He leaned forward. "In fact, as soon as I can find somebody to do it for me, I'm going to post the recipe on my website. And I'm giving a copy to the *Bay Blurb*. I hope they run it on the front page."

Angela wouldn't be happy about that, but there wasn't much she could do about it. It wasn't like there was any way to prove her recipe was the first.

Franco rose. "I've taken enough of your time, ladies. Here's your pizza. Do you need another pitcher?"

We both shook our heads as the steaming cheese-fest was set in front of us. Brenda and I were still on our first glasses. At this rate, we'd leave most of the pitcher on the table.

And come to think of it, Brenda seemed to have curtailed her drinking. A lot. It had been customary to see her making her Dumpster rounds with a little buzz on most of the time. Well, good for her. Maybe she realized she needed a clear head if she wanted to expand her business empire.

A Killer Kebab

After all the appetizers and the salad, I could only eat one slice of pizza. We asked the waitress to box up the rest and I sent it home with Brenda. I paid, leaving a generous tip even though the server probably didn't deserve it, and we left the Casa. Brenda went toward her apartment, I headed for the drugstore.

My shopping basket soon contained my overnight essentials: toothbrush, trial-size toothpaste, fresh package of unattractive but serviceable underwear, and a souvenir T-shirt to sleep in. I tossed in a bar of dark chocolate and a trashy gossip magazine. Hopefully, my mother, the famous television actress, would not be featured in this issue. Since her injuries a few weeks ago, she'd been staying at my friend Liza's spa, located in the castle on Valentine Island just a short boat ride away from Bonaparte Bay. Liza would be closing up the Spa at Thanksgiving, so Melanie—I still couldn't bring myself to call her "Mom"—would have to find some new digs. Guilt pricked at me. I had the whole Bonaparte House to myself for the winter. I should invite her to come and stay with me. In fact I had, but Melanie, who was perhaps not quite as self-absorbed as I'd thought, told me she preferred to stay at the Spa, where she could pay people to take care of her. And by doing so she was giving me space to process having her back in my life.

I placed my items on the counter and the teenage cashier began ringing them up. "Hey, Georgie," a voice said behind me.

◈ FOUR ◈

I turned around to see Steve Murdoch. His jaw was set and a furrow deep enough to plant corn creased his brow.

"Steve? Are you okay?" Clearly, he wasn't. The tiny black cloud I'd noticed surrounding him earlier at the Bonaparte House was now a full-blown thunderstorm. The skin of my arms broke out into goose bumps.

"Okay?" His voice was hard and bitter. "In less than thirty minutes, as long as it takes me to get squiffed, I'll be just fine."

I glanced down. He had one hand in his jacket pocket and the other held a six-pack of beer. Crap. Steve was a recovering alcoholic with a lot of years of sobriety under his belt. Was I supposed to remind him of that? What if I said the wrong thing? I had no idea who his Alcoholics

Anonymous sponsor was, which might have been a good thing because now I wouldn't have to make a decision about whether to butt in. There were probably guidelines about this situation somewhere on the Internet, but there was no time or means to look anything up. So I just said, "Do you want to talk?"

He emitted a bitter snort. "Talking sounds good. Right after I drink this six-pack."

"Can I . . . call someone for you?" *Lame, lame, lame.*

Steve eyed me. "Like who? My wife?" He pulled his hand out of his pocket and held up a disk about the size of a half dollar. His sobriety chip. He tossed it and it sailed along the bank of cash registers like a Frisbee, then hit the counter and landed in front of the jewelry display. "She's home crying over Jim MacNamara. I'm glad that son of a bitch is dead."

I heard the cashier suck in a breath. Steve's tone was low and menacing.

I took an involuntary step away from him. I couldn't help the thought that popped into my head. Steve clearly hated Jim MacNamara. He had access to my ladies' room and to my kitchen. Could he have killed the lawyer while I was out getting my hair done? "Where's Ewan?" I said softly.

A look of horror replaced the rage on Steve's face at my reference to his son. He blinked, his eyes traveling from the cashier, who had her hand on the phone, to me, then down to his own hand. His fingers relaxed their grip and he reached around me to set the six-pack on the counter. "I won't be needing this," he said, and trudged toward the glass doors.

I handed the cashier my credit card, my foot tapping as I willed her to hurry. While she ran the card, I went to the jewelry counter and picked up Steve's chip. I rubbed the edges and read the number: fifteen years. How bad would things have to get before someone would throw away fifteen years of sobriety? I signed the electronic pad, grabbed my bright orange plastic bag, and left the store.

Steve was leaned up against the brick building. His chest rose and fell as he breathed deep and exhaled in turn, emitting frosty clouds that glowed white in the exterior lighting.

"I'm a cheap date," he said with a small laugh. "In the old days it would have taken at least a two-fer to get me where I needed to be."

He used the Canadian phrase for a case of beer. I couldn't imagine downing twenty-four beers in one sitting. Twenty-four dark chocolate bars? Maybe.

Steve filled the silence. "Ewan isn't home. He's off visiting a friend in Utica for a couple of days. So at least he didn't see his mother bawling her eyes out over a man who was just using her."

Cold sliced through me. I pulled my knit hat into place over my ears and adjusted my scarf around my neck. "Are you going home?" I asked. None of my business, but it didn't seem like a good idea for him.

"Home?" He gave a brittle laugh. "No, that hasn't been

a home for a while now. Even though she told me it was over with MacNamara and like an idiot I believed her. But nothing was ever the same."

Awkward. I wasn't close to Jennifer, but we'd always been friendly with each other. I reached out for Steve's hand. He looked startled. PDAs were probably not his thing. I pressed the sobriety chip into his calloused palm. "You might want this," I said.

He stared at the disk, then rubbed the surface and placed it in his pocket. "Thanks," he said, and strode off across the parking lot.

My breath came out in a frosty whoosh as I watched Steve get into his truck. A plume of exhaust blew out the tailpipe. He didn't wait for the truck to warm up before he left. I wondered where he was headed.

The stars sparkled in the night air as I went in the opposite direction. It was only a two-block walk to the Camelot, but I wished I had my Honda. Not so much for protection from the cold, though that would have been welcome, but because it had been a long, long day and I was bone tired. And even though I'd walked this stretch of sidewalk hundreds of times, there hadn't been a killer out there. Now there was. And I wondered if I'd just seen him heading out of town, maybe out of the country.

And selfishly, I wondered, if Steve had killed Jim Mac-Namara, who was going to fix my bathrooms?

A thin layer of ice covered the concrete sidewalk. I walked as fast as I dared. Last thing I needed was to slip and break a wrist. I checked into the Camelot and texted

Jack and Liza so somebody would know where I was. After locking my door and window, I climbed into a comfortable warm bed, broke into my chocolate bar, and looked at my phone messages. Sheldon Todd had left me a voice mail, probably while I was in the bathroom. *Staying at River Rock. Can you meet for breakfast tomorrow, nine a.m.?*

The River Rock was a 1960s-era hotel on the opposite end of town. Too new to have vintage charm, too old to appeal to the younger crowd, it sat in limbo waiting for someone to infuse a whole lot of cash into sprucing it up. Or burn it down so some big investor could come in and build a brand-spanking-new resort on the property. The three-story boxy building was covered in wooden shingles, weathered to a dark brown over the years. Curls of white paint peeled from the trim around the front door. There wasn't a spot of color anywhere. Angela could have at least put up a wreath of fall-colored silk flowers or something, or hung a bright "Welcome" sign.

Inside I had my pick of tables, so I sat by the windows overlooking the water. The sun's weak November rays warmed me through the glass, but I still shivered. The water was gray and choppy this morning. The server set a carafe of coffee and a little metal pitcher of half-and-half in front of me, just as a man approached the table.

I'd never met Sheldon Todd in person, only talked to him on the phone. "Georgie?" he said.

"Mr. Todd? Nice to meet you," I said, extending my

hand, which he grabbed and pumped up and down before lowering himself into the chair opposite me. He pushed his chair back a bit to allow room for his round, Santa-esque belly. "Coffee?"

"Thanks." Sheldon flipped his cup over in its saucer and I poured from the carafe. I watched, fascinated, as he methodically opened five sugar packets and dumped them into his cup, then began to swirl his spoon until he created a syrupy whirlpool. No cream, just a whole lot of sugar, the way the Greeks like it. But Greek coffee is very strong, stronger even than espresso, and can stand up to the sweetness. This was pure American stuff, probably brewed in a Bunn-O-Matic like I had back at the Bonaparte House. My teeth hurt just watching.

After Sheldon had taken a good long draught, eyes closed, he set the cup down and looked at me. "Normally this would be confidential between me and my client, but your mother said she wasn't feeling well, so I should call you." The voice was clipped and businesslike.

Melanie Ashley, formerly known as Shirley Bartlett. Soap opera star and my estranged mother. She'd only been back in my life for a little while, but she was already dumping things she didn't want to deal with off on me. Not feeling well, my eye. Her gunshot wound had healed nicely and she would have no lasting effects from her splenectomy, other than some scarring from the surgery. Now she was living in the lap of luxury at an exclusive spa, with a personal assistant at her beck and call twenty-four/seven.

Still, I was interested to hear what Sheldon had to say.

"I'm working on a new lead," he said, not waiting for my reply.

My heart sank. My genealogy had turned out to be a can of big fat lethal worms and people had died because of it. Much as I was thrilled to find out that I had family still living, it was a big adjustment. Not to mention there was a lot of money involved due to a complicated trust that was going to vest in a few months. And there was another complication, one I hadn't thought about before. With Jim MacNamara dead, who was administering the trust?

"Don't tell me you've found another branch of the family." I unfolded my napkin and put it in my lap, even though we hadn't ordered yet. My fingers itched to refold the napkin into the rosette shape we used at the Bonaparte House. Restaurant origami.

"Let's order, then I'll explain."

A reprieve. I opened the menu. Inch-high letters at the top of the first page read, *Home of the One and Only Thousand Island Dressing!* Curiosity tempted me. What could I order at nine in the morning that would be good with a sauce? Eggs maybe? That sounded a bit nasty. It was too early for a burger. There were bottles of premade dressing at the front, by the cash registers, so my taste test could wait for another time. I settled on scrambled eggs and local sausage, with a side of buttered raisin toast, and vowed to have salad for lunch.

We gave our orders to the server, then closed up the

menus and put them back into the metal holder on the table. Sheldon took a sip of his coffee, then leaned back.

"As you know, your great-great-great-grandfather, Elihu Bloodworth, was a bit of a player."

That was putting it kindly. More like, he was a bit of a criminal, with two wives in different places and children by each one. "Right," I said. "And my mother and I are descended from one of his children by his second, bigamous marriage. My friend Liza is descended from one of the legitimate children." I was glad to repeat this information. It helped me keep it straight in my own head.

Sheldon folded his hands over his belly. "Correct. And your mother, the delightful Ms. Ashley . . ." His eyes took on a far-off expression. My nipped, tucked, enhanced, and Botoxed mother seemed to have that effect on a lot of men. ". . . hired me to trace the genealogies of all of Elihu's children down to the present generation, with help from her assistant."

I knew all this. Caitlyn Black, my mother's minion, was a pretty good researcher, as well as being extremely loyal. "And Liza, my mother, my daughter, and I are the only ones left."

"That we know of."

Well, nertz. Elihu Bloodworth, lumber king of Northern New York after the Civil War, had given each of his children a set sum of money, then tied up the rest of his millions in a generation-skipping trust that would be ending legally next February. My mother and Liza were the beneficiaries of the trust. My daughter and I had no immediate interest. But upon my mother's death, anything she hadn't spent would come to Callista, which was how Melanie had set up her will, and which was fine with me.

"Have you traced all the descendants?" I swear I wasn't worried about anyone else sharing the trust. Large sums of money seemed to be within my grasp lately, but disappeared almost as quickly as they came, and I was mostly okay with that. Not that I would turn it down if some of that money made its way to my bank account, but my life was pretty good and I had everything I needed and almost everything I wanted. And not everything I wanted could be bought.

But not everybody felt as I did. The trust was reputed to hold multiple millions of dollars, due to compounding over the last hundred years or more. It was a pile of money, and people had died because other people had gotten greedy. If it was just Liza, Melanie, Callista, and me left, I could feel safe. We weren't about to kill each other.

The waitress set our plates down in front of us. I picked up a piece of raisin toast. Disappointing. I'd hoped for better, but it turned out to be a droopy triangle of grocery store bread drenched in margarine. Not even real butter. The two points flapped like the wings of an unhealthy bird as I set the bread back down on the plate and sighed.

Sheldon, however, attacked his plate with gusto. The fork clinked against the plate as he speared a piece of ham and a hunk of fried egg, dripping with yolk. I wished

I could take him back to the Bonaparte House and give him a real breakfast. Which would mean I could get one too. But who knew when I'd be able to return?

He swallowed and wiped his rather fleshy lips with the napkin. "I've traced all but one of the children from both marriages and your daughter is the last of the line, as far as I know. But I've reached a dead end with one line, which is why I'm in town. I'll be digging through documentation at the newspaper, the library, the village and town historical societies, as well as some private sources."

So this might not be over. No. No more heirs will be found, I told myself firmly. Still, I had to ask. "Do you expect to find anyone?" I fiddled my fork into my scrambled eggs. They looked dry and hard with an unappetizing brownish skin attesting to the fact they'd been cooked in too hot a pan and had probably been sitting under a heat lamp too long.

"I've traced the line down to the 1940s. Your distant cousin Percy disappears from the records at that time. He's the one I need to confirm. After that, I'm confident we'll have everyone accounted for."

There was something I'd been wondering about. "Wouldn't the lawyers have been keeping track of who the descendants were? I mean, the MacNamaras have been overseeing the trust since it was formed."

Sheldon nodded. "It would certainly help if I could see the lawyer's files, at least the genealogy charts, which they must have if they're at all competent. Can you ask them?"

I had, and Jim MacNamara had told me rather snootily that he wasn't at liberty to say, since I wasn't his client for this matter. And my mother couldn't be bothered to ask. Or if she had, she hadn't told me. When it suited her purposes, she could withhold a lot of information. Of course, the point was moot now that Jim MacNamara was dead. I wondered again who would take over managing the trust. Presumably Ben, the son who was only a couple years out of law school.

"When will you be finished?"

He grinned. "With you, my lovely company, or with breakfast? This was so good I might just order a second helping."

On my mother's dime, no doubt. I hadn't really learned anything new from this meeting, except that Sheldon was not exactly a gourmand, and there was one line of descent that had to be ruled out. Sheldon could have given Melanie or her assistant, Caitlyn, that information in an e-mail or phone call instead of wasting my time. Although you could never predict whether Melanie would talk or not, so I guess this meeting over breakfast, if you could call this pitiful meal that, had been worth it.

My cell phone buzzed in my purse. Saved by the vibration. It was rude, but I pulled out the phone and looked at the display. My cook, Dolly, had sent me a text. "Excuse me, would you, Sheldon? I've been, uh, waiting for this."

He nodded as I rose. "Don't worry about the bill. I'll put it on my expense account. You going to eat that raisin toast?"

"Take what you want. And let me know what you find." I walked toward the display of souvenir items and selected a bottle of salad dressing. "Put it on his tab, please?" Angela Wainwright, who owned the River Rock, had appeared behind the counter.

"You're not going to try to replicate my secret recipe, are you?" Angela's smile didn't quite reach her eyes. She'd never really had the Three Musketeers attitude most Bonaparte Bay business owners had. All for one and one for all. Not a team player. Not a member of the Chamber of Commerce.

I laughed insincerely. "Good to see you, Angela. No, my palate's not sophisticated enough to do that, though I could probably guess a few ingredients." I didn't owe her an explanation, so I didn't say anything more. She apparently wanted the sale more than she wanted to know what my intentions were regarding the dressing, because she simply nodded.

I made my way out the doors and onto the porch. The sun was bright but it wasn't enough to warm the air, which assaulted me like an iceberg hitting the *Titanic*. I thought about Liza and my mother over on Valentine Island and wished Liza had closed up early this year. No one should be out on a boat in weather this cold, and eventually they'd all have to move back to the mainland.

Finally, I looked down at the cell phone in my hand and tapped the icon to retrieve my text message. Call me ASAP. My gut clenched. Dolly rarely texted me, knowing I wasn't good about keeping my phone charged, something I was trying to be better about. That "ASAP" bothered me. My fingers tingled with cold as I dialed, then shoved my gloveless hand into my pocket.

"Hello?" Dolly rasped, her voice roughened by years of cigarette smoking although she had finally quit.

"Dol, it's me. Georgie. What's going on?" My teeth chattered and I moved to another spot on the porch, where the landscaping might provide a windbreak.

"It's that idiot son of mine. Russ has gone and gotten himself arrested."

Well, it wouldn't be the first time. During the years Russ had worked for us as a dishwasher, and most recently just a few months ago, he'd had a number of scrapes with the law. Mostly petty stuff, like public urination. Brawling. "Forgetting" to pay his tab at the Island Roadhouse. Largely alcohol-related. "What for?" I asked.

"Murder."

◈ FIVE ◈

"Jim MacNamara's murder? Oh, Dolly. I don't know what to say."

I could almost see her pursing up her bright pink lips. "They arraigned him last night. Said his fingerprints were on the murder weapon, you know, the spit where we roast the gyro?"

Wow. That had been fast. Of course, if the police had recovered a print, all they'd need to do would be to run it through the database. At least, that's what they did on the television cop dramas I watched over the winter. And they must have confirmed that the spit came from my kitchen. My stomach rolled.

"But he was our dishwasher for years. His fingerprints are probably all over the Bonaparte House," I finally said.

A fit of coughing overtook her, deep, wet, and rattly.

Next time I saw her, I was going to insist that she see a doctor. When she recovered, she said, "There's more."

I held my breath. "What?"

"Somebody overheard the dope arguing with the lawyer. Russ threatened to shoot him."

"What were they arguing about?" I couldn't imagine many scenarios where Russ and Jim MacNamara would cross paths, even in a village the size of Bonaparte Bay. It wasn't like they played golf at the country club together.

"Oh, hell. You know that property out in back of Russ's house? Well, it's been for sale for years. Russ always wanted to buy it, but he could never put together enough scratch, especially after he lost his job with you." Her tone was matter-of-fact, not accusatory.

"I had to fire him after what he did to Spiro, you know that, right?"

"Oh, yeah. I don't blame you for that. Sometimes I'd like to fire him from being my son, but it don't work that way." She gave a rattly laugh.

"So what does the property have to do with Jim Mac-Namara's murder?" I hated saying the word. "Murder." His death couldn't have been an accident. Unless he committed some kind of Greek hara-kiri and skewered himself, somebody else must have killed him. But Russ? I could see him getting into a fight or driving drunk and accidentally killing someone. And I knew all too well he was capable of other criminal activities. But I didn't think he had premeditated murder in him.

"Last week the lawyer put in a purchase offer on the

land and it looked like Old Lady Turnbull was ready to sell."

I pictured the fields behind Russ and Dolly's house. "But that's all old overgrown pastures and dense woods, isn't it? Why would Jim MacNamara want that property? He isn't—wasn't—the farming type." Unless he'd planned to become some kind of preppy feudal lord.

"True. It was the old Turnbull farm. But there's also close to a mile of waterfront on Silver Lake."

Now it made sense. "MacNamara wanted to develop it."

"Yup. And not just put up a few camps either. He was talking about putting up humongous summer houses, like those big camps in the Adirondacks? I heard Murdoch was going to be the builder."

About the same time as the elaborate mansions were being built on the St. Lawrence in the nineteenth and early twentieth centuries, huge rustic lodges were being built to the east in the mountains by people who had more money than they knew what to do with. If Jim had succeeded in his plan for Silver Lake, only the very wealthy would have been able to afford his modern vacation homes.

"So why did Russ want the property so badly?" I thought I knew. People who could afford lakefront McMansion-Camps would not take kindly to Russ running his ATV through the neighborhood whenever he pleased, as he was used to doing. But I was only partly right.

"Russ has been hunting that property his whole life.

Me too, back when I still hunted. Old Lady Turnbull never cared as long as we brought her a package or two of backstrap and some stew meat for the winter."

One thing about the North Country. You didn't get between a man—or woman—and his hunting territory. "And that's what Russ and Jim argued about?"

"Yup. The lawyer told him he was going to put up 'Posted' signs all around the property and he was going to enforce them. I admit it, Russ was madder than a wet bobcat."

A sharp breeze stabbed at my cheeks, reminding me I was standing outside. "And someone overheard the argument and reported it to the police. Do we know who?"

"Yep, and nope. Don't know who it was who ratted him out. But I wouldn't want to be that person when Russ gets out of jail. I just hope that public defender knows what he's doing."

Me too. I had no idea what a private lawyer would charge to defend someone accused of murder. Did I have enough saved up to help if Dolly asked? That would make a big dent in my Buy-the-Bonaparte-House-Someday Fund. But I would do it for Dolly. Not for Russ, but for Dolly.

"And no," she continued. "Don't offer me money for a lawyer. He got himself into this mess. He can get himself out."

I wished I could hug Dolly through the phone. She'd been a friend as well as an employee to me over the years. Despite her rough exterior and no-nonsense demeanor, she had to be upset. Having your son on probation, or fined for jacking deer, was one thing. Having him arrested for murder was quite another. And Russ had a temper. If he'd gotten angry enough—and make no mistake, his way of life had been threatened . . . Well, maybe I had to reconsider whether I thought he was capable of killing someone, even though I'd given him the benefit of the doubt.

"Call me if you need anything," I said. "Oh, and I know this might not be the best time to tell you this." I bit my lip. The idea had been kicking around in my head for a while now. "If the restrooms are finished, I was thinking about reopening the restaurant, just for one Thanksgiving seating. Of course I'll find somebody else to cook. You already work all the warm-weather holidays."

She cut me off. "Don't you dare. I'd have to cook at home anyway, so we can all just eat at the restaurant." She pronounced it *rest-runt*. "Turkey and all the trimmings. Prepping and cooking'll keep my mind off Russ."

We'd have to add a few Greek dishes. Some tiropita as an appetizer and a traditional Greek dessert or two, at the very least.

"I'll let you know when we can go back into the kitchen. And I'm sorry about Russ," I said, and rang off.

From where I stood on the porch, I could just see the Bonaparte House. I was at odds. What was I going to do with myself until I could go back to my home? Stay in my room at the Camelot? That had already gotten old. I was used to being busy. Take a walk? It was awfully cold and that couldn't be healthy. I could go visit Liza and Melanie at the Spa, but that would require finding someone with a boat, or having Liza send someone over from the island to pick me up. And that just seemed like too much trouble. If the crime scene people would let me have my car, I could drive to Watertown and have an early lunch after my dismal breakfast, then do a little early holiday shopping. Maybe see a movie.

My heart clenched. It would be so much nicer if I had a friend to go with me. I missed Sophie, my soon-to-be-ex-mother-in-law, who was back in Greece for the winter. I missed my daughter, who was due back soon but hadn't told me yet when she was flying from Europe.

And most of all, I missed Jack Conway. A Coast Guard captain, he was off doing . . . something. Something he wouldn't, probably couldn't, tell me about. After twenty years of a marriage of convenience with Spiro, I'd spent the last couple of months learning how to have a relationship with a man who preferred women. But Jack's job took him away, sometimes for weeks at a time. And it wasn't clear what exactly he did. And I wasn't exactly sure how I felt about that. I'd spent a lot of years with a man who was usually present, but not there for me. And now I'd taken up with a man who was there for me, but wasn't always *here*.

I descended the steps and walked the few blocks to the parking lot behind the Bonaparte House. The building was barricaded with yellow crime scene tape, but my car sat all by its lonesome. I crossed the gravel, just as a New

York state trooper's car pulled in and rolled to a stop in front of me, cutting off my exit.

A man stepped out of the car, six-feet-plus of bulky muscle encased in a perfectly fitted jacket and crisp-pressed pants. He took off his mirrored aviator sunglasses and let his steely eyes come to rest on my face. I squirmed. This wasn't my first rodeo with Detective Lieutenant Hawthorne, but it never got any easier. Nor did it matter that I was completely innocent. Given the chance, the man could intimidate the Pope.

"We have to stop meeting like this," he drawled, popping a cherry Life Saver into his mouth. He'd apparently eaten another one earlier, because his lips were a slightly unnatural shade of red. I pictured him interrogating suspects then sucking their blood. For fun.

"Isn't there somebody else they can send to question me? People are going to start talking." My attempt at flippancy was not nearly as successful as his had been and I wished I could take it back.

"I asked for this job," he said with a grin that showed very white teeth. Possibly the first smile I'd ever seen on his face. If I wasn't already, maybe, sort of in love with Jack, and if the detective wasn't a little bit, uh, scary, I might have set my toque for this guy. "This address is preprogrammed into my GPS unit. Saves time."

I unset my toque. "You think I like this? You think it's my fault somebody died in my restaurant? Think again." Despite the cold, I could feel heat rush to my cheeks and my blood pressure tick up.

"Settle down, Georgie. We know you didn't have anything to do with this. At the time of the murder you were at the accountants' office and then at the hair stylist. Who did a very good job, by the way."

My knit hat was still on my head, so I knew he was just trying to soften me up. "Let's just get this over with," I snapped. "Can I use my car? When is this"—I swept my gloved hand in a semicircle toward the yellow tape—"going to be finished?" Then my ever-present guilt reflex kicked in. No matter what kind of a jerk Jim MacNamara had been in life, he still deserved justice in death.

A flicker of amusement crossed Lieutenant Hawthorne's face.

"So glad you find this funny." My guilt evaporated and annoyance came rushing back in to take its place.

The detective reached into his jacket pocket and pulled out a spiral-bound notebook. "Do you want to do this here, or shall we go inside where it's warm?"

"*Can* we go in? We can use my office, I guess. It should be familiar to you since you've been here before." I sincerely hoped this would be the last time he ever visited me.

He led the way to the door, then lifted the crime scene tape for me to duck under. Such a gentleman.

I'm not sure what I expected to find. A passel of white-suited technicians dusting for fingerprints and inspecting surfaces for hair and fiber samples maybe. But in fact, we passed only a couple of people and I didn't even have to put on paper booties to get to my office.

Lieutenant Hawthorne explained without my asking. "We're not really expecting to find much useful forensic evidence. This is a public business and it would be basically impossible to rule out every hair or fingerprint we find from every customer and employee who's been here."

They'd found Russ's fingerprints, though, and that, along with the witness's account of hearing Russ and Jim arguing, had been enough to make a very quick arrest. Maybe too quick? My gut was telling me there might have been a rush to judgment.

"Sorry I can't offer you anything while we talk," I said. "My kitchen's not available to me." My tone was probably a teeny bit snarkier than was strictly necessary. Why this man always irritated me so, I couldn't say. It didn't seem to bother him.

"No baklava? Then just tell me about the day of the murder and describe what you saw," he said, pen poised over his notebook.

My eyes closed as I gave him an account of everything I could remember. Which wasn't much. I hadn't stayed very long once I saw Jim's body lying on my ladies' room floor. An image that was probably burned into my memory banks forever. "Did you look in the kitchen cabinet I told you about? Was it my gyro spit sticking out of Jim's back?"

"It was. That's where we got Russ Riley's prints." He consulted his notebook. "Anything else relevant?"

Should I tell him about Steve? He'd been pretty angry last night talking about Jim and the affair with Jennifer. I decided to go the indirect route.

"Have you interviewed Steve Murdoch and the guy working for him? Zach Brundage? They were the ones here with Russ."

He tilted his head to one side, ever so slightly. "Yes, of course."

Then there was no need for me to put any suspicions in his head about Steve. If the police had done their homework, they would have known about Jennifer's affair with Jim and come to their own conclusions. It was all over town, even though I was apparently one of the last to learn about it.

"Then I can't think of anything else."

"Well, if you do, you'll be sure to call." It was an order, not a request. He rose, towering over me. "The techs should be done here by tomorrow morning, so you can come back then. In the meantime, if you need anything upstairs, I can accompany you to get it. And you can take your car."

If I hadn't needed clean clothes, I would have declined. "Come on, then," I said, and led him through one of the three dining rooms, up and around the spiral staircase, and into our living quarters on the second floor.

"Wait here," I told him, pointing to a couch in our little family room—really just an open landing at the top of the stairs with some seating and a coffee table.

"You're not going to invite me in?" He folded up his bulky body and sat down on the couch, then picked up a magazine, which he began to thumb through. Funny, he didn't seem like the kind of guy who'd be interested in recipes and housekeeping tips, but then again that was the only magazine available.

I twisted the doorknob. "Nope." With those red lips from the cherry candy, it would be like inviting in a vampire. And we all know what happens when you do that.

Inside my room I threw fresh underwear, jeans, a T-shirt, and a sweater into an overnight bag. If the crime scene techs had been in here, it didn't show. Everything appeared to be in the not-quite-neat-as-a-pin state I'd left it.

Lieutenant Hawthorne followed me back downstairs and out to the kitchen. A glance at my prep counter showed Gladys Montgomery's recipes still in piles on the stainless steel surface. I felt bad leaving them there unprotected, but had to think Gladys would understand. It wasn't as though I had a choice.

A knock sounded at the kitchen door. The evidence techs both inclined their heads toward the sound, and Detective Hawthorne strode over. He opened the door and said to whoever was on the other side, "This is a crime scene."

A tremulous voice said, "I know."

The detective seemed to relent because he held the storm door open and stepped back to allow a young woman to cross the threshold.

"Don't go any farther than where you are," he ordered. "What's your name and why are you here?"

◈ SIX ◈

I recognized her. It was the not-so-hot waitress who had served Brenda and me last night at the Casa di Pizza. She shook her head so her long, straight hair fell around her shoulders in a glossy wave. I wondered what kind of shampoo and conditioner she used. The cold dry winter air of the North Country always gave me staticky flyaways.

"Piper," the woman said. "Piper Preston. I'm supposed to bring this to Georgie." She reached into her bag and I saw the detective stiffen and put his hand automatically on his sidearm. I resisted the urge to roll my eyes. This girl could barely serve up salad and pizza without help. She couldn't possibly be dangerous.

You've been wrong about people before, that obnoxious little voice in my head piped up. Fine. A little caution wouldn't hurt.

Piper reached farther into her giant purple Coach bag so that her entire arm disappeared into the depths—which was saying something, because she was quite tall and had correspondingly long appendages. What could a young woman of her age possibly need a bag that big for? At least it wasn't carrying a little dog, that I could tell. It seemed to be mostly empty, but she finally came up with a piece of paper.

"I'll take that," Detective Hawthorne said in a voice that would scare the Crypt Keeper. Piper didn't seem to notice, but handed him the paper. He scanned it, turned it over to examine the other side, then held it out to me. "Salad dressing," he said in the same tone he might have said, "Murder."

I reached for it and read the title. Ah. Franco's Thousand Island dressing recipe, the one he'd found in one of the unused upper floors over his restaurant. I scanned the first couple ingredients. As I'd suspected when I'd tasted the dressing, this recipe was a little different from the one we served here. A little thrill ran though me. Was this it? The smoking gun of salad toppings? The Maltese Falcon of the Thousand Islands? The concoction that would force the tour boat guides to change their spiel?

"Thanks for bringing this over," I said to Piper. "And thank Franco for me, will you?" It was all I could do to not pull out a stainless steel bowl and start mixing up a batch right then.

Piper gave her gorgeous hair another toss, then adjusted her creamy white hand-knit hat to the perfect slouchy angle. "No problem. It's nice to get out of the restaurant for a while. I wish I could think of another errand to run." She cut her heavily fringed eyes to Detective Hawthorne. "Uh, can I go now?"

A tiny muscle in his jaw twitched. "Yes," was all he said. Piper threw the straps of her bag up over her shoulder and left.

I folded the photocopied recipe into quarters and put it in my pocket. It would be wrong of me to let it go public before Franco had a chance to take the credit for finding it. But tomorrow, when the Bonaparte House was turned back over to me, there was a salad on my personal menu.

Detective Hawthorne zipped up his jacket and shoved his hands into black leather gloves, then headed for the door. "Till next time," he said.

Was it illegal to throw something at a state trooper? Probably. But he was outside before I could find anything within arm's reach. I donned my jacket, grabbed my purse, and followed him out.

A few minutes later my little blue Honda and I were motoring out of town, headed toward Watertown, the North Country's biggest city, population twenty-five thousand or so. Located just a few miles from Fort Drum, home to twelve thousand Army personnel and their families, Watertown was where most everybody, Army and civilian alike, came to shop. Most of the major retail and restaurant chains were here, but if you couldn't find what you wanted, the next big stop was Syracuse fifty miles farther south.

And if you couldn't find it there, well, you'd probably just order online and have somebody else do the driving.

I pulled into a parking space at the Salmon Run Mall and shut off the engine, which also killed my 1980s music in the middle of a Bruce Springsteen song. In addition to doing some early holiday shopping, I needed to outfit my car for the upcoming winter. Jumper cables were in a plastic milk crate stored in the hatchback, along with deicer. I'd need to pick up a second can to store in the house. If my locks froze, the can in my car would be useless since I wouldn't be able to get to it. My list also contained a case of water bottles. Half a dozen was a good number to keep in the car, opened and with some of the contents poured out so the bottles wouldn't crack when the water inside froze and expanded. A box of protein bars, a new ice scraper and snow brush combination, a couple of bottles of dry gas, an extra hat and gloves, some cat litter—poured under a spinning tire, it would provide enough traction to get moving again on slick ice or snow if I got stuck. I already had a couple of blankets stored back there as well. Winter came early, hit hard, and stayed late this far north, and it paid to be prepared.

My shopping for essentials didn't take long. Since I couldn't go home, I stopped in at the department store, shopped for a while, and picked up a very cute pair of black leather dress boots, along with a cherry red cashmere sweater that was cut a little lower than my normal clothes. A look in the dressing room mirror told me the sweater was flattering and fit me perfectly, and the soft, delicate knitted fabric was darn near irresistible.

Cal would approve, I thought. She'd been trying to unfrump me for years. It wasn't that I didn't care about my appearance. It was just that during the spring and summer, my jobs were so varied at the Bonaparte House, from reservations clerk to supply orderer to line cook, that clothes had to be cool, practical, comfortable, and easily washable. And during the winter, well, clothes had to be warm in my drafty two-hundred-year-old home. So like most everyone else in northern climes, I wore a lot of fleece and flannel.

I paid for the boots and sweater, wincing only slightly at the price as the clerk ran my credit card. I loaded up my arms with bags and headed for the parking lot.

The air was cold, colder than before I'd gone into the mall. My breath came out in a frosty whoosh as I placed my bags in the car, then raced around to the driver's side to turn on the engine and let it warm up. A thin layer of frost had formed on the windshield while I'd been inside. I could let the defroster melt it off, or I could scrape. Since my gloves were currently residing on the passenger seat, scraping was out. I shoved my hands in my pockets and got inside, even though it was no warmer in there yet than it was outside.

Shivers ran through me in waves as I waited. Finally, two circles of clear glass appeared on the windshield, fanning out slowly until a view of the parking lot presented itself. A woman in a long dark blue coat was walking briskly past my car, pulling a fur-trimmed hood up over her head as she did so. I'd only gotten a glimpse of her before the hood went up, but I thought I knew who she was. And I needed to talk to her.

I put the window down a crack and left the motor running as I followed the woman, who was walking at a good clip. Not that I could blame her. Did I mention it was *cold*?

She ducked into a late-model white Beemer, one I'd seen around Bonaparte Bay, just as I caught up. She started when I knocked on the window, but rolled it down halfway.

"Georgie! You shouldn't sneak up on people." She relaxed and gave a little laugh.

"Hi, Lydia. I thought I recognized you. Doing some shopping, like everybody else in the North Country?" Lydia hadn't been carrying any bags. In fact, I hadn't even seen a purse. Well, maybe she was a minimalist and carried only a wallet and phone, which could be stowed in pockets. Good idea, frankly.

Her face darkened as her lips twisted down into a frown. "My new *boss* decided part of my job description was driving to Watertown to buy socks for his dead father. Apparently nothing he has—had—are good enough to be buried in."

I knew I didn't like that little brat, Ben MacNamara, and here was a concrete reason why. Lydia Ames had worked for his father for at least ten years, and instead of giving her the day off when the man died, he sent her on a ridiculous errand. I wondered what would happen to her, whether Junior would keep her on at the law firm, or if she'd even want to stay. It wasn't necessarily easy to find a job in Northern New York, so people tended to stick around, even if they weren't happy. I glanced down at the Beemer. She'd married well—and divorced well—a few years ago and she'd gotten a nice settlement, if rumors were true. Maybe she *could* leave if she wanted to.

"Did you find the socks?" I shivered and pressed my hands farther down in my pockets, hunching my shoulders against the wind, as if that would do any good. "You don't have any bags."

Lydia rolled her eyes. "Penney's doesn't carry the specific brand anymore, so now I have to go to the men's store across town. At least I'm getting paid mileage in addition to my exorbitant salary."

"Will the office be open again soon? I hate to ask, but I need a copy of the Bloodworth Trust file. It's kind of important." The sooner we knew for sure we'd identified all the potential heirs, the sooner I could breathe easier.

She tilted her chin down and looked up at me. "I can't give it to you. You know that."

I blew out a breath. "Yes, I know. It was worth a shot. As I said, it's important to me. What do I have to do to get it?"

"Have Melanie and Liza sign an authorization saying you can pick up a copy of the file. I'm manning—womaning—the office and Junior will be in and out. It'll take me a couple of days to copy everything—some of the original documents are probably old and fragile—and I'll have to get it approved by him, of course. Even if you produce an authorization, I'm just an underling. It's not my place to make decisions of any kind." The frown returned to her face. She reached over and turned the heater on full blast. Her hair blew back over her shoulders. What I wouldn't have given for a little of that heat right about then.

"Thanks. Should it say anything special, or just that they give you permission to release the file to me?"

She rattled off instructions, which seemed easy enough to remember.

"I suppose you all want to know how much money the trust is worth? You already know it will dissolve in February of next year."

"Since the money isn't mine, it doesn't really matter how much there is, does it?" I laughed. My words belied the reality. I was dying to know. In fact, it was a little surprising that Melanie wasn't curious enough to ask herself. But my mother was an oatmeal raisin on a tray of chocolate chip cookies. Odd. She hadn't been back in my life long enough for me to know what she was made of. Or maybe she had asked, already knew, and just chose not to tell me.

"Well, I'm curious myself," Lydia said, echoing my thoughts. "Jim MacNamara always kept the trust file in a locked cabinet in his office. Only he had the key, and he did his own filing on it."

Interesting. Was there some kind of confidentiality

requirement in the trust that would keep even longtime office personnel from accessing the records? It seemed like overkill, frankly, although of course, data security was a big deal these days. Not that it would have been when the trust was created. Just what was in the trust file? I was even more curious than I'd been before.

"The office is still open for now. It'll be a couple days until the medical examiner releases the body and the arrangements are made. Junior's been there dealing with the detectives and the crime scene techs. He's frazzled. This is awful of me to say, but I don't know if he's upset about his father, or if he's worried about actually having to work, now that the law firm is his."

So as I'd assumed, Ben MacNamara would be taking over. "Were Ben and Jim close?" A wet drop, then another, landed on my cheek. Snow.

"Not especially. I think Ben was always closer to his mother. Not surprising, since she babied him, treated him like the Crown Prince of the Kingdom of MacNamara, and still does. But personality-wise, he and Jim were an awful lot alike."

I blinked rapidly as a snowflake landed on my eyelashes. The sky was the dull gray of a Navy battleship, which signaled a storm coming in. Time to wrap this up and get home. Well, not home. Back to my room at the Camelot, at least for tonight. "Where is Ben's mom these days? I never really knew her."

"Rosemary? Last I heard, she was living in the Carolinas with her new husband. She calls Junior on the office phone all the time instead of just calling his cell. I think she gets a snooty thrill out of having her calls go through an underling, also known as me."

"None of my business, but are you planning to stay on?" The snow was picking up. Last question. Even if I'd had more, I would have tabled them for now.

Lydia looked thoughtful. "Honestly, I'm not sure. My house and car are paid for, and I've got money left from my divorce settlement. But I'll stay on for a few months at least. Not for Junior. Jim MacNamara was a player, but I respected him. And a lot of people in Bonaparte Bay were his clients. It's going to take a while for Junior to get up to speed on all our files and he's going to need my help. I can't just walk away and leave everyone in the lurch."

I nodded. Lydia had a work ethic I could relate to. "It's been great talking to you. I'll get you that authorization."

"Drive safely," she said as the window rolled up between us.

The snow was coming fast and furious by the time I got back to my car, which was still running. I shook the loose snow out of my hair and brushed off my coat, again wishing I was wearing one of the two pairs of gloves currently inside the vehicle. I opened the door and got in, instantly grateful for the warm air blasting out of the vents, which would dry me off in no time. I unzipped my coat so my arms were less constricted, buckled up, and reached into one of my shopping bags on the passenger seat for the bar of dark chocolate I knew was there.

Huh? The bag was empty. In fact, all the bags were in disarray, with the contents strewn on the seat, underneath a layer of plastic shopping bags, which was why I hadn't immediately noticed. These bags had not just fallen over and the contents spilled. Somebody had been pawing through them. I checked the backseat. Empty, the same as I'd left it, but the floor mats were askew. I took a deep breath and engaged the lever to pop open the hatchback, bracing myself to go back out into the snow. Yup, the milk crate was overturned and one corner of the carpet covering the spare tire compartment was lifted up. In the ten minutes or so I'd been talking to Lydia just a few yards away, somebody had tossed my car.

◈ SEVEN ◈

Of course, it was my own fault. The car had been running and unlocked. When the weather got cold in the North Country, it was common to do just that. Theft was a risk we took in order to have a warm car to get into.

But I'd done a quick inventory as I surveyed the mess. Nothing appeared to be missing. My purse had been looped over my shoulder as I talked to Lydia; I wasn't quite *that* trusting to leave it in an unlocked vehicle. And other than emergency supplies, there was nothing of value in the car. I shrugged, righted the milk crate, and got back inside. It was probably just someone looking for money, which they weren't going to find. Since there were no ashtrays in cars anymore, I didn't even keep spare change around, preferring instead to just toss it into the bottom of my purse until it got too heavy to lug around.

Other than trespassing, no crime seemed to have been committed, and whoever had done it was either long gone or hidden among the cars in the full parking lot, so there was nothing for me to do except head back to the Bay.

And lock my doors next time.

By the time I reached Route 12, the snow was falling harder and faster and visibility was only a few yards filtered through a descending curtain of white flakes the size of quarters. This kind of wet, heavy snow piled up fast, but I was lucky to get behind a plow. It was slow going, but it was relatively safe, and I traveled along on the layer of chemical salts the plow was spitting out in front of me. The chemicals were tough on cars, causing them to rust out sometimes sooner than the loans were paid off. But replacing cars frequently was one of the costs of living here. We North Country residents complained, but we put up with it.

A set of headlights cut though the falling snow behind me. I couldn't discern the make or model through the whiteness, but in the rearview mirror I could see the headlights gaining on me. "Back off," I said out loud, though of course the driver couldn't hear. The car was clearly traveling too fast, and definitely too close, for these conditions.

I concentrated on the plow and the road ahead. It was all I could do. I couldn't control anyone else's car but my own.

My shoulders tensed and my jaw clenched. As cold as I'd been when I was talking to Lydia, I was now sweating and wished I'd taken my coat off completely instead of just unzipping it. It was hot as the pizza ovens at Franco's in here. I kept my eyes on the road ahead but risked taking one hand off the wheel to adjust the temperature. My face was damp but I didn't dare wipe it.

The headlights in my rearview flashed bright, and I didn't need to turn around to know that the vehicle was only a couple of yards behind my bumper. What the heck was the driver doing? This was insanity. One wrong move by either of us and we'd collide and be off the road.

There didn't seem to be much choice but to keep going. It would be crazy to pull over or take a side road and lose the plow. I moved my jaw from side to side, trying to work the tension loose, leaving a dull ache in the joint in front of each ear. The car was still right on my tail, ironically too close for me to make out any details such as the color or size of the vehicle. And the driver's face was an anonymous blur behind the veil of white. Was someone deliberately trying to rattle me? If so, it was working, but it wasn't actually a great tactic. Messing around on slippery roads was just as dangerous for the mess-er as for the mess-ee, no matter how good a driver someone was.

And then there was the why? Jim MacNamara's murder flashed through my mind. But it made no sense. Sure, he'd been found at my restaurant. But nobody could think I had anything to do with it. My alibi was airtight. The trust? I had no immediate financial interest in it, and it was pretty much common knowledge at this point, with

Melanie in town, so if there was a connection, it escaped me.

The plow continued to spew out chemicals on the road in front of ahead and a wall of snow off to the shoulder. The car continued to bear down on me from behind. I concentrated on my driving.

A set of lights approached, opposite from me in the southbound lane. As it got closer, the black-and-white color scheme of a Jefferson County Sheriff's Department SUV materialized. The driver behind me apparently saw the vehicle too, because the car dropped back, not to what I'd call a safe distance but certainly a more reasonable one. The cruiser passed us, but didn't put on its lights. Up ahead, I could just make out the exit for the village of Theresa (which we pronounced with a soft consonant, like "three"). I was almost home.

My fingers, which had been close to creating dents in the steering wheel, finally relaxed. I stretched and wiggled them, feeling a rush of warmth as the blood returned. I glanced in the rearview again. The car turned off at the Theresa exit. I still couldn't get a good look at it. Once a car is covered with a haze of New York State road salts, it can be tough to figure out even the color. I drew in a deep breath, then another, and returned my attention to the road ahead.

What had just happened? Normally I'd chalk it up to an operator who thought a little too highly of his or her winter driving skills—par for the course in this area. I'd been known to take a few chances myself when I'd been in a hurry. But I had to put it together with the fact that someone had been snooping through my car, and had apparently not found anything worth taking. It all seemed to add up to something, but I didn't know what it was.

I finally arrived, somewhat worse for the wear, at the Camelot. I sorted through my bags, leaving the emergency supplies in the car. Honestly, if someone was in dire enough straits to need to steal an ice scraper and some cat litter, they could have the stuff. The other bags I looped over my arm, then grabbed my purse and braved the snow for the few yards it took me to reach the covered front portico from the parking lot.

Inside, a cheerful, crackly fire on the hearth greeted me. The air was warm and it felt wonderful to be out of the dampness. The clerk behind the counter nodded at me as I lugged my bags and my stress-weary body to my home away from home, Room 16.

I fitted my key into the lock—no magnetic-strip plastic key cards here—but to my surprise, the door snicked open. I immediately went back on high alert. It was possible I, or housekeeping, had not engaged the lock fully when one of us was last in here. But considering the last couple of hours, it paid to be cautious. I gave the door a tap and it swung slowly open, giving a tooth-buzzing creak. Someone was coming in my direction, probably a guest, so I stepped into the room. If something happened, at least the door would be open and the guy would hear me scream.

But everything appeared to be in order. I'd only bought

the barest minimum of clothes and the toiletries from Kinney's drugstore, so other than the room's regular amenities, there wouldn't have been much for a thief to go through. Housekeeping had come in and made the bed, but it was impossible to say if anything else had been touched. I checked the bathroom, the tiny closet, and under the beds. It seemed I was alone.

Room service. All I wanted was room service, a warm bed, and a novel. Romance, not mystery. I'd had enough mystery and intrigue lately to last me a lifetime.

Fifteen minutes later a knock sounded at the door. A waiter I didn't recognize handed me a tray. I handed him a tip and shut the door. Even from under the metal cloche covering the plate, something smelled delicious. When I lifted the cover, my troubles evaporated on a whiff of my dinner, at least temporarily. Bacon, tomato, and three kinds of melted cheese on butter-grilled sourdough bread. A bottle of hard cider and a glass full of ice accompanied the sandwich. *Come to Mommy.*

It was eight a.m. when I finally rolled out of bed—practically midmorning. I pulled back the heavy drapes and looked outside. In one of those magical transformations that I'd seen a thousand times, but still marveled at, the sky was blue, and the sun made the surface of yesterday's snowfall sparkle like an expanse of pavé diamonds. The contrast from yesterday's leaden sky and dense atmosphere made the scene all the more remarkable.

I took a leisurely shower. Plenty of hot water and plenty of water pressure, unlike anything the antiquated plumbing at the Bonaparte House could offer. Maybe next winter I would spend some more of Sophie's money by getting that updated.

An hour later my hotel bill was paid and my car was parked in the employee lot behind the big limestone octagon that was my home and my business. The crime scene tape had been removed, and there was no sign of the techs, so I assumed it was safe to go in. I had to make a couple of trips with the bags from my shopping trip and the coffee and bagel with homemade honey-walnut-raisin cream cheese I'd picked up from the Express-o Bean. I set everything on the counter by the dishwashing station and hung up my coat.

There were a few things on my must-do list for today. It was too early to call Melanie about the authorization— no way would she be up at this time. Her glued-at-the-hip assistant, Caitlyn, probably would be, but I hadn't talked to Melanie in a few days and I needed to bring her up to speed on my conversation with the genealogist. So I dialed Steve Murdoch instead.

"Murdoch Kustom Kontracting, Steve here." Steve sounded tired. I couldn't blame him. He had a lot going on.

"Steve, it's Georgie." I pulled the plastic lid off my caramel double-shot macchiato and slurped a little whipped cream off the top. Yum. No need to get a fancy coffee setup here while the Bean was around. In Bonaparte Bay, each business filled its own symbiotic niche, and for the most part we didn't poach on each other's territory.

"Morning," he said. "You calling to tell me I can go back to work?"

"Looks like it." I hesitated, not wanting to pry, but a little worried about him. "You okay?"

He gave a soft laugh. "Yeah, I'm fine. Sober, thanks to you, and no thanks to my wife." A sigh came through the receiver. "Sorry. This can't be about her. It's all about me. My choices. But you don't want to hear about this. I'm going to be shorthanded without Russ, so your restrooms might take me a little longer than we'd originally discussed."

"It's no difference to me, honestly." Actually, I was a little relieved. With Russ behind bars, at least for now, I wouldn't have to worry about him trying to sabotage the project and I wouldn't have to listen to his snarky comments. Still, my guilt-meter ticked up a notch. I wasn't entirely sure the authorities had the correct murderer in custody. But I had nothing concrete to base that on, so for now there was no point in saying anything.

"No worries. I'll have you open in time for Thanksgiving. Don't look for me today, though. I wasn't sure how long the restaurant would be closed to me, so I told Liza I'd go and look at some things she needs done at the castle."

An idea popped into my head. "You wouldn't happen to have room for a passenger, would you?" Melanie could hardly avoid me if I was right there in front of her. And

Liza was sure to have something delicious on the lunch menu. It was hard to work up much enthusiasm for cooking just for myself.

"Sure. Meet me at the docks at eleven. Dress warm. There won't be many more days we can get over to the island safely." He rang off.

My prior suspicions about Steve flitted through my mind. But the police must have checked him out due to his wife's connection to Jim MacNamara. And he must have passed, because otherwise they'd have him in custody. I was worrying needlessly. It didn't take long for me to plan out my Thanksgiving menu and fire off an order to my suppliers. I threw in a load of laundry, then returned to the kitchen.

Gladys's recipes still sat in disarray where I'd left them on the prep counter. The project would need to be started again from scratch, since the crime scene techs had clearly been shuffling through the random bits of paper. I began to sort again, separating the recipes into categories. So far, the pile I called "Casseroles Made with Canned Cream Soups" was the biggest. Hardly surprising. Gladys was a 1960s housewife. As unglamorous as it was, I was, myself, guilty of a hankering for an occasional tuna noodle casserole with a crispy top crust of crushed potato chips.

Finishing the sort of what was on the counter, I reached into the shoe box for another handful and spread out the contents. A small envelope among the grease-spotted index cards and yellowing newspaper clippings caught my eye.

"Formica Cleaner" was penciled on the outside in a spidery hand. The flap was unsealed and I lifted it gingerly. The envelope contained a slightly yellowed piece of paper, folded into a square. I left the paper inside and put the envelope into the "Miscellaneous" pile, along with "Hair Conditioner" (a mix of eggs and mayonnaise, yuck) and "Hand Cream" (no idea what some of those ingredients were).

After an hour, I sat back and raised my arms over my head in a stretch. About two-thirds of the recipes were still in the box, but the piles on the counter had grown. I'd made a good dent and I was having fun. But it was time to go meet Steve at the docks.

❖ EIGHT ❖

My teeth chattered as I made my way over the side of the boat, none too gracefully due to the big puffy parka I was wearing. Steve offered me a hand, then led me into the little pilot house, a five-by-five-foot-square room situated toward the bow of the boat. I went inside and sat down on a cushioned bench. It was none too warm, but compared to being out in the frosty wind, it was almost tropical.

"Welcome aboard *Witch of November*," Steve said.

"Do you change the name every month, or is it just a coincidence?"

Steve laughed. "No, it would be too complicated to change the marine registration and have the name restenciled on the stern that often." He throttled up. "Just sit back and relax."

Relax. Right. While I'd recently learned to drive a boat, out of necessity, I would not have had the confidence or experience to take one out myself this late in the season, so I was both slightly nervous and very grateful for the ride. And I couldn't help thinking about the song the boat's name had come from. Seemed like bad luck to name a boat from a line in a song about a tragic shipwreck. But maybe it meant something else. Maybe his wife, Jennifer, had been born in November.

A light chop on the water made the ride a little bumpy. Later in the winter, the river would freeze over, becoming a layer of ice over liquid water beneath, where the fish and other aquatic creatures somehow survived the frigid temperatures. It was common for the air above to reach twenty degrees below zero, and sometimes it went even colder. But right now the water was clear of ice.

"So," I said, raising my voice to be heard above the whine of the twin outboard engines. "What does Liza have you doing at the Spa today that can't wait till spring?"

Steve smiled. "There's no shortage of repairs and maintenance that need to be done in a property that old and that large. But she wants me to inspect the integrity of the building and the roof, on the castle and on all the outbuildings. It'll take me a couple of hours, as long as the snow didn't stick. I hope you don't need to get back for anything right away."

Er, no. I'd braved it out this morning, but a murder had been committed in my home and business. I wasn't all that eager to go back, truth be told. "Nope. You take your time."

Steve assessed me. "I wouldn't want to spend too much time there alone either. Have you got someone to come and stay with you?" He was matter-of-fact, not looking for an invitation.

"Oh, I'll be fine." *Woman up, Georgiana Gertrude.* I'd have to make peace with staying there soon. Might as well make it now as later. "I'll lock myself in my room tonight."

"Well, we've got spare rooms now that my two older sons are off on their own. One of which I'm currently occupying." Ouch. His brow furrowed. "On second thought, if I were you, I'd stay in the house where a murder was committed instead of mine right now. It'll be pleasanter."

Poor Steve. He was such a decent guy, and his wife had dumped all over him. I wished Jennifer were here right now so I could give her a piece of my mind. But of course, it was none of my business. My new mantra.

"Don't worry about me." I hoped my words were convincing. "The . . . cleaning company has apparently been in and taken care of . . . everything. It's all gone."

Steve stared off into the distance, his thoughts clearly elsewhere. "Uh, oh, yeah." He gave his head a small shake. "Almost there," he said.

Ahead of us I could see the turrets and peaks of the Valentine Island Spa, my best friend and newfound cousin's ultra-exclusive resort. It was not the only castle in the

Thousand Islands, Boldt and Singer castles being more famous and open to tours, but Castle Grant was impressive all the same. Liza had inherited the property in a state of disrepair fifteen years ago, and by hard work and acute business savvy had brought it back to its former glory. Catering to the rich and famous, the Spa was a popular place for Hollywood actresses and billionaire trophy wives to come and lose a little weight, get some expert skin care with Liza's proprietary homemade products, or hide out in luxury while they recovered from plastic surgery.

Right now, the Spa was home to my mother, television actress Melanie Ashley. Someday, I hoped, we might have a good enough relationship that I could tell her how ridiculous her stage name was. For now, I just called her Melanie. We were still figuring out our relationship but I thought it might work out. Someday.

Steve pulled up at the dock and cut the engines. He tossed a rope over a cleat on the dock and pulled us in close, then secured the bow and stern with a few deft sailors' knots. We climbed up onto the boards, which seemed to be made of some kind of composite decking material, not wood. She'd have to pull the dock soon, or it would be frozen in until spring.

Steve offered me an arm and we made our way up the stone walkway to the big double doors of the castle. He opened the door and gestured me in. "Tell Liza I'm here and looking at the outbuildings and the exterior while the light is still good."

"Of course." I ducked inside before any more cold air blasted in. I shuddered to think about the heating bill for this place, though by this time of year there were only a handful of guests, so Liza had shut down and blocked off most of the rooms to conserve energy. Even so, it had to be expensive, if the bills for the Bonaparte House were anything to go by.

The big entrance hall had a tile floor done in an intricate black and white pattern. The walls of the round space were wainscoted in oak, which had darkened over the years to a rich deep brown. Overhead, a massive crystal chandelier sparkled over a round oak table set with a large silver bowl filled with bright green apples and sprigs of rosemary. Very pretty. And it wasn't like Liza could get fresh flowers this time of year. The gardens were long cut back and covered for the winter.

Liza came from behind one of the oak doors that lined the space to greet me, elegant as always with her blond hair pulled back into a ponytail and understated makeup on her flawless skin. She wore a long-sleeved rust-colored sweater over black leggings and knee-high black boots with bronze buckles and a medium-sized heel. I felt a bit, as I always did around her, like a roadside daisy next to a hothouse orchid. But my general unstylishness never seemed to bother Liza. She loved me anyway.

"I am so glad to see you," she said, giving me a hug. "Come on in and warm up." She took my coat and hung it up in a closet concealed behind one of the other oak doors, then handed me a pair of slippers. I kicked off my boots and put on the warm slippers gratefully. "Come on out to the kitchen. There's soup and salad. I'm down to a skeleton crew so I can't serve you in the dining room."

"That's fine, of course. You know I'm not fussy."

"And I know you're never happier than when you're in a kitchen."

She knew me so well. We traipsed down twisty corridors for what seemed like forever but was only a few minutes at most. Like most houses of this size and importance, the kitchens were far away from the living and entertaining areas so as not to disturb family and guests with such mundane details as where their food was being prepared. The last hallway finally opened up into a large, bright room with what seemed like miles of stainless steel counters, some with cabinets underneath, and punctuated by the occasional sink and a huge commercial range. Dozens of copper-bottomed pots and pans hung from black iron racks suspended from the high ceiling. It was similar to the kitchen at the Bonaparte House—if the Bonaparte House were pumped up on steroids. And yet, though I'd never say this to Liza, I preferred the smaller, cozier atmosphere of my restaurant, with its mismatched cookware and white, utilitarian walls.

I parked myself at a stool at one of the counters. Liza placed a steaming bowl of velvety orange soup in front of me. "Butternut squash?" I asked, hoping I was right.

"Yes. It's vegan." She set down another bowl in front of me, this one containing crispy onions, which I spooned on top of the soup, then took a bite. The combination of sweet, savory, and crunchy hit every right note with me, making me forget that it was healthy. A Perrier with a twist of lemon, and a simple green salad with toasted pecans and a sprinkle of bleu cheese (decidedly not vegan) in a light vinaigrette, completed the meal.

Liza sat down across from me and tucked into her soup. Her trim frame belied a healthy appetite. Of course, she owned this spa and had personal trainers and state-of-the-art fitness equipment available at any time during the regular season, so she could eat pretty much whatever she wanted.

"How's Melanie?" I couldn't decide whether I liked the soup or the salad better, so I alternated bites. "She's not returning my calls."

Liza looked at me with her big blue eyes, then caught her lower lip between her teeth. "You know I value confidentiality here above all things."

What was coming? I had no idea, but braced myself. "Yes, of course. Your clients expect and deserve that." Had I just said that? What if she decided not to tell me now?

"Well, for any other client, I would never divulge this without express permission. But now that we know we're all family, that changes things a bit." She stirred her soup as she spoke. "Melanie made me promise not to tell you this, and I only agreed because she swore she'd tell you herself."

Now my curiosity was piqued. "I have no idea what you're about to say."

"Oh, it's not that big a deal, really. She and Caitlyn have been sick for a couple of days. Some stomach bug. So I moved my few remaining spa guests over to another wing and left the two of them to recuperate privately."

I relaxed. So my mother and her assistant had tummy troubles. Big deal. "Why wouldn't one of them tell me? I mean, everybody is under the weather once in a while."

"Well, there's an . . . intestinal component to this bug. I don't think it's a secret so much as it's just . . . nasty, and Melanie doesn't want to talk about it."

A little snort escaped my lips. "She probably doesn't want somebody reporting it to the tabloids. You know how they love her."

"That was my take on it too. Don't tell her I told you, but if you were to, say, head for her suite without my knowing about it, you could check on her." She forked up some salad and a pecan fell back onto the plate.

"Yes, if you don't mind, I may just do a bit of exploring of the castle after lunch." I smiled. "Oh, by the way. I ran into Lydia Ames yesterday. You know, Jim MacNamara's assistant? We need to get a copy of the trust documents to see if there's any kind of genealogy in any of the files."

Liza looked thoughtful. "You know, that's a good idea. Let's put this to bed once and for all so we can all breathe easier. The last thing we need is another cousin popping out of the woodwork and ending up dead, all because of some hundred-year-old legal maneuverings by a bitter, vindictive old man who wanted to stick it to his heirs." She tapped the handle end of her fork on the counter.

"And frankly"—she glanced around, even though we'd been alone the entire time we'd been here in the kitchen—"I'd like to know how much money we are talking about. I'm pretty sure Steve Murdoch is going to come back in here and tell me that my roof needs repairs and all my masonry needs repointing."

I whistled softly. "That's going to set you back some."

"It will cost a fortune," she said matter-of-factly. "Probably in the six figures. I've got money, of course. You know I don't live extravagantly, and my clients pay extremely well to stay here. But I'd hoped to build an indoor pool in the spring, and maybe hire a celebrity chef next summer, just to shake things up."

"A celebrity chef?" I leaned forward, eager to find out more. "Which one do you have in mind?"

"Oh, maybe that tall, gorgeous blond one—the Australian?"

Brilliant. I knew I liked Liza for a reason. "Get him, and I'll leave Sophie and Dolly in charge of the Bonaparte House and camp out here for a week."

She grinned. "Yes, I'm pretty sure my clients would appreciate his . . . cooking."

Footsteps sounded from the direction of the back door. "Hi, Steve," Liza said over my shoulder. "Come on in and have something to eat?" He was back early, which might mean nothing—or everything—needed to be replaced or repaired.

He looked over the remains of our lunch and smiled ruefully. "That looks, uh, delicious. But no."

"How about some stew made from grass-fed beef and organic potatoes?" Liza inquired playfully, giving her head a little tilt that caused her ponytail to swing. Interesting.

"Well, if you put it that way . . ." He plunked himself down at the counter. "We can talk about what I found outside."

Three seemed to be a crowd, and it was time I went upstairs to see my mother anyway. "Liza, Steve, I'll leave you to talk about, uh, whatever. Send me a text when you're ready to leave and I'll meet you in the foyer."

I made my way back through the maze of hallways and to the grand carved staircase that led to the guest rooms and suites on the second floor. Because my mother had been staying here, recuperating from surgery for several weeks, the route through this part of the castle was firmly embedded in my memory banks. I went down the long upstairs hallway, past the Clover Room, where I stayed when I spent the night here, and stopped two doors down. I took a deep breath, and knocked on the door. When no one answered, I knocked again, then gingerly opened the door and stepped inside.

This two-bedroom suite had creamy white walls and was decorated in shades of rose and gold. Elegant, feminine, and pretty. I crossed the sitting area and knocked on my mother's bedroom door. There was the sound of movement, then a weak voice said, "Come in."

Melanie lay propped up on about eight pillows under a pink puffy comforter. She was wearing a satin bed jacket, a thing I'd never seen outside of old Doris Day movies. Her normally big hair was flat on one side, as if she'd been lying on it, and her grayish pallor confirmed it—she really was ill.

If she was surprised to see me, she didn't show it.

"Melanie, why didn't you tell me you were sick?"

"And if I had, what would you have done? Come over here and caught whatever this plague is from me?"

She had a point. But still, she could have at least taken my calls and let me know.

"Where's Caitlyn?"

Melanie sat up and took a sip of water from a crystal glass on the night table. "She's in her room with the same illness." That was hardly a surprise. Caitlyn was on duty with Melanie twenty-four/seven. She'd never taken a day off, let alone a vacation, in all the months I'd known her.

"I won't stay long, and I'll check on her before I leave."

Melanie nodded weakly, then looked as though she might be about to throw up. There was a basin at the ready on the floor by the bed, I noted with relief. "Can I get you anything? Some ginger ale maybe, or some crackers?"

She did a dry heave, which made me feel a little queasy myself. "No, thanks," she said when she recovered. "Liza either comes herself or sends somebody"—another dry heave—"to check on us every couple of hours."

"Where's your cell phone?"

Melanie looked at me blankly. "What?"

"Your cell phone."

She pointed to the drawer in the night table. "In there."

I retrieved the phone to make sure she had charged it. The battery was half full. I plugged it in and set it on the night table. "Keep this out, right here, not in the drawer. Then if you need to call someone, you can."

She nodded, and her eyes drifted closed, then opened again slowly. I hated to ask her to do anything when she was so sick, but this couldn't wait any longer. I reached into my bag and pulled out the authorization form I'd written and printed off back at the Bonaparte House. "Mel—"

"Don't call me Mel," she whispered, then prepared to doze off again.

"Fine. *Melanie*. Sheldon Todd, the genealogist, needs to see some documents out of the Bloodworth Trust file so he can finish up his work. You need to sign this so I can get copies made. You understand what I'm asking you?" This was probably illegal, no matter how you looked at it. She was clearly not of sound body, and her mind was wandering. But it had to be done.

"Jim . . . he's dead. In your restaurant."

The news was a couple of days old, so it shouldn't have been a surprise that she knew. I sighed. "Yes, I found the body. They've arrested Russ Riley, Dolly's son, who used to work at the Bonaparte House?"

Her chin dropped toward her chest again. "Be . . . careful. I'll sign."

She scrawled her name on the line I indicated. I folded the paper in half and stuck it back into my bag. Now I just needed Liza's signature and I could get this ball rolling.

"Thanks, Melanie," I said, brushing a lock of hair back

from her sweaty brow. "I should fax this in and stay with you till you're on the mend."

"No. You go. I'll be okay in a day or so." I pulled the comforter up around her neck as she settled down into a prone position.

"If you're not significantly better tomorrow, I'll have Liza call in Dr. Phelps. Maybe he'll make a house call for a medical emergency. You don't want to get dehydrated, so keep drinking."

"Yes, Mom." Her lips curved up into a wan smile. "Check on Caitlyn. Call me tomorrow." She dozed off.

I stared at her, wondering how she'd picked up this sickness on an island where no one else seemed to be ill. At least Liza hadn't mentioned anyone else, and I knew it had been a couple of weeks since Melanie had been on the mainland. Not that I understood anything other than the basics about disease transmission. Maybe this particular strain of bug had a long incubation period, and she'd been exposed to it weeks ago.

Should I stay? It was tempting, and I was worried about Melanie. It had been a long time since I'd seen anyone that sick. But I really did have to get this authorization over to Lydia and I wasn't sure if a fax copy would be sufficient, or if she'd need the original. Liza was keeping an eye on Melanie and Caitlyn, and I trusted she would let me know if their conditions worsened.

I left Melanie's door open behind me, and looked in on Caitlyn. Her tiny frame was dwarfed by the king-size bed, just her head visible on the pillow. Her black-framed hipster glasses were on the nightstand next to a cup of water, and a basin identical to the one in Melanie's room lay on the floor. She was out cold, but since she seemed to be breathing, there was no need to disturb her. A little twinge of maternal sympathy rippled through me. Caitlyn wasn't much older than my daughter. I wondered if Caitlyn had a mother or other family I should call. I could only hope that wouldn't be necessary and tomorrow would be a better day for both her and my mother.

I made my way back downstairs. I texted Liza, and she told me to come to her office. When I arrived, Steve was sitting in an armchair across from her desk. She appeared to be writing him a check.

"Just as I thought," she said ruefully. "Repointing and a new roof. I could buy a whole new house on the mainland for what this is costing me." Liza looked over at Steve and smiled as she said it. He smiled back at her. She ripped the check along the perforations and handed it to him. "Here's your down payment, balance due when the work is done next spring, as we discussed."

He folded the check and zipped it into a pocket on his fleece coat. "I'll do the calculations and get the supplies ordered and delivered here before the snow flies again. We can store the materials in the carriage house, right?"

"Carriage house, boat house, pick an outbuilding. It doesn't matter to me."

Steve rose and held out a hand to Liza. "Good to see you again, and thanks for the business."

The business. I didn't like the thought that popped into

my head. With Jim MacNamara's death, the development project out at Silver Lake was in limbo. And Steve had had the contract to build those luxury waterfront camps. He was out a lot of money. I hoped he wasn't scamming Liza by telling her the castle needed more work than it really did. But that was hardly a suspicion I could voice without concrete evidence to back it up.

"Georgie, are you ready to go? I'll meet you at the boat." He left.

Liza watched him go, a thoughtful expression on her face. "He's cute," she finally said.

"Cute, but still married," I reminded her.

She waved her hand. "Pish. If he and Jennifer reconcile after what she did to him, I'll eat one of my Ferragamo sandals."

"Liza, before I go, I need you to do something for me."

"Of course." She closed up the checkbook and put it into a drawer, then locked it.

"I need you to sign this authorization, so I can get a copy of the trust documents. For the genealogist."

She took the paper I handed to her, read it over, and nodded. She pulled out a pen and signed her name. "I asked Jim MacNamara for this information a couple of weeks ago, but he never got back to me."

Lydia hadn't said anything about that. But of course, she might not know. If MacNamara kept the file in a locked drawer and had the only key, it stood to reason that he wouldn't tell her about Liza's request. Now I was more curious than ever to see that file.

"So you think Jim's son, Ben, might be more responsive?"

"Let's hope so. And while we're hoping, let's hope for multiple millions in that trust. It's going to be an expensive year." She handed the paper back to me. "A very expensive year."

❖ NINE ❖

Steve dropped me at the docks. There was no time like the present, so I didn't stop at the Bonaparte House but walked right on to the offices of MacNamara and Mac-Namara. Or just MacNamara, singular, now. Lydia was sitting at her desk, typing away. She nodded toward an interior office door. "Junior's in there," she whispered.

I handed her the authorization. "Here you go. I know you've got your hands full, but I'd appreciate anything you could do to expedite this."

"I'll try," she said. "But it'll depend on Junior giving me the go-ahead. And of course, I've never seen the file, so I have no idea how big it is or how long it will take to copy."

The interior door burst open and James Benjamin MacNamara Jr. stepped into the outer office. He stared at me. "Can she help you?" he said, pointing at Lydia.

"I'm Georgie Nikolopatos. From the Bonaparte House? I'm so sorry about your father."

He ran his fingers through his perfectly barbered short brown hair and frowned. "You . . . found him." His voice was tight, forced out as if an unseen hand were putting pressure on his throat. If he was experiencing any emotion other than agitation, which was rolling off him in currents, it was hidden under a well-schooled preppy demeanor.

I gulped, remembering the skewer—my skewer—sticking out of Jim's back, and felt a wave of sympathy and revulsion. I hadn't been to prep school to learn to squelch my feelings. "Yes. I found him. I—hope he didn't suffer."

"According to the medical examiner's preliminary reports, Dad died pretty much instantaneously after that bastard Riley stabbed him. The skewer pierced his heart." His face took on a purplish cast. "He killed him over hunting land. *Hunting land.* As if anyone else couldn't just come along right now and offer Old Lady Turnbull money for the property and he'd lose it anyway. The idiot. And Dad was poised to make some serious money on that deal."

I wondered how much of that money Junior expected to share, then chastised myself. The young man had just lost his father. Grief made people act in unusual ways. Although my gut feeling was that Ben MacNamara was a spoiled, entitled brat.

Lydia looked at me, then at Ben. "Georgie and her family need a copy of the Bloodworth Trust file. She brought an authorization from her mother and Liza Grant."

Junior stared at me. "Why do you need that? You'll all

see it when it vests in February." He picked up a paperclip off Lydia's desk and began to twist it into an unusable shape, then back again.

Grief-stricken or no, Junior was getting on my nerves. And that response was suspicious. "My mother and my cousin are your clients regarding this trust, and they want me to look at that file. I am also your client, because you are handling my divorce. So maybe you'd like to lose all three of us? I'm certain I can find a lawyer in Watertown to represent us in both these matters and then you'll be turning over that file anyway. What's in it that you don't want me to see?"

My question hit home, as I'd intended it to. Lydia shot me an amused look, which I hoped, for her sake, Ben didn't see. Ben slumped into one of the visitor's chairs and put his face in his hands. Lydia's smile turned into an expression of mild surprise.

Ben looked up. "Look, I'm going to level with you."

I wasn't so sure about that. My truth-o-meter was ticking up into the Horse Apples zone. "Yes?"

He took a deep breath. "My father was the only one who ever handled the Bloodworth file, and my grandfather and great-grandfather before him always handled it personally, to my knowledge. I guess Dad figured since the trust was going to vest and dissolve in a few months, there was no point in bringing me up to speed on it. I've never even seen the file, so I couldn't hide anything from you if I wanted to." Ben's fingers gripped the armrests.

"And?" I had no idea what was coming next.

"Well, uh, the file was always kept in a locked cabinet in his office. I think he kept other personal papers there too, which I'm going to have to go through eventually. And he always kept the key on him, and as far as I know, there was only one. But his key ring wasn't recovered from his body or at the crime scene. I know, because I asked for it and that Detective Hawthorne told me there were no keys."

So the killer had presumably taken Jim MacNamara's keys. That could mean anything. Russ had a predilection for taking cars on joyrides, stinking up the interior with his Akwesasne Mohawk Reservation discount cigarettes. If he had committed the murder, of which I still wasn't completely convinced, he could have taken the keys and hidden them somewhere or discarded them when he was done. The killer—whoever it was—could have wanted the keys for any number of purposes. To gain access to this office. To gain access to Jim's home. To find something. To destroy something. Without more information, this was all just speculation.

"Okay," I said. "The keys are gone. So you just call a locksmith and have him or her open the cabinet, then I can get what I need." I softened. "Look, Ben, I know this is a tough time for you. But you've got obligations now. Your dad would have wanted you to step up to the plate, otherwise he wouldn't have brought you into the family law firm." I hoped I was right about that, and Jim hadn't just brought Ben in out of obligation, or because he'd paid for Ben's law school and wanted him to work off the tuition.

Lydia's eyebrows rose and she gave me an almost

imperceptible nod of approval. She'd probably wanted to say something like that to him for years, but never dared. But I was paying him, he wasn't paying me, and I was almost old enough to be his mother, so I felt entitled to say more or less what I wanted.

Ben stared at me, clearly unused to being given orders. But he wasn't angry or defensive. He just looked . . . relieved? "Uh, yeah. Good idea. Lyds, can you find a locksmith?"

"Socks, locks, I can do it all," she said, and tapped at her keyboard. "Don't forget you're supposed to go meet with Clive at the Bay Funeral Home at four." She clicked at her mouse. "Eureka. There's no locksmith in Bonaparte Bay, but there's one in the area. I'll give him a call. I assume as long as the price seems reasonable I can book him?"

Ben nodded. "Thanks, Lyds." I wondered how many times in his short career he'd said *thank you* to Lydia Ames.

Just as Lydia was picking up the phone, the front door opened and a rush of cold air and a whiff of expensive-smelling perfume preceded a woman, who stepped over the threshold.

Jennifer Murdoch.

She unzipped her North Face parka and shook out her long mane of expertly highlighted hair. Having just had the process done myself, I knew she'd spent a small fortune on it. She had at least three subtly blended colors that looked perfectly natural yet too perfect to be natural, if such a thing were possible. Her posture was erect, and I just knew she had a flat stomach and long, lean muscles under her well-fitting clothes, likely from hours of Pilates and yoga.

Jennifer marched over to Ben and shoved her long manicured nail toward him, stopping just short of his chest. "I need to get into your father's house."

Three sets of eyes stared at her. Three mouths were speechless. Ben came around first. Maybe he wasn't as hopeless as I'd thought. "Excuse me?" he said. "Do I know you?"

Jennifer's eyes narrowed, but she lowered her arm. "Don't play coy with me, James Benjamin. You know I was seeing your father."

"How does Steve feel about that?" My response was automatic. I liked Steve. But the little doubt that had been niggling at me resurfaced. Steve Murdoch had just as much reason to want Jim MacNamara dead as did Russ Riley. Maybe more, since his family was threatened. Although why anyone would risk their freedom to kill over this high-maintenance shrew was beyond me. *Witch of November*, indeed.

She turned to me and glared. "You. You have a reputation for sticking your nose in where it doesn't belong."

Well. If people I cared about needed my help, I would continue to stick my nose in anywhere I pleased.

"If you don't want me involved, why are you having this conversation in front of me?" My voice dripped sweetness like a fresh square of baklava. I saw Lydia put her hand to her mouth, clearly trying not to laugh.

Ben's lawyer training kicked in. "What do you want, Ms. Murdoch? I have an appointment shortly, so please get to the point."

Her eyes narrowed again, to the extent I wondered if she could actually see anything through the lids. "I told you, I need to get into your father's house. Now."

"Have you been past the house? It's a crime scene." Ben folded his arms across his chest. "You can't go in until the scene is released."

She blew out a sigh. "I know that, you little snot. But they'll let you in, and I figured I could go with you."

Whoa. I actually thought Ben was a bit of a snot myself, but if she wanted something from him, calling him that was probably not the best way to go about getting it.

Ben raised his eyebrows. "Do you know why crime scenes are sealed, Ms. Murdoch? It's to keep people who don't belong there from contaminating any evidence that might be present. By the way, I suppose you've been questioned by the police?"

Her face darkened. "Yes, and my alibi checks out." Her features cleared as an idea seemed to dawn. "If you won't get me in, then you can get what I need for me. It'll only take a minute."

"If I were to do this for you, what would I be looking for?" Ben was maybe a better lawyer than I'd given him credit for. He hadn't outright turned her down in an effort to keep her talking.

She leaned toward him. "There's a, um, video camera. In the nightstand drawer. It's mine, and I want it back."

Double whoa. If she wanted it that badly, it was safe to assume there were more than videos of her kids on the machine.

A muscle began to tic in Ben's jaw. "Ms. Murdoch. Are you suggesting that I remove evidence from a crime scene? I could—no, *would*—be disbarred for that. Now, if there's nothing else, as I told you, I have an appointment. So it's time for you to be going."

Her face purpled. "Don't you care about your father's reputation?"

Ben smiled. "My father was a grown man who made his own choices. Clearly some choices were not as smart as other ones." He looked at her pointedly.

She stuck that finger back toward his chest. "You listen to me, kid. I want that camera. I promise you will be sorry you ever crossed me," she hissed. The door slammed behind her.

We looked at one another. "Ten to one," Ben said, "the cops have already found it and are watching the tape over coffee right now. Lyds, go ahead and call that locksmith."

"I'll call you when the copies are ready," Lydia said to me. She picked up the phone and dialed.

Ben was already putting on his topcoat, presumably to head out to his meeting with Clive at the funeral home, which was my signal to leave as well. "Thanks," I said, shrugging into my coat and putting on my hat and gloves.

We parted ways on the front stoop. It was only a couple of blocks to the funeral home, and Ben went off on foot.

I went in the other direction, toward the Bonaparte House.

When I reached the parking lot around back, I hesitated. The back door with its squeaky hinge loomed above me. The huge stone octagon house always seemed friendly and welcoming to me, even through the events of a few months ago. But Ben's reminder to me of how his father had died made me leery of going inside. *It's your home.* Yes, it was for now at least, until my mother-in-law, Sophie, decided to up and sell it out from under me, or threw me out because I was divorcing her son.

The sky was gray and overcast, which only added to the gloomy unappeal of the Bonaparte House. Maybe I wasn't ready to go back yet. I decided to give myself a few more hours, then if I still felt creeped out, I could go back to the Camelot for the night.

My car started right up, for which I said a little prayer of thanks to the Car Battery Gods. Between November and April, due to the cold climate, it wasn't always a given that one's car would start. As the car warmed up, I dialed my cell phone with slightly numb fingers. "Dolly? You home? Can I come out for a visit?"

Her cough started up again. When she got it under control, she said, "Come on over. There's scalloped potatoes and ham for dinner. Harold did the cooking. I ain't feeling so good. But I supervised and pulled a pie out of the freezer."

"Need anything from the drugstore? I'll be right over."

◈ TEN ◈

Dolly lived just outside of town, so the trip was short. Her place was one of a row of houses that lined a short street. Behind the houses was a big hayfield, now covered in snow, and beyond that was a copse of dense woods that obscured Silver Lake from view. I kept on driving. A glance at the sky told me that maybe fifteen minutes of light were left, and I wanted to see the Silver Lake property for myself. The Tyvek wrap was still flapping in the wind on the enormous unfinished garage Russ Riley had constructed last summer between Dolly's house and his own. The place was quiet, and I wondered who was taking care of Russ's half-dozen beagles while he was in jail. And I wondered if he'd ever be able to use that enormous garage for hanging his more-than-strictly-legal haul of deer.

Half a mile past Russ's house I turned left onto Silver

Lake Road. Ruby Turnbull's farmhouse stood by itself, a two-story building made of pale beige stone, probably built before the Civil War. A huge weathered wooden barn on a rough rock foundation lay behind the house, flanked by smaller outbuildings in various states of repair. Last I heard, Mrs. Turnbull, who had to be in her eighties, was still tending her own few cows and chickens, and raising a vegetable garden every summer. She drove into town in her ancient Ford pickup for breakfast once in a while. Why now, after all these years, was she ready to sell off the Silver Lake frontage? If she'd been planning to move south, she would have done it by now.

I slowed and turned left again, this time onto a dirt path. A sign in front of me said, "Seasonal Road. Not Maintained After December 1." Thankfully, it was only November, and a plow and/or sander had been here before me. Otherwise I never would have risked this trip with my compact car. The woods on either side of the road were covered in a thick mix of hardwood trees. A stump here and there showed that someone had been cutting firewood, a common way to heat homes in the North Country, wood being cheap and plentiful.

The road twisted and turned, following the natural ridges and hills of the terrain, until it finally ended at a level spot with a plowed turnaround. A beautiful expanse of lake opened up in front of me. There were seasonal camps on the other end, small utilitarian one- or two-story cabins, in stark contrast to the elaborate Victorian mansions just a few miles away on the St. Lawrence

River. But where I stood now, the woods and shore and water were undisturbed. Pristine.

I could understand why someone would want a vacation home overlooking this lovely bit of nature.

I could understand why someone else might not want that lovely bit of nature to change.

If it were up to me, though it pained me to think it, I'd have to side with Russ on this one.

The car was still warm as I got back in and headed back out the way I'd come, grateful for my snow tires on the small hills that had to be climbed, driving slowly to be sure the car stayed on the road on the sharp curves.

Just as dusk fell, I rolled to a stop in Dolly's driveway, behind her metallic green Ford LTD. She hadn't driven it since the snowfall, because it was covered with a couple inches of white stuff. Her lawn ornaments were put away for the winter, but she had a silver foil Christmas tree set up on the covered front porch. The blue lights twinkled, and the silver gleamed against it. Dolly loved anything shiny, sparkly, and bright.

A chorus of muffled yips and barks sounded behind the blue-painted door. Russ's dogs, no doubt. "Shuddup!" came a male voice as the door opened. "Not you, Georgie. Come on in where it's warm."

Six or seven small brown and white dogs with floppy ears rushed toward me. Dolly's live-in boyfriend, Harold, ordered, "Down!" and herded them toward a side room. He slammed the door before any of the beasts could escape, then brushed his hands on his faded jeans. He took my coat and hung it on a coat tree just inside the front door. Not only would I be warm inside, I would be sweating. Thanks to a woodstove combusting away, it was over eighty degrees in here. "Sorry about the animals. Russ's dogs, you know."

"Hey, Harold. That's okay." I lowered my voice. "How's Dolly? That cough of hers has me a little worried." I handed him the six-pack and bottle of wine I'd picked up in town.

Harold's weathered face wrinkled into a frown. "I've been after her to go see Doc Phelps. She won't listen. Maybe you can try? I'll go put these in the fridge." He inclined his head toward the living room. "She's in there. Go on and sit down. Supper'll be ready in fifteen minutes."

Dolly was sitting in a green leather recliner, wrapped in a brightly colored granny square afghan. "Long time no see," she said, pointing the remote control at the television and turning down the volume, but leaving the screen on.

"I heard there was pie, and I couldn't stay away."

She emitted what must have been a laugh, which immediately sent her into a fit of coughing. Her trademark high blond hairdo, however, barely moved. I observed her closely. Clearly she was not suffering from whatever Melanie and Caitlyn had, and she wasn't acutely sick, but her general appearance told me she might be soon if she didn't take care of herself.

"Dolly, will you let me call the doctor and make an appointment for you? I'll drive you if Harold can't."

She waved a hand in the air. "Don't worry about me. I'll be fine."

I wasn't so sure about that. This didn't look like an ordinary cold. She'd smoked for thirty years before giving it up, and she'd almost certainly done some major damage to her lungs. At the very least, especially with winter already here, she should be checked out for bronchitis or pneumonia. I would have to be more subtle to get her to agree to a doctor's visit; that much was clear.

"Any news about Russ?" No need to be subtle about that. Dolly and I were practically family.

"He's lawyered up, some public defender from Watertown," she wheezed. Her next words were harsh. "And he's got his work cut out for him."

"How so?" From what I'd heard, the evidence against Russ was enough to warrant an arrest, but frankly it seemed like a decent lawyer could establish reasonable doubt.

"You know about the fingerprints and the threats he made, right?" She coughed again.

I nodded. "But the fingerprints don't convince me. Russ worked at the Bonaparte House for years. And people get into arguments all the time." Maybe they didn't threaten out loud to kill other people, but threatening and actually doing were very different things.

"Well, that's all they got, at least that's all they're telling us. She rolled her eyes. "But he's acting like an idiot in jail. Went after a guard. Threw stuff around his cell. Complained about the food." This set her off into another fit of coughing, and this time it sounded painful.

There was a glass of water sitting on the small table between us. I handed her the drink. Her face was red and her breathing was ragged. I cursed Russ for causing this poor woman such pain, as if he had directly triggered this attack. Dolly's demeanor was tough and no-nonsense, but Russ was still her son and she loved him. Even if he didn't deserve it. Maybe she loved him *because* he didn't deserve it. Me, I wished I had a piece of him right now.

"Dinner's on," Harold's voice rang out like a chuck wagon cook. "Come and get it."

Dolly threw the afghan over the back of the recliner, then led me to the kitchen. The conversation about Russ was clearly over.

We sat down at the kitchen table. On a trivet in the center of the table sat a thirteen-by-nine-inch Pyrex dish, which was emitting a savory aroma that made my mouth water. Chunks of pink ham peeked up from the surface of the browned and bubbly casserole. I was willing to bet there was not a canned cream soup in sight when this had been made. "Dig in," Harold said, clearly proud of his efforts. I scooped some onto my plate, then added some buttered green beans. Low calorie? Nope. Heart healthy? Regrettably, no. Perfect on a cold November night with good friends? Heck yes.

I passed the serving spoon to Harold, who solicitously filled a plate for Dolly, then filled his own. Finally, I could take a bite, even though Dolly and Harold wouldn't expect, or even want, formal dinner etiquette. The food was everything I could have wanted and more. Rich with milk and butter, the potatoes were tender, coated in little flecks of onion and surrounded with nuggets of sweet ham.

A few bites later, when I came out of my brief, comfort-food-induced coma, I asked, "Is this your recipe, Harold?"

He smiled. "My mom's. She taught me how to make it. Of course, it ain't as good as hers."

Dolly laughed, her pearly white dentures on full display. "That's the only thing he cooks, other than venzun." *Venison*, if you lived outside the North Country. "But he does a pretty good job." She patted the sleeve of his flannel shirt. My heart warmed. I was so glad Dolly had found love again after her first husband died. She deserved to be happy.

I speared a piece of ham and some saucy potato. "Silver Lake is pretty this time of year. I drove down there to take a look before I got here."

Harold eyed me. "What made you want to do that? You could have gotten that little car stuck."

"And she would have called us and you would have gone to pull her out," Dolly piped in. "But I know what this is about." She took a sip of her hot tea. "Russ and the lawyer and that damned land."

"Why does Mrs. Turnbull want to sell now, after all these years?"

"Last time I talked to her, she said she had a granddaughter who wanted to go to medical school, and she wanted to help out. It's not like she ever used the water frontage or the lake for anything. Though she never minded if we put our boat in there or fished off the shore."

"And the woods were going to go with the property? Would you pass the pepper?" I added.

Dolly handed me the shaker. "Yeah, I guess they were supposed to be a buffer zone from us riffraff." She gave a little snort, which set her off coughing into her napkin.

"Did Jim MacNamara have any buyers lined up?"

"Not that I know of," Harold said. "Nothing was definite yet about the sale anyway."

I shook a little pepper on the potatoes and looked up. "I thought the sale was in the works? That a purchase order had been signed and Steve Murdoch was lined up to do the construction."

"Nah," Dolly said.

Harold nodded. "Old Lady Turnbull hadn't made up her mind."

"About selling?" I chewed on a green bean.

Dolly and Harold looked at each other. "No," Harold finally said. "About who she was going to sell *to*."

Huh? I looked up from my plate. "There was another potential buyer? I assume the police know this?"

"They do if they've talked to Old Lady Turnbull, and I saw a cruiser out there yesterday," Dolly said, answering my second question first.

"So who else wanted the property?" I leaned forward. So help me, if one of them said it was my mother, I would scream.

"Steve Murdoch," Harold said.

Pieces started falling into place. Suddenly, my earlier suspicion about Steve took on a new dimension. Steve had been in competition with Jim MacNamara for his wife's affections. But he'd also been in competition with him for a construction project that would have made one of them rich. Steve would have made money as contractor for the Silver Lake development project. But if he owned the land, as well as undertook the project, his profits would be doubled, tripled, or even more.

I sat back in my chair. Steve, who was struggling with his sobriety. While I was out getting my hair done, he could have helped himself to his booze of choice from my bar, and when MacNamara came to the Bonaparte House for whatever his errand was, Steve saw his opportunity. And took it. And set Russ up to take the fall.

"Russ's public defender knows all this?" As much as I secretly, sort of, wanted Russ to be guilty so he'd be out of my hair for a couple of decades, I couldn't let him go to prison for a crime he didn't commit. There were no doubt plenty of other crimes in his future that he could be caught for, which cheered me a little.

"Yup," Dolly said. "He's working on getting Russ released." She waved her fork and made stabbing motions in the air with it. "But they can take their time. It'll do his butt good to have it parked in jail for a few more days."

I reviewed what I knew so far. Nope, no need for me to go to the police. If what Dolly and Harold said was true, and I'd never had reason to doubt either of them before, the police had all the information I did. Good. The fewer meetings with Detective Hawthorne, the better. I just had to let justice take its course.

"So," I said, giving Harold a little wink, then turning to Dolly. Harold's pale blue eyes twinkled. "You still want to work Thanksgiving? Assuming the restrooms are finished?" If Steve turned out to be guilty, I'd have to find a new contractor, but it wasn't a huge project so it might not be too hard. I looked out the window into the night. Snow fell, illuminated by the light on the garage.

She stared at me. "And who else would you get to cook for you?" Her tone was indignant.

"Oh, I don't know. Paloma maybe?" Paloma was the cook Dolly would be training in the spring to work at Spinky's. Paloma had been working in the high school cafeteria for a few years but she had no experience as a restaurant cook.

Dolly's face flushed. "What? She ain't ready for that." I hoped she wouldn't start coughing again.

"Well," I said innocently. "If you're sick, you can't cook."

"I'm not sick!" she said, then coughed.

Harold pressed his lips together, clearly stifling a laugh.

"Then you won't mind going to see Doc Phelps just to make sure." I smiled at her. "Because you know I can't let you cook for me unless you get checked out."

Dolly's eyes went from me, to Harold, then back again. They narrowed, then she sighed. "Fine. You got me. I'll call in the morning."

"And I'll drive you," I said.

Harold looked out the window. "Speaking of driving, you're not going anywhere tonight, you know that?"

I glanced out at the snow, which was falling at a pretty good clip. It wasn't a long drive back to the Bonaparte House, but the plow hadn't been back through yet. And to tell the truth, the prospect of sleeping alone in that big old pile of rocks didn't exactly frost my cupcakes.

"You'll stay," Dolly ordered. "Hope you don't mind the couch. The dogs are in the spare bedroom."

"I'll take you up on that. And I'll clean up from dinner." In the morning, I would call and make that appointment for her myself. I stood and began clearing plates. Harold smiled up at me. "How about some coffee? We can take it in the living room with our pie."

"Harold! Georgie's a guest in our home." I realized she hadn't eaten much. Her face was pale. I hoped whatever she had wasn't contagious.

"She's no guest," Harold countered. "She's family."

I had to smile. That was one way to get me to do the dishes.

❖ ELEVEN ❖

The next morning I found myself on the couch, swaddled like a mummy, if the Egyptians had crocheted afghans and velour blankets. It was toasty warm, and my cheek brushed the flannel pillowcase. Maybe just a few more minutes of shut-eye.

A chorus of yips and barks sounded from somewhere in the house and my eyes flew open. What sounded like a few hundred feet thundered across the floor in the next room. "Hold on and I'll let you out, you little devils!" The front door opened, then shut a few seconds later, and the barking was muffled again. Harold had apparently let the dogs out. Woof.

Dolly appeared, wearing a big pink bathrobe and fuzzy slippers. There were dark circles under her eyes, but her hairdo was somehow perfect. No idea how she made that happen. Probably a boatload of hairspray, applied over days between visits to the salon for a set and comb-out. "Mornin'," she said.

"Good morning, Dolly. How did you sleep?" I disengaged myself, regretfully, from the blankets, stood, and put my hands in the pockets of the flannel pajama pants she'd lent me last night—camouflage in a pink color scheme, which would bode well for the deer if these clothes had actually been designed to wear for hunting.

"Eh, all right." She cut her eyes to me. "Let's have some breakfast and get this over with. I can't fight both of you."

I knew what she meant. I wasn't a fan of doctors either, but it had to be done. "I'll call and make the appointment."

An hour later we'd eaten—eggs and toast, prepared by me, not that I minded a bit, since Harold had to work. The sky was a bright winter blue, and the sun sparkled on the crust of the snow that had fallen last night. Harold, bless him, had cleaned the snow off my car and turned on the defroster before he left, so the car was ready for us as we piled in to make the trip back into town.

Dr. Vernon Phelps had been practicing medicine since approximately World War One. Well, perhaps that was an exaggeration. Probably more like the Korean War. His office was located in a long, low building attached to the back of the Bay's small hospital. I dropped Dolly at the entrance to the offices, parked, and headed through the big glass doors.

The familiar smell of antiseptic reached my nostrils as I sat down in a molded orange plastic chair and picked up a gossip magazine. Dolly was already at the sliding window, talking to the intake nurse and handing over her insurance card. She came and sat down beside me. She'd been uncharacteristically quiet on the ride here, and she didn't appear to want to talk now. I patted her arm. "It'll be all right."

She looked up at me, her big brown eyes locked on mine. Good golly, Miss Dolly. She was *afraid*. Never in the more than twenty years I'd known her had I seen this side of her. My gut clenched. If the bravest person you'd ever met was afraid of something, it stood to reason there was something to be afraid *of*.

"What if they . . . find something?" she whispered.

My heart flew up into my throat. This was no unreasonable fear that I could just *shush* away. Decades of smoking, given up only a few months ago, made it an undeniable possibility that something *was* seriously wrong. I cursed Russ Riley for causing his mother any more stress than she was already under. I swallowed my heart back down, then took her hand and looked into her eyes.

"If they find something—and that's a big, fat *if*—Sophie and I will take care of you. But there's no sense borrowing trouble. One thing at a time. Do you want me to come in with you?"

She hesitated, then nodded. It cost her.

"Dolly?" A nurse stood in the door across from us, holding a clipboard. "Come on in, hon."

We stood together and went in to face whatever this was together.

The nurse deposited us in an examination room, the walls of which were covered in sage green and peach wallpaper that clearly had not been updated since the years of New Wave music. "Undress from the waist up, and put this johnny on," she instructed with practiced efficiency, turned on her heel, and left. I pretended to busy myself by studying the ceiling while Dolly changed, then gave her a hand up onto the examining table.

A knock sounded at the door, then Dr. Phelps entered, clipboard in hand. I amended my prior assessment. This thin little man with the snowy comb-over and neatly trimmed mustache had probably been practicing since the Spanish-American War. He was, however, still sharp as a tack, a fact that was reinforced when he spoke.

"Dolly Riley," he said. "What brings you in to see me today? I don't suppose you brought me lunch?" He chuckled.

"Dolly's not feeling so well," I butted in.

He eyed me shrewdly over the tops of his glasses. "People don't usually call for same-day appointments if they're in the pink," he said. "How's that mother-in-law of yours?" Doc's wife was long dead, and he'd never remarried.

"Back in Greece for the winter."

"Pity," he said, and turned to Dolly. "What seems to be the trouble?"

Dolly sat there, her arms folded across her chest. Finally, just before I was about to answer for her, she said in a small voice, "I've got a cough that won't go away. And my chest hurts." She hadn't told me that part, and I squelched a fresh throb of worry.

The doctor consulted something on his chart, then spoke matter-of-factly. "You quit smoking? Good. Very good." His tone was nonjudgmental. He stuck the ends of his stethoscope into his slightly hairy ears. "Let's have a listen."

He held the amplifier end in his hand for a moment, presumably to warm it up, then placed it inside Dolly's gown and on her chest. "Breathe in, as deep as you can," he said, listening intently. "And again." Dolly's chest rose and fell with the exertion, fatigue and worry written on her face. The doctor moved the stethoscope around to the back and listened for a few more breaths, then pulled out the chestpiece and let it drop over his own chest. He shined a light into her eyes, then peered intently down her throat.

"I think," he said, "you've got bronchitis." Dolly visibly relaxed, and I breathed a sigh of relief. "I'm going to put you on an antibiotic, and you're to rest for at least a week, then come back and see me. If you're feeling worse at any time, call again or just come in to the ER and I'll come over and see you."

She nodded. He continued. "Before you go, we're going to give you a chest x-ray. And I'm ordering some tests, which I expect you to have done next week when you're feeling better."

Dolly's face fell. "Chest x-ray? Why do I need tests?" Her voice was small, and I reached out to take her hand.

He eyed her. "Just to rule out . . . pneumonia," he finally said.

Right. Pneumonia.

An hour later Dolly had been x-rayed and we'd filled her prescription at the drugstore. I took her arm and walked her into the house, then sat her down in her recliner and covered her up while I fetched a glass of water. Her Adam's apple bobbed as she swallowed her medication, then she settled back into the cushions.

"You want me to make you some lunch?" A long, dull afternoon of television watching stretched out before us, until Harold got home, but I was prepared to do it for her.

"Naw," she said, yawning. "I'm going to take a nap. There's homemade chicken noodle soup in the fridge and I'll just heat up some of that later. You go on home now. You've done enough for me for today." Her eyes drifted closed.

I debated, then went out to the kitchen to make a phone call. Dolly's daughter, Brandy, who cleaned for me at the Bonaparte House, both upstairs and down, thanked me for getting her mother to see a doctor, and said she was on her way over.

Before I could put my phone away, a text came in. File copied. Pick up when ready. My heart leapt. Lydia must have gotten the locksmith there last night or early this morning, and had managed to copy it already. If the answers about my genealogy that I hoped for were contained in the file, Melanie, Liza, and I could all rest easier tonight.

Finally. This was almost over and I'd know my family was safe.

Once I verified that there was, indeed, homemade chicken noodle soup in the refrigerator, and Brandy arrived and assured me she was there for the duration, I wasted no time getting myself to the offices of MacNamara and MacNamara.

Lydia was at her usual spot in the reception area,

typing away. She stood up and stretched when she saw me, and gave me a smile. "Come on in," she said. "I have the file all ready for you."

How big was a hundred-year-old file? Lydia handed me a manila envelope a couple of inches thick. "I took the liberty of only copying the important documents. There was a lot of extraneous stuff that you're welcome to come back and look at, but I didn't think you'd need."

The envelope weighed about five pounds. "I'm really only interested at this point in the financials, so I can report to my mother, and anything to do with genealogy and the heirs."

Lydia smiled. "All there. And if you need anything else, just let me know."

"Thanks for doing some of my work for me. Where's Ben?"

She rolled her eyes. "Like he tells me where he's going. I know he was here late last night, after the locksmith left, going through that filing cabinet."

I didn't have a growing reputation for sticking my nose in for nothing. "Did he find anything? If you can tell me, of course?"

Lydia let out a giggle. "Well, I don't know if Junior took anything, but when I looked—you know, for *your* file—I found one of the drawers filled with underwear, deodorant, cologne and, well, other things that make me want to never sit on the leather couch in that office again."

Ooh, interesting. So Jim might have used his office for his romantic trysts. My mind raced backward. Had *I* ever sat on that couch?

"Well, thanks again for this, Lydia. I'm sure we'll talk again soon."

"Later, Georgie."

I tossed the envelope onto the passenger seat of my car. Were there any other errands I could run? Anyone else I just had to see? I sighed. It was ridiculous to be afraid. Time to put on my big girl undies and go home.

The Bonaparte House was quiet as, well, the dead when I got there. Of course, if there'd been noise, I'd have been even more uncomfortable, since I knew I should be alone. The prep counter was still full of recipes, so I took the attorneys' file to my office and sat down. The metal clasp on the mustard yellow envelope opened easily. Lydia hadn't bothered to tape the opening.

I pulled out a stack of papers. Lydia had thoughtfully put sheets of colored paper with labeled sticky note tabs in between the different sections. On top was "Trust Documents." I knew more or less what was in there—or at least I thought I did—so I removed that section and set it aside.

"Info re: Heirs." Now this was more like it. I took a deep breath. *Please let it say that all the heirs have been identified*. I flipped over the divider page and began to read.

A half hour later, I turned over the last page of genealogical charts and blew out a sigh. Damn. The lawyers had apparently lost track of my umpteenth-removed cousin Percy, the one who disappeared in the 1940s, so Sheldon knew more than they did. I wished I could get those thirty minutes back. This little exercise had netted me exactly nothing. Just in case I'd missed something an expert would have recognized, I put the whole stack into the document feeder of my scanner, and sent it off to Sheldon. I didn't know what kind of office setup the gene-alogist had at his room at the River Rock, but he'd figure it out. On Melanie's dime.

I turned to the last section of papers. Maybe this would make this all worthwhile. The money.

The oldest information was on top. It appeared to be a ledger, with monthly debits for attorneys' fees and expenses, and in a separate column interest paid, all written in an old-fashioned hand. The starting balance was more than ten million dollars. *Not too shabby, Grandpa Elihu.*

I thumbed through the pages until I hit 1929. The num-bers, which had been steadily increasing up to that point, suddenly took a nosedive, then, as the years approached World War Two, started to creep back up. I eagerly turned more pages. How much money were we talking about here?

As I flipped, my eagerness turned to confusion, then disbelief. Somewhere in the last twenty years or so, about the time the ledgers switched from typewritten to computer generated, the balance got lower, and lower, and lower.

I stared at the bottom line, the one from the ledger dated a couple of months ago, closed my eyes, and opened them again. No change.

Unless I was misreading the final document, the Elihu Bloodworth Trust, the one people had been killed over, was now worth the decidedly nonprincely sum of six thousand dollars.

❖ TWELVE ❖

No. It couldn't be. This had to be wrong. Not that whatever was in this account was mine, but I was ripping angry. My family was in danger over this? People had been killed for this? Just a few thousand bucks? I threw the paper down in disgust. How had the lawyers blown millions of dollars that had been entrusted to them for other people?

Had it been bad investments on the part of the Attorneys MacNamara, past and present? I looked at a random page. The debits for legal fees and expenses seemed reasonable, so poor investment strategy had to be the answer. If this was an example of the care with which the MacNamaras handled their clients' cases, it was time for me to find another lawyer for my divorce, no matter how close it was to being finalized.

I dialed my accountant. "Kim? It's Georgie. Hey, can I hire you to take a look at something for me?"

"Sure," she said. "Send it over."

"Thanks. I'll e-mail it to you in a few minutes. And Kim? Keep this between us, will you?"

"My lips are sealed." She rang off.

It was quick work to scan and send the information. I wasn't quite sure how to break this news to Melanie and Liza. *Hello? You know those millions of dollars you thought you were inheriting? Fuhgeddaboutit!* Not that Melanie or Liza was ostensibly hurting for money. But, though she'd assured me the rumors were untrue, Melanie was in one gossip magazine or another—I knew, because I read them—every few weeks under suspicion of being almost bankrupt. And Liza, well, as far as I knew, she was well off due to shrewd financial management of her business, despite having some very expensive castle repair bills coming up next spring. Still, they must have had plans for that money, and I was willing to bet that some charities were the intended recipients of some of it. The charities were probably the biggest losers here.

The bubble of anger grew in my stomach. Jim Mac-Namara had managed to lose almost all the money, either through ineptitude or maybe even willful misconduct, then got himself killed. Before I could go after him myself. There was a special place in hell reserved for people like him. Suddenly, I felt relieved for Old Lady Turnbull out at Silver Lake, who'd never sealed the land development deal with him. She probably didn't know how close a call she'd had. Her granddaughter would get herself through medical school, one way or the other.

Russ Riley was sitting in jail on suspicion of murdering MacNamara. And what about Steve Murdoch? Just how many times had MacNamara screwed him over? It begged the question, of course: how many other people had Mac-Namara taken advantage of? People who might have wanted him dead. Even his own son didn't seem that broken up about his father's death.

I sat there stewing, and was just about to get up and go see if I could find something to cook to take my mind off it, when my cell phone buzzed in my pocket. The display read *Liza*. "Hello?"

"Hey, Georgie. I just called to give you an update on Melanie and Caitlyn."

Call me the World's Worst Daughter. I'd meant to call earlier, but had gotten caught up with making sure Dolly got to the doctor and now this stupid trust. "How are they?"

"I've been keeping an eye on them, like I told you I would, and there's nothing you could do, so stop feeling bad." She must have heard the guilt in my voice.

"Are they any better?" *Please let them be on the mend.*

There was a slight pause on the other end of the receiver. "Not better. But not worse either. I've called Dr. Phelps. He's having one of the other doctors take over his afternoon patients, and coming over here."

Relief washed over me. Doc Phelps would take care of them. "He's making a castle call?"

Liza laughed. "Yes, and I'm making a rather sizable

donation to his favorite charity, Doctors Without Borders."

The charities. I felt awful and angry again. Should I tell Liza about the trust accounting so she could adjust her expectations? No, better to let Kim Galbraith corroborate my interpretation of the numbers, then break the news to her and Melanie together, once Melanie felt better.

"Should I come over?"

"As I said, nothing you can do here, and they're both sleeping. Let's wait to hear what Dr. Phelps has to say, then you can decide."

"Okay," I said tentatively. Of course she was right, but it felt . . . wrong.

"Don't worry. I'm sure they just have the flu or something."

That didn't look like any flu I'd ever seen, but I didn't comment. "I'll talk to you later. Call me when he gets there."

"I will. Bye-bye." She rang off.

Now to keep myself busy for the next few hours. The recipes. That ought to do it.

I fixed myself a cup of coffee using the single-serving machine Cal had given me for my birthday last spring. When the restaurant was open, the machine wasn't practical, since we needed full pots of coffee going all the time. Of course, there was the Bean, but it was cold outside, and it just seemed like too much trouble to get bundled up and walk down there. So today I was grateful for my little plastic cup of cinnamon-hazelnut-vanilla.

The recipes were still spread out on the prep counter,

where Dolly and I would be chopping meat and vegetables and assembling Greek and other dishes come spring. But for now, it was the perfect big, flat surface to sort. I had placed a spoon over each of the piles already started, to keep the contents from shifting or blowing away. The Bonaparte House was old, and sometimes drafty, even the newer addition that housed the kitchen.

I took a moment to review the categories I'd already sorted recipes into, then reached into the shoe box for a handful. The work went quickly as long as I didn't stop to read more than the titles. Next to the pile of cream soup casseroles I started a new one for molded gelatin salads. The definition of the word "salad" had definitely changed in the last few decades.

That got me thinking. *Thousand Island dressing.* Why wasn't it Thousand *Islands* dressing, with an *s*, which would have made more sense grammatically? I stuck my hand into the pocket of my jeans and pulled out Franco's recipe, the one his waitress had delivered, then opened it up and smoothed out the creases. Good thing it was a copy, because those creases were permanent.

Sophia's Sauce. Written in different script at the bottom was a notation: *Received from Sophia LaLonde at July 4th celebration, 1910.*

I reviewed what I knew—or thought I knew—about the dressing. The most widely held belief, perpetuated from close to a century of tour boat operators, was that the recipe had been cobbled together a century ago from ingredients aboard a St. Lawrence River yacht. The owner of the yacht was George Boldt, wealthy manager of the Waldorf Astoria hotel in New York City, and the builder of the destined-to-be-unfinished Boldt Castle, which was located farther downriver across from the town of Alexandria Bay, and which remained the most popular tourist destination in the Thousand Islands. The story went that the dressing was created for Boldt, his boss, by the famous chef Oscar of the Waldorf, who also created the now-classic dishes Veal Oscar and Waldorf salad. The tourist industry along the St. Lawrence got a lot of mileage out of George Boldt, that was for sure.

But there were other origin stories. A chef at a Chicago hotel, the Blackstone, claimed he, not Oscar, had invented it. But why would a Chicago chef name a sauce after the Thousand Islands?

A restaurant owner a couple of towns over claimed he'd found the original recipe in a safe when he bought his building forty years ago.

Angela Wainwright at the River Rock Resort claimed she had found the original recipe hidden in a coffee can on a shelf in her pantry. She was now bottling the dressing on a small scale and selling it at her hotel.

And then there was Sophia LaLonde, the wife of a fishing excursion captain, who was rumored to have invented the sauce to accompany her husband's shore dinners. When I thought about it—and I'd not ever really given this any thought before, but now it seemed like a no-brainer—Thousand Island dressing was a combination of ketchup-based cocktail sauce and mayonnaise-based tartar sauce, both of which go perfectly with fried fish. Suddenly, Sophia seemed like a pretty good candidate. And Franco's recipe was attributed to someone named Sophia. That couldn't be a coincidence.

I went to the small refrigerator and pulled out the bottle I'd bought from Angela the other day after my less-than-memorable breakfast with Sheldon Todd. The label listed a dozen or so ingredients. I compared the label to Franco's recipe. There were a few differences, but the general idea was the same: ketchup or chili sauce, mixed with mayonnaise and pickle relish. The recipe we served at the Bonaparte House—no idea where that had come from originally—was similar, though we added chopped green olives in addition to the pickle relish. The Bonaparte House was a Greek restaurant, after all.

Franco's recipe called for lemon juice, which accounted for the brighter, fresher flavor I'd tasted at the pizza restaurant. Suddenly, I couldn't wait any longer. A taste comparison was definitely in order. I whisked up the ingredients, covered the bowl with plastic wrap, and set it in the fridge. Then I put a couple of eggs in a pan of cold water and turned on the burner.

The eggs would need to cook and cool before they could be peeled and chopped, so I sat back down at the counter and grabbed the last handful of loose papers from the shoe box.

Just as the last clipping went into its stack, a knock sounded at the back door. "Come in," I called out of habit, then realized when the handle started to jiggle that I'd locked it. I made my way to the door, shutting off the flame under the eggs as I did so. They would sit there for six minutes, no more, no less, then go into an ice water bath, and they'd be perfectly cooked.

Someone began pounding on the back door. "Georgie!" The voice was muffled. The pounding started again.

That wasn't impatience. Whoever it was, was in trouble.

I made it to the door and looked out the window, my hand on the knob. I could see a crown of red hair that could only belong to Brenda Jones. She looked up, and her face was dead serious. I flung open the door.

Brenda stumbled across the threshold. She wasn't alone.

Her arm was around a man, who was leaning heavily on her. He was on his feet, but bent at the waist and holding his arm across his middle. I flew to one side of the man and grabbed, relieving Brenda of half his weight. Together we managed to bring him inside and sit him in Sophie's armchair along one interior wall of the Bonaparte House kitchen.

Panting with the exertion, I ran back to the row of pegs near the back door and grabbed a fleece jacket. The man wasn't wearing a coat, and he must have been freezing. I covered him. He gave a moan, then looked up. The right side of his face was covered in a bruise the color of the merlot I kept in my desk drawer, and a gash over one eye was covered in crusted blood. A single drop oozed from one end of the cut. The man groaned, then began coughing, which clearly brought on a fresh wave of pain.

Franco.

◆ THIRTEEN ◆

"Have you called an ambulance?" I said over Franco's head, tucking the coat tighter around him. I got some ice from the freezer and wrapped it in a towel, which I applied to the lump I could see swelling up on his head.

Brenda shook her head. "Not yet. I found him out back of the Casa di Pizza when I was on my rounds. I didn't know if it was safe to take him back into the restaurant, so I brought him here."

I nodded. "Good thinking." She couldn't very well have left him outside while she waited for an ambulance, not in this weather, and there were no other businesses open between here and the Casa. I just hoped Franco hadn't done any further damage by moving. Still, he'd managed to help get himself here, and that had to be a good sign. I didn't go through 911 this time. Honestly, if

I had to listen to Cindy Dumont one more time, I might scream. So I dialed the Bonaparte Bay Volunteer Fire Department directly.

When I was assured that help was on the way, I turned back to my temporary patient.

"Franco? The ambulance will be here soon. Do you remember what happened?"

"I . . . I was in the kitchen. Someone . . . came up behind me and hit me on the head." He winced, as if remembering the blow. "I must have blacked out. I fell. Or was pushed. Because when I came to, I had this cut on my forehead, and there was blood on the corner of the prep counter. And I think—" He winced again, then took a deep breath. "I think my arm is broken."

"Why would anyone do this to you?" I said. "Was anything taken? It's the wrong time of year for a robbery. No tourists in town spending money, so it's only locals coming in for lunch or dinner, right?"

Franco shifted in the chair. I removed the ice pack until he found what appeared to be a more or less comfortable position, then reapplied it. "I just about break even, sometimes operate at a loss, by staying open all winter. So no, there aren't huge bundles of cash lying around. I don't keep anything valuable at the restaurant." I thought of my mother-in-law, Sophie, who kept large amounts of cash hidden under a floorboard under her bed during the tourist season. But whatever she'd had stashed away, she'd taken with her when she went back to Greece. Franco had just denied keeping money at the Casa, but then again he was hardly likely to admit it if he did, even to me.

Sirens sounded from the parking lot behind the Bonaparte House. "I'll go get them," Brenda said, heading for the door.

"We should call the police," I said. I would do some more bypassing of 911 by directly calling Deputy Tim Arquette, who had quite a bit more on the ball than our illustrious village police chief. "I'm sure the person who did this is long gone, but we should have the Casa checked out."

Franco nodded. My hand holding the ice mirrored his movement. "Can you call my daughter too? Send her over to the ER. If she hears about this on the scanner first, *I'll* never hear the end of it."

The back door opened and the same set of EMTs who had taken Jim MacNamara's body away came in. They headed straight for Franco and began their initial assessment. I took the towel over to the sink and shook out the ice, then laid the towel over the rim of the sink to dry until I could do laundry. Brenda came to stand by me.

"Any theories?" I said.

"Can't be personal, otherwise they would have hurt him worse."

I was inclined to agree. Which meant whoever had done this wanted something. If it was money, the thief was going to be disappointed. If Franco was bringing in a couple hundred dollars a day this time of year, he'd be lucky. What else was there? Ten pairs of matching salt and pepper shakers? A few pounds of premade pizza dough?

My thoughts were interrupted by the EMTs, who were helping Franco to a standing position. They had placed a sling over his arm, then wrapped a blanket around his shoulders.

"I'll call Marielle and the police," I said.

"Thanks," he ground out, breathing heavily with the effort of movement. The door caught on a gust of wind that blew into the kitchen.

After I saw Franco loaded into the ambulance, I dialed the Bonaparte Bay police station and asked to speak to Tim Arquette. While I was on hold, I said to Brenda, "You want a drink? There's soda in the fridge. Could you grab me a Diet Coke?" When Tim came on the line, I told him what had happened. Brenda popped the top and handed me a can.

"So you need to go over to the Casa and check it out. See if it looks like anything's been taken. Franco doesn't know much. He was mobile, but dazed, when Brenda brought him here." I took a sip of the soda. "No, Tim, I'm not telling you how to do your job." Well, maybe I was, just a little. It wasn't like the BBPD had been much help to me over the last couple months. I clicked off.

I turned to Brenda. "You wouldn't happen to know Marielle's number, would you?" It was going to be difficult to call Franco's daughter. Was her last name even the same as her father's?

"Naw. But doesn't she own that exercise studio over by Fort Drum?"

Right. Now I remembered. I'd heard Marielle was some kind of health nut, which was ironic considering the amount of cheese and fried food that her father's restaurant served. I used my phone to Google local gyms. Brenda leaned over the screen.

"Try that one," she said, pointing. "Buff and Ready, over by Evans Mills."

I looked at the address. Same plaza where my almost-ex-husband's partner, Inky LaFontaine, had a tattoo shop. I tapped in the number.

"May I speak to Marielle?" I asked when someone picked up.

"She's just centering herself for her next yoga class. Can I help you?"

"This is Georgie Nikolopatos, from Bonaparte Bay. Her father asked me to call. It's important."

There was a silence on the other end of the line, as if the receptionist was making a decision. Finally, she said, "Okay. Just a minute."

It was not more than that minute before Marielle spoke. "He's had a heart attack, hasn't he? All that cheese, all that half-and-half in his coffee. I should have tried harder to make him exercise and eat better."

Franco was a big boy and could presumably make his own health choices, but her concern was nice, just the same. She clearly loved her dad. "No, it's not that. But he is at the emergency room in Bonaparte Bay."

"What happened?"

I told her what I knew.

"I'll get someone to take my classes and be right over. Thanks for letting me know."

When the call ended, I turned to Brenda. "You busy? You want to take a walk up Theresa Street and see if any other businesses have been broken into?"

Brenda smiled. "Sounds like our civic duty. And as it happens, I didn't finish my rounds this morning. You could help."

That was easy enough to agree to. There weren't any tourists in town, which meant that any bottle and can retrieval Brenda would be doing would be minimal. And frankly, I didn't want to hang out here by myself, waiting to get hit on the head by some unknown assailant who was targeting the shops of Bonaparte Bay.

Brenda rinsed out the two cans we'd been drinking from and put them inside a bright orange plastic bag she'd produced from her canvas purse, which I hadn't noticed she'd had strapped across her ample chest when she came in with Franco. "Seeds," she said, and dropped the cans inside the larger bag.

We bundled up and headed out.

Brenda and I were the only people on the street, which was hardly surprising. Brenda scanned for cans, which I don't think she really expected to find, and I looked into each business window as we passed. No broken glass. No open doors. We gave special scrutiny to Spinky's and Tat-L-Tails, the closed-up tattoo shop. All seemed to be in order, so I didn't need to bother Spiro or Inky on their vacation.

Finally, we reached the Casa di Pizza and went around

back. One of Bonaparte Bay's two police cruisers was parked there, idling and emitting a plume of blue smoke into the cold air. Deputy Tim Arquette sat in the driver's seat, taking notes. He rolled down his window when he saw me.

"Why are you here?" he said. He looked around. "Is your mother with you?"

I resisted the urge to roll my eyes. Another Bonaparte Bay male with a crush on my daytime-drama-star mom.

"Uh, no. I'm just helping Brenda with her rounds." I nodded toward my companion, who was pulling a half-full bag out of a trash can. Franco must have let her set up a collection station back here. "Did you find anything?"

Tim shook his head. "Whoever it was, was probably looking for money. They jimmied open the cash drawer and cleaned it out. He was gone before I got here."

Franco didn't know how long he'd been blacked out, so Tim was probably right. "I don't like this," I said. The off-season was usually quiet in Bonaparte Bay.

"I wouldn't worry. I'll patrol downtown when I get done here. But my guess it was just a quick hit by someone from out of town."

That made some sense. Why would someone local take the chance that Franco would recognize and remember him? At least we knew it wasn't Russ Riley. He was in jail, so he was off the hook for this.

I glanced at my watch. It was nearly four o'clock and the sky was beginning to darken. In fact, it looked like more snow might be coming in. Brenda came toward me. Her collection bag wasn't much bigger than when I'd seen it a few minutes ago.

"You all set?" she said. "I'm gonna head home. I've gotta get up early tomorrow. Going to the boat show in Syracuse if the weather's okay."

"I'm fine." Brenda was brave. I could be too. But a feeling of unease continued to creep over me. Russ was in jail for murder, but I wasn't all that sure he'd done it, despite the fact that my gyro spit was the murder weapon. Which meant a killer could still be out there. And now this break-in at Franco's. I couldn't see any possible connection between these two crimes, yet the fact remained that they'd happened, close in time, in my little town.

"Then I'll see you around," she said, and headed back toward her apartment over Margie's T-Shirt Emporium.

Movement inside the squad car caught my eye. Tim must have finished his notes, because he said, "You want me to come check out your restaurant?"

I thought of the Bonaparte House—a big, drafty pile of rocks with a lot of rooms. I thought about saying no. But common sense got the better of me. "Yes. Yes, I guess I do."

Tim smiled. "No problem. I'll cruise by there as soon as I get a hot cup of coffee from the Bean."

"I could make you some," I offered.

"Naw. I want one of those blueberry muffins. Hope they've got one left, this time of day." He rolled up his window, then picked up his radio, probably calling Dispatch to give them an update.

As if in sympathy, my own cell phone gave two short vibrations in my coat pocket. Before I looked at the display, I assumed it was Liza texting to give me an update on herself, Melanie, and Caitlyn. But the caller ID read *Kim Galbraith*.

Call me. We need to talk.

◈ FOURTEEN ◈

An icy wind chose that moment to gust up and slice through me. I shivered, then glanced at Tim, who appeared to be waiting for me to leave the parking lot before he did. Which I appreciated, on the off chance that whoever had broken in was still around. I walked back out onto the street and into the relative shelter of the doorway of Inky's tattoo parlor. I could have waited until I got back to the Bonaparte House, but I wanted to give Tim a chance to get there first.

I pulled off my glove and dialed Kim, then switched the phone to my other hand and shoved the bare one deep into my coat pocket. "Galbraith Accounting," Kim said.

"Hey, Kim. It's Georgie. What's up?" My teeth chattered between the words.

"I've taken a quick glance at those documents you e-mailed me."

"Pathetic, aren't they? I'm no accountant but even I could see the bottom line." I felt a fresh stab of disgust at the dead Jim MacNamara, then hunched down as another gust of icy wind swirled around inside my three-sided shelter.

"Are you at the Bonaparte House? I'd like to come over."

"No, but I'm headed there now."

"I'll be there in fifteen minutes," she said.

Tim's cruiser pulled out of its spot in front of the Express-o Bean, then headed toward my home and restaurant. By the time I traversed the block and a half, Tim was already walking the octagonal perimeter of the building. He held a flashlight and shone its beam into the shrubs out front, then in a broader arc around the small front lawn. I met him at the emergency exit on the side, and we walked together around to the employee parking lot.

I unlocked the door and it swung open. Tim entered in front of me. He made a perfunctory visual sweep of the kitchen, checked the walk-in, then headed for the dining rooms.

I hung up my coat and exchanged my boots for a pair of slippers I kept by the back door. Now that I was in the warmth of the building, the shivers came back, probably an involuntary attempt by my body to regulate its temperature. My eyes fell on the gas burner. A saucepan sat there. It wasn't like me to leave a dirty pot on the stove, even in the off-season.

Right. Before Brenda had brought Franco in, I'd put a couple of eggs on to boil. They were still sitting there. The water was ice cold now—at least I'd remembered to shut off the flame—but the eggs were no good. Aside from the fact that they had sat out, unrefrigerated, for a few hours, they had not gone into their ice bath at the proper time, so would have developed an ugly green—and not so tasty—ring around the yolk. I emptied the water into the sink and tossed the eggs into the trash. I washed out the pot, refilled it, added two fresh eggs, and started the process again. This time I filled up a bowl with ice and set it on the counter to be ready.

Headlights shone in through the window in the back door, then blinked out. A moment later, Kim's face appeared near the glass. She waved when she saw me. I hustled over to open the door.

"Is everything all right?" she demanded, peering around me.

"Huh? Oh, yeah, everything's fine. Here at least. Tim Arquette's just checking out the place for me. Did you hear about Franco?"

She nodded. News traveled fast here. "Is he going to be okay?"

"I think so. Maybe a broken arm, possibly a concussion. You hungry? I just realized I never ate lunch and I'm famished." We could hear doors opening and closing upstairs. Tim was being thorough, which I appreciated.

My room wasn't quite as neat as it could have been, but I consoled myself with the thought that he'd probably seen worse.

"I wouldn't say no," Kim said, unwinding her long fringed scarf from around her neck and hanging up her coat. "Pete's gone to a Rotary event tonight. I was just going to heat up a Lean Cuisine."

"How about a burger?" I said. "There are rolls from Kelsey's Bakery in the freezer. It'll only take a few minutes to defrost and toast them up."

"Sounds heavenly." Kim inclined her head toward the hallway that led to the dining rooms. She dropped her voice. "He won't be much longer, right? I'll tell you what I found after he's gone."

Seemed like a smart plan. The beneficiaries of the trust, my mother and Liza, my friend and distant cousin, didn't even know yet that the trust was basically empty. No need to give it a chance to leak out now. The timer dinged. I fished out the eggs with a slotted spoon and set them inside their icy bath.

I turned on the flat-top grill to preheat, then pulled out some ground beef and set about forming a couple of patties. I added salt, pepper, and a sprinkle of our house Greek seasoning to the meat, pressing the spices lightly into the top and bottom surfaces.

"Can I help?" Kim offered.

"You want wine?" When she nodded, I sent her down to the bar to choose what she liked.

By the time she came back, I'd washed my hands,

sliced up some tomatoes—which didn't look too bad, considering they were now out of season—and added some prewashed romaine lettuce to a small platter. The rolls were wrapped in foil and heating in the oven. She came back at almost the exact moment as Tim.

"The place checks out, Georgie," he said. "Just make sure you arm your alarm system before you go to bed." His eyes moved from the raw burgers to the plate of simple fixings.

"Should I put one on for you?" I asked, hoping, inhospitably, he'd say no. Curiosity about what Kim had to tell me was growing.

He sighed. "I wish. But my mother-in-law's making her special split pea soup tonight and my wife ordered me to be there on time." The way he said "special" made me think his dinner might not be all that special to him. Tim left.

I slapped the burgers onto the hot surface, where they hit with a sizzle. Much as I loved Greek food, on a night like tonight, with a storm coming in, there was nothing like the hearty smell of American beef. I began to peel the eggs, as Kim set a water glass of merlot in front of me. Nothing fancy, which suited me fine.

"So," I said, pausing my peeling and chopping to sip the wine. "Did you find something?"

Kim sat down on a stool on the other side of the counter. "Let me start by saying that I didn't have time to do a full analysis."

"You know I didn't expect that, and I still don't." I

resumed chopping the egg until it was in a tiny dice. Although I had planned to pay her for her time—or even better, I could have Moneybags Melanie pay her. I was spending other people's money with abandon lately.

"No, no, I was intrigued. I wanted to see what hundred-year-old financials looked like."

I wiped my hands on a clean kitchen towel, retrieved the bowl of Thousand Island dressing I'd prepared earlier, and folded in the egg.

"There's only five or six thousand dollars left, right? Out of millions. How does that happen?" I flipped the burgers and pulled the rolls out of the oven. They sent up a yeasty fragrance like a genie emerging from a bottle, ready to grant my every carbohydrate wish.

"That's what the bottom line says. So as you know, the trust was funded with about ten million dollars. I didn't do the calculations, but in 1900 money, that was *a lot*." Her face was thoughtful as she swirled her wine around in her glass.

"It's a lot now. But I know what you mean. My however-many-great-grandfather cut down a bunch of trees," I said. "He was probably speculating in other busi-nesses too." I sliced the rolls and set a burger on each bottom half. "You like Thousand Island dressing?"

"Of course. Load 'er up."

I put a big dollop of the dressing on each burger, then piled on lettuce, tomato, and the top of the bun. I sat down on my stool, and Kim reached for her plate. We each took a bite.

"This is heaven, you know that, right?" Kim said.

It was pretty delicious, if I did say so myself. The burger was juicy, seasoned just right, the bread was everything the aroma had promised, and the dressing . . . was good, but didn't taste quite like what I'd had at Franco's. I pulled the spoon out of the bowl of dressing and tasted, then set the spoon down on my plate. Something was definitely missing. Had I forgotten an ingredient? The Worcestershire. That was it. I'd add it next time.

"So what do you think happened to the money?" I asked. "I figured mismanagement. Bad investments."

"I'm sure there was some of that. The MacNamaras have not been Warren Buffetts. The portfolio took a dive with the stock market in 1929, as you'd expect, but fortunately wasn't completely wiped out. Whichever MacNamara was in charge of it then shepherded it back into a steady climb through the war years, until it reached a peak during the Reagan Administration. At that point the money was mostly in mutual funds, and it was valued at over a hundred million dollars."

I nodded. "That's more like what my mother expected to be there. But from what I could see, the balances started dropping again until we get to now, when it looks like there would be just about enough to cover the legal fees of dissolving the trust." My mother had told me that she was leaving her entire estate to my daughter, Callista, which was fine with me. But it was my daughter, and the charities, that were being cheated. And that stuck in my craw.

Susannah Hardy

Kim chewed and swallowed. "After we eat, I'd like to take a look at your original documents."

"The scan wasn't clear? The originals are still at Mac-Namara's, by the way. I only have photocopies."

"Well, I'd like to take a look anyway. I want to know if I'm seeing what I think I'm seeing."

Our eyes met. "What do you mean?"

"I think," Kim said, "the trust financials have been altered."

"Altered?" I set my burger down and let Kim's words sink in. "What do you mean *altered*?"

"I'll show you when we look at your copies. But something isn't right."

◈ FIFTEEN ◈

We finished our dinner and cleaned up in record time. Kim was just as eager to show me the documents as I was to look at them. Since the prep counter was still covered with Gladys Montgomery's recipes, a project that looked like it wasn't going to get completed anytime this winter, we spread out the financials in date order on the counter we'd just eaten at.

Kim pointed to the earliest ledger. "Here's the inception of the trust. The numbers, labels, and notations are all handwritten, as you'd expect. There were typewriters back then, but not everyone was using them for accounting."

"Okay, I see that."

"By the 1940s, they'd switched over to the typewriter. This must have been some tedious work for the typist.

Not to mention annoying. Every time she—or he, though I'd guess it was mostly women doing this kind of work then—made a mistake, she had to fix it manually."

"Pain in the butt," I said. "Every typewriter has its own signature, right? Like rifling on a gun barrel, or fingerprints." Watching all those cop dramas over the long Bonaparte Bay winters was definitely paying off. "Here's where they got a new typewriter. You can tell because the font looks different."

Kim nodded. "Keep going. I want to see if you come to the same conclusion I did."

I studied the ledgers. Every few years the font changed, presumably because the office got new equipment. By the 1980s, the records were kept individually, one year to a page or pages, instead of in a running tally, and there was an unmistakable switch to a dot matrix printer, so the records were now being generated with a computer, probably stored on floppy disks. In 1986, the font changed again, this time to clearer, darker, more uniform letters.

I continued to flip through the pages, then went back to 1986. "This is where the balances start declining," I said. I flipped some more, going all the way to the last page, which showed the paltry six-thousand-dollar-and-change balance. "How long," I wondered, "has Jim Mac-Namara been practicing law?"

Kim nodded. "He joined his father's practice in 1982. But his father died—"

"Let me guess—in 1986."

"Yup. Pete and I bought the accounting business ten

years ago, but the prior owners had been doing taxes and payroll for the MacNamaras for decades before that. We inherited all the records, so those dates were easy enough for me to check."

"Okay," I said, thoughtful. "So Jim MacNamara was young and inexperienced, and he made bad investments. Lost the money over the course of the years."

I thought back to the genealogy Sheldon Todd had shown me. By the mid-1980s, the only beneficiaries of the trust—great-great-grandchildren of my nasty ancestor, Elihu Bloodworth—were pretty young, including my mother. And if Jim conveniently didn't send statements to the beneficiaries, if they didn't know about the trust, or know enough to ask about it, they couldn't monitor the balances.

I thumbed through the last few dozen pages again, then looked up at Kim. She was watching me expectantly.

"The fonts," I said. "From 1986 on, they're all the same. They look like they were all made on the same printer."

She nodded. "That's what I thought too. And what office keeps the same printer, and uses the same font, for more than thirty years?"

"You said you thought the financials had been altered. You think somebody went back to 1986 and retyped all the information—inserting new, reduced figures?" It made some sense, but there could be other reasons. A recent attempt to standardize the files, make them look nice and uniform, without altering the numbers? But Kim clearly hadn't told me everything yet, because she was eyeing me over the rim of her wineglass.

"Yup," Kim said, taking a sip of her wine. "And the only reasons to alter the documents would be—"

"To cover up mismanagement. Or theft." Jim MacNamara. I had a feeling she was right, even though the documents in front of me were hardly proof. "So which do you think it is?"

"In his personal life, Jim was a good investor. Had a nice, diverse portfolio making a more or less steady positive return, at least from what I could see from his tax records. So I think it's unlikely he didn't know what he was doing when it came to the Bloodworth Trust."

Damn him. "Which leaves us with theft. He was skimming the trust money, then he produced these fake financial reports, probably recently, since the trust would be dissolving—expiring—in a couple of months and he knew he was going to have to give Melanie and Liza, the beneficiaries, something." Still, this was all just speculation. There was no real evidence here, nothing I could take to the police.

Kim seemed to have read my mind. "We need more, though. It might help if we could see the original documents these photocopies came from."

That made sense. We'd have a lot better idea if the records since 1986 were a single printout. "I could ask Lydia, who'd have to clear it with Ben. But I'm not sure how I'd do that without letting them know why. Not sure I'm ready to start casting veiled accusations against Jim."

"I agree. But I do have something. I looked up one of

these supposedly failed mutual funds, and guess what? It was actually making money during the time period where these financials show a loss. So I'll do some more digging on the other funds and get as much as I can for you. That's solid information."

Now, maybe, we were getting somewhere. "Yeah. Go ahead. Keep track of the hours you spend on this and get me a bill. I'll make sure somebody pays it." Me, my mother, Liza—maybe we could bill MacNamara's estate? "But even if we find fraud, what do you think the chances of us actually recovering any money are?"

Kim set down her glass and looked me in the eye. "Impossible to say. He could have spent it, given it away, diverted it to some anonymous foreign bank account, converted it to cash and stuffed his mattress—"

"Mattress." The word made me think of Jennifer Murdoch and the affair she'd been having with Mac-Namara. Was she mixed up in this somehow? Was Mac-Namara stockpiling money so he could run away with Jennifer? Maybe she was putting pressure on him? Did he need money to put the Silver Lake real estate deal together? Maybe. But he'd been skimming for years, if our theory was correct, and Jennifer and Silver Lake had only come up recently. Still, it bore consideration.

And how much did Jim's son, Ben, know? He'd said his father always handled the trust himself. They'd needed a locksmith to open the filing cabinet. I supposed Ben could have staged that, but it seemed like overkill.

There was another question that needed to be asked,

not that I expected Kim to have an answer. "Do you think Jim's death had anything to do with the money?"

"I don't know," she said. "But money is a powerful motivator."

Didn't I know it. Suddenly, I wished I was back in my nice, safe cocoon of a few months ago, neatly dividing my life between the tourist season and the off-season, mothering my daughter, being Sophie's daughter-in-law and Spiro's wife, at least on paper. I'd never heard of the damned Bloodworth Trust. And people didn't die because of it.

But there was a little thing—okay, a big thing—called justice. I'd never really thought about it till now. But figuring out what was going on here, then taking it to the police, was the right thing to do.

And I was done with people messing with my family. Fed up with dishonesty and greed and violence and death. Tomorrow I'd light a fire under Sheldon, the genealogist. The sooner I confirmed what was in the legal file about the descendants of Elihu Bloodworth, the sooner I could check that, at least, off my mental list.

My cell phone rang, pulling me out of my thoughts. Across the prep counter, Kim was picking up the documents we'd laid out. I connected the call. "Hello?"

"Georgie? This is Marielle Riccardi."

Franco's daughter. "Yes. How's your father?" My heart rate began to tick up. I hoped she had good news.

"He's got a concussion and a dislocated shoulder. He'll be all right. I wanted to thank you for helping him. And to ask you a favor."

"Of course." I realized, too late, that I probably should have waited to hear what the favor was before agreeing to it.

"We're still at the hospital, and they're going to keep Dad overnight. I don't want to leave until he's settled for the evening. Would you mind going to the Casa di Pizza and putting a note on the door that the restaurant is closed for two weeks? There's not enough business this time of year to justify trying to find a temporary cook to take Dad's place so we'll just close up."

"I'll do it tonight," I said. I'd ask Kim to accompany me, on the off chance Deputy Tim Arquette was wrong about the assaulter not still being in town. "Is there anything else you'd like me to do? If you're going to be shut down, someone should go over and clean the perishables out of the fridge and straighten up, at least, so anybody looking in the window doesn't see the mess and look at it as an invitation to break in."

"Would you?" Marielle sounded relieved. "Dad will probably be discharged tomorrow. I'll be bringing him home with me and I need to fill prescriptions and get extra groceries and get my house set up. And, oh yeah, run my business."

"Not a problem," I said. "I'm happy to help." It wouldn't take long, and I was pretty sure Franco would do the same for me.

"I'll drop the keys off in the morning, if that's okay. And Georgie, thanks." She clicked off.

I filled in Kim about Franco's condition. We packed up the trust documents and she followed me to my office, where we typed up a sign and printed it off. I located a plastic sheet protector and some duct tape, then we bundled up, checked and double-checked the alarm, and headed off in Kim's car for the Casa.

The wind was even colder than it had been just a couple of hours ago, a thing I wouldn't have thought possible if I hadn't lived through a few decades' worth of North Country winters. Snow from the recent storm we'd had blew up in a white whoosh against the car as we pulled up in front of Franco's restaurant. I envied Sophie—and my daughter, Cal—in Greece right about now. I wondered when Cal was coming home. She was supposed to call when she got her flight, but I hadn't heard from her yet.

"Want me to help?" Kim said.

"No sense both of us freezing our butts off. Keep the heater running and I'll be right back." I braced myself, then opened the door.

Tearing off the four pieces of tape required me to take off my gloves, and my hands were numb by the time the sign was on the door. I jammed my hands into my pockets and looked in the window, but it was too dark to see anything. I returned to the car, shut the door, and leaned forward in my seat to put my hands over the heating vents, which were blasting precious hot air.

"Ready to go home?" Kim put her hand on the shifter.

"May as well," I said. "Do you mind driving me around back? I just want to double-check that Tim locked the door after he was finished."

Kim drove to the end of the block, then up Vincent Street. "Scene of the crime," she said without humor. We were nearing the building that housed MacNamara and MacNamara. The sign over the door, which hung on an old-fashioned wrought iron rod perpendicular to the exterior of the building, swung violently in the wind. A light was on in the office. I checked my watch. It was nearly eight o'clock at night—way past business hours. Now that he was in charge, had Junior developed a work ethic?

Just as we passed the building, the door opened and a figure came out onto the street. The cut of the coat was definitely feminine. Whoever it was had her hat pulled way down and her scarf pulled way up. She stood at the curb, apparently intending to cross the street. Kim pulled to a stop to let the woman cross in front of us. The headlights illuminated her, but it was impossible to make an identification, bundled up as she was.

Kim spoke first. "A bit late for a legal appointment, especially with Jim MacNamara not even in the ground yet. I wonder who that is?"

The woman got into a light-colored compact car parked a few yards in front of us. The lights blazed up, cutting through the November darkness.

"It's not Lydia," I said. "That woman is too tall." She was about the same height as Jennifer Murdoch, though. Had Jennifer come back to harangue Ben about the videocamera?

Kim started forward again. She drove as slowly as she

could past the parked car. I looked into the windows but they were opaque, still defrosting. I didn't recognize the vehicle.

"Do you have to get home right away?" I said. "Let's drive around the block and see if we can figure out where she goes."

"Ooh, are we on a stakeout? Count me in," she said gleefully.

"I honestly don't know. But I don't trust Junior."

Kim drove up Vincent Street to the next intersection, made a right, then increased her speed and made another right back onto Theresa. She pulled back onto Vincent. The taillights of the vehicle were visible up ahead. I glanced at the law office as we passed for the second time. The lights were now off. Ben must have parked around back because there was no other vehicle on the street.

We followed the car at a distance, which wasn't difficult since the streets were empty. A few minutes later, the car pulled in at the River Rock Resort.

Kim parked and turned to me. "Now what?"

"Beats me." Sheldon Todd was staying there, so I supposed I could follow the mystery woman in on the pretext of my needing to speak to him. But it was late enough that Angela, or whoever she had at the front desk, would think it odd, my showing up now. And what would I say if I ran into the woman? "Excuse me, but who are you and why were you meeting with Junior MacNamara after hours?" I didn't have that kind of moxie.

We stared up at the shabby façade of the River Rock.

There were half a dozen cars in the lot. The lobby was lit, but there were only a couple of upstairs windows illuminated. We watched, but another window didn't light. Which didn't necessarily mean anything. The woman might not have gone directly to her room, or she might just be checking in, which would take longer. Had Jennifer and Steve Murdoch had another fight? That would explain her checking into the River Rock. If it was her.

"You may as well take me home," I said. "We aren't going to find out anything else tonight, and you'll want to get home to Pete."

Kim dropped me at the back door of the Bonaparte House, then waited while I went inside before driving off. I locked up, then went straight to bed, too tired to even be creeped out about sleeping here, where a murder had occurred one floor down. It had been one heck of a long day.

◆ SIXTEEN ◆

I slept later than usual the next morning and was still in my slippers and fleece pajamas and drinking my first cup of coffee in the restaurant kitchen when a knock sounded at the back door. It was Marielle, dropping off the keys to the Casa di Pizza.

"Coffee?" I asked.

"Tempting, but I need to get to the hospital. I really appreciate this." Her expression was apologetic, as though she wasn't used to asking for help. Which was something I understood.

She handed me the keys and left.

Sufficiently caffeinated, I reviewed my mental to-do list for the day. I had a number of phone calls to make, which I would do before I went to the Casa. I started out by texting my daughter, asking her for a status on her flight information.

And then I texted Jack. I miss you. He probably couldn't respond—he hadn't been able to call me last night—but it made me feel better to let him know I was thinking about him.

Next, I dialed Dolly. "How are you feeling?" I asked when she picked up. "Do you need anything?"

"Hey," she rasped, then set off in a short fit of coughing, which sounded less intense than yesterday. When she caught her breath, she said, "Better. And no. I think the prescription Doc Phelps gave me is working." There were shades of her usual upbeat self in her words.

"Well, don't overdo, okay? You want me to bring you dinner?"

"We're all set here. Harold and Brandy are taking good care of me. I'll be up and around to cook your Thanksgiving."

Whether there would be a Thanksgiving dinner remained to be seen. My restrooms were all torn up, my cook was going to need a clean bill of health before I could let her into my kitchen, and I hadn't even thought about the menu, let alone doing any local advertising. Oh, and a murder had happened here. That might bring people in, or it might keep them away.

"Any news from Russ?"

She gave a dry snort, but managed to keep herself from breaking into another fit of coughing. "You mean, from the slammer? Brandy went to see him, but he wouldn't talk to his own sister. Just asked about his dogs."

"Do you want me to, uh, ask around? See if I can find out anything?" I wasn't very enthusiastic about that offer since, like his mother, I thought it wouldn't hurt Russ to cool his heels in jail for a while, whether he was guilty of murder or not. He'd been guilty of plenty of other things in the past that he hadn't been prosecuted for. Still, if he was innocent—and that was a big *if*—I'd get involved for Dolly, if she wanted me to.

Fortunately, she didn't, because she simply said, "Nope."

We said our good-byes and disconnected.

Next I sent a text to Liza. Normally she'd be up by now and I would have called, but I knew she was under the weather too, maybe in the early stages of whatever Melanie and Caitlyn had, so I didn't want to disturb her if she was sleeping in. I wondered what, if anything, Dr. Phelps had diagnosed. But if it had been anything serious, Liza, or somebody on her skeleton staff, would have called.

My eyes fell on the pile of Gladys's recipes still on the prep counter. Beginning to read through them would be a good project for this afternoon. I drained my coffee, rinsed out the cup, and went upstairs to get dressed.

As I put on my jeans, I realized there was something in the pocket. I pulled out a folded piece of paper—the photocopy of Franco's Thousand Island dressing recipe, the one he thought was an original. I opened it up, set it on the bed, and wiped my hand across the surface to flatten it.

Huh? I read through again. The recipe was labeled "Sophia's Sauce." I read through the ingredients, then thought back to the dressing I'd made yesterday from it. I *had* followed the recipe—this recipe, at least—exactly. But my dressing didn't taste like the one Franco had served me and Brenda at the Casa, what seemed like weeks ago but was really only a few days. Franco's dressing had contained Worcestershire sauce. The recipe I was holding in my hand did not.

And what else had Franco said? Something about . . . grammar? Punctuation? *Sophias Sauce*, he'd said. *No apostrophe*.

Well, the title of this recipe contained an apostrophe.

And this was clearly not Franco's recipe, the one he'd said he planned to post on his restaurant's website and send to the local newspaper, the *Bay Blurb*.

I hadn't asked for the recipe. He'd offered, and he was planning to go public with it. So why would he send his server over with a fake? It made no sense.

Unless it wasn't Franco who'd sent it.

I thought back to that server. I'd never seen her before. During the busy season, that wouldn't be unusual. The restaurants and bars and other businesses in town were heavily staffed by college students who needed summer jobs. But by this time of year, when almost everything was shut down or running on minimum power, it *was* unusual to have a nonlocal on staff.

Had she altered the document? But why?

I sat down on the bed, shivering. I realized I was still

in just a T-shirt so I pulled my cardigan over my arms, grateful for the immediate warmth.

What was it with all this document altering anyway? First the Bloodworth Trust documents, and now this recipe. If there was a connection, it escaped me.

Unless it was Jim MacNamara. But he was already dead when that waitress dropped off the recipe. And Franco had said he used a Watertown lawyer, not Jim. So any similarities had to be a coincidence.

Another shiver ran through me, despite my warm sweater.

Other people had an interest in Thousand Island dressing, beyond making a choice as to what they would put on their salads. There was that guy a couple towns over who claimed he'd found the original recipe in a safe.

And there was Angela Wainwright at the River Rock.

Franco had been assaulted in his own restaurant. What if the reason hadn't been money? What if someone had been looking for his recipe?

I pulled out my cell phone. Suddenly, the prospect of cleaning up at the Casa di Pizza alone didn't seem all that appealing. I could call the BBPD, get one of the deputies, like Tim Arquette, to come over while I worked. But according to Tim, they thought it had simply been someone looking for money, someone who was long gone.

Lieutenant Hawthorne from the State Police? No. Just No.

Brenda had said she was going to the boat show today. I looked out the window. The sky was dark. Gray.

Ominous. That storm we'd been promised was coming in today. I dialed Brenda anyway.

"You home?" I said.

"Yeah. I decided not to go to Syracuse. Looks like I could get there, but it's the getting back I'm worried about. What's up?"

"Meet me at the Casa in twenty minutes?"

She agreed.

Brenda was already there when I arrived. The air was so damp and heavy, I felt like I'd trekked miles, though it was only a block and a half. I unlocked the door and we went inside.

"So why are we here?" Brenda asked. "Place is a mess."

"I told Franco's daughter I'd come in and straighten up." I began to right chairs and reposition tables and Brenda joined in.

"And in case whoever did this comes back, I'm expendable?" She gave a good-natured laugh.

"More like, I'm a wimp and I need moral support." Brenda was also tough—she needed to be in her line of work, prowling the streets of Bonaparte Bay at night during the tourist season—and I would not have been surprised if she'd been packing. Maybe not a gun, but something.

"You're no wimp. But I'm glad you called." She righted the salt and pepper shakers and brushed the spilled spices off onto the floor.

I felt a little surge of pride. She didn't think I was a

wimp! Even if I wasn't quite sure I believed it, it was nice to hear.

"The refrigerators need to be emptied. You want to help with that, or keep going out here?"

"Out here," she said. "And I'll keep my eyes open."

Back in the kitchen, I opened the extra-large refrigerator door. Franco didn't have a big walk-in like we had back at the Bonaparte House. I found what I expected: dairy products, including a half-dozen giant blocks of mozzarella shrink-wrapped in heavy plastic from the factory near Ogdensburg, a few towns downriver. I checked the expiration dates. Other than one that was opened, which I set aside, these would be fine for a couple of weeks and I replaced them on their shelf. Several large tubs of red sauce, whose handwritten labels indicated they'd been made a couple of days ago. They'd still be good today, but I wondered if he'd want me to donate or freeze them. Deciding to err on the side of caution, I made room on the freezer side of the unit and put them in. When he did reopen, the sauce would be one less thing he'd have to worry about.

My mind wandered as I got into the rhythm of the work: pull, check expiration, sort into freezer, fridge, throw away, or donate to the First Methodist Food Pantry.

In the background, I could hear Brenda moving things around, but it barely registered. Suppose someone did want Franco's recipe. What could he or she do with it? My understanding was that a recipe itself couldn't be copyrighted or patented, which I'd found out when Dolly had once asked me about protecting her special pie crust recipe. But it could be trademarked, like Toll House® chocolate chip cookies.

Could someone be trying to trademark Thousand Island dressing? That would explain why someone would give me a fake, and why my car and this restaurant had been ransacked. Maybe someone was looking for all the copies of the original. But that seemed naïve on the part of whoever was behind this. Who was to say Franco hadn't already sent a real copy to the *Bay Blurb* or to his Aunt Tillie in Kokomo?

Still, the bigger question was why. Thousand Island dressing recipes were a dime a dozen. There were bottles of the pink, lumpy stuff on every supermarket shelf in America, manufactured by several different companies. Nobody really knew which recipe was the first one, though I thought Franco had a pretty good case for his. How valuable could it be? My guess was not very. There was an awful lot of competition out there.

The sound of Brenda's voice brought me out of my thoughts. I wiped my hands on a kitchen towel and headed for the front of the restaurant.

A woman was there, talking to Brenda, who had her arms folded over her chest. Brenda cut her eyes to me.

"Can I help you?" I said to the woman, suddenly realizing I knew who this was. "You're the waitress, right?"

"Yeah," she said. "I came in for my shift last night, but the police sent me home without telling me anything.

Franco's not answering his phone, and I saw the 'Closed' sign out front. What's going on?"

No sense trying to be discreet. News of the attack would be all over the Bay by now. I was only surprised she hadn't already heard about it. But then, she didn't appear to be a local.

"Franco was attacked yesterday. He'll be all right in a couple of weeks. In the meantime, he's closing the restaurant until he's well enough to come back."

Her lips, glossy as though she'd just applied makeup, turned down. "Great. And I've got a car payment due." She must have recollected herself, thought about how that sounded, because she added quickly. "I mean, I'm sorry about Franco. Two weeks? I guess I can pick up a shift or two somewhere else."

Even though she'd been insensitive, I couldn't really blame her. Jobs were precious in the North Country.

I stuck out my hand. "I'm Georgie Nikolopatos. From the Bonaparte House. And this is Brenda Jones. We're here helping Franco temporarily close up."

"Piper. Piper Preston." She gave my hand a tentative shake, then dropped it.

"You brought me an envelope the other day. Thanks." I watched her closely. Her face was expressionless.

"You're welcome. I, uh, gotta go. If you see Franco, tell him I hope he feels better." She turned to leave.

"Say, Piper," I called to her back. "Who gave you that envelope to give to me? Franco? There was no name or note inside."

She stopped, then faced me. "I just found it on the counter with a sticky note addressed to me, telling me to deliver it to you. I assumed it was from Franco, but we didn't talk about it." Piper left.

The woman was either lying, or somebody had used her. For what purpose was anybody's guess.

❖ SEVENTEEN ❖

I bagged up the items to be donated and made a list for Franco for tax purposes, which I left in a drawer near the point of sale machine, then realized I'd need to go get my car to deliver everything to the food pantry. So the bags went back into the refrigerator for now. I made a run to the Dumpster out back with anything too close to its sell-by date to risk giving to the church. By the time I completed these tasks, Brenda had finished straightening up the front of the house and was waiting for me.

"We done?" she asked.

"Yeah, the place looks good. I'll lock up and come back later to get the food. Thanks."

"Call me if you need me again," Brenda said. She left through the back door.

I locked up and was right behind her.

Within a half hour, I'd retrieved my car, picked up the food, and delivered it. Before I left the church parking lot, my cell phone rang. I put the car into Park again and answered.

"Georgie," Liza said. "I wanted to give you an update." Her voice was weak, breathy as though each word cost her. My worry meter ticked up. My friend and cousin was getting sicker.

"Did Dr. Phelps make it over there yesterday? What's wrong with you all?" A little knot formed in my stomach in sympathy.

Liza drew a ragged breath. "He did. Thinks it's some kind of food poisoning. He took . . . samples for testing."

Food poisoning. Two words that struck terror into the heart of any restauranteur. And I had no desire—or need—to know what kind of samples had been taken. "But you developed your symptoms after Melanie and Caitlyn. Do you know what caused it?"

"Not yet," she said. "But we're all living on canned chicken broth and ginger ale now. I've sent the staff and the last couple other guests home."

"I'm coming over there now. Brenda hasn't pulled her boat from the water yet. I'll borrow it and come get you."

Liza let out a weak cough. "Dr. Phelps wants us to stay here. Says the motion of a boat ride or helicopter ride will make us even more nauseous than we already are."

"Then I'm coming to stay. I can take care of you." I'd just bring in my own food.

"Love to have you, but no need. The doctor is

arranging for a visiting nurse. She'll be here in a few hours. We'll be fine until then. Trust me," she said. "You want a professional dealing with these . . . symptoms."

I remembered that I'd promised to take Dolly to her follow-up appointment tomorrow morning so Brandy and Harold wouldn't have to miss time from work. "Are you sure?" I was torn. A lot of people I loved needed me right now. How was I supposed to choose?

"I'm sure. We'll be okay for a few more hours."

"All right. But the minute that nurse gets there, I want her to call me so I can talk to her." I wasn't at all happy, but at that point, nothing could make me so. Liza was sick, but she seemed functional at this point, so presumably whatever bug they had just needed to work its way out of their systems.

"I will. And don't worry. As soon as the doctor says we can move, we will. You could do me a favor, if you want."

Finally. A way to help. "Of course. What?"

"Can you call Steamie's and have them clean the carpets in my mainland condo and e-mail me a bill? I'm too tired to look up the number."

"Good idea. Your place will be ready when you are. And Melanie and Caitlyn can come stay with me until they head back to California. Now go get some rest. And have that nurse call me," I ordered.

Liza gave a soft chuckle. "Yes, ma'am." The call disconnected.

Food poisoning? Of course it could happen in any

kitchen, home or professional, no matter how careful someone was. But it was rare. I was grateful, for Liza's sake, that she didn't have a castleful of guests, only Melanie and Caitlyn, who could presumably keep it quiet. Based on the timing of the illnesses, it seemed like Liza would be able to figure out what the culprit was by process of elimination without too much difficulty when she was feeling better. Although at this point, it probably didn't matter. She was closing up, and all the perishables would presumably be discarded. Anything sealed would be donated, just as I had done with Franco's food.

While I had my phone out, I sent another text to my daughter. Why wasn't Cal answering? I hoped she wasn't going to show up here to try to surprise me. I'd had enough surprises to last a lifetime in the last few months.

I pulled out of the lot and drove to the River Rock Resort.

The building hadn't gotten any nicer since the last time I was here. A fresh coat of paint would have done wonders for the place, at least the exterior. I'd never seen the guest rooms. As I walked toward the front steps, I thought about the woman I'd seen coming here the other night. Today the parking lot had only a handful of cars, which was to be expected this time of year. None of them looked like the car the woman had driven, but then again, it had been dark and I hadn't gotten a close look at it.

I entered the lobby. Quite a difference between this place and the comfortable, understated feeling of elegance the Camelot engendered. And it was light-years away from the foyer of Liza's Castle Grant, but maybe that wasn't a fair comparison. Still, Angela Wainwright could have done a better job here, even if she was on a low budget. The rack of Thousand Island dressing bottles was full, indicating either that she was vigilant about restocking, or she hadn't sold any since I'd been here last. I was betting on the latter, since there was a thin coating of dust on most of them. I still had a bottle back at the Bonaparte House and it hadn't even been opened.

And where was Angela anyway? I'd been here at least five minutes waiting for Sheldon Todd to come down from his room. Five minutes might not seem like a long time, but if I'd been a paying customer waiting for someone to rent me a room, I might have left and tried somewhere else in that time.

Angela. Could she have been behind the break-in at the Casa di Pizza? Bonaparte Bay was a small town. I didn't know who else Franco had told about his discovery of the very old—quite possibly the oldest—recipe for Thousand Island dressing, but it was a safe bet other people knew about it and it could have gotten back to Angela. And Brenda had said something about Angela trying to capitalize on it somehow.

My thoughts jumped to my trip to Watertown the other day. Someone had tossed my car in the mall parking lot, the same day the fake recipe had been delivered to me by Piper, Franco's waitress. Could someone have thought Franco had already given me a copy? Followed me to Watertown then followed me—too closely—home?

But I still couldn't see what Angela, or anyone, would have to gain from the recipe. If someone wanted to make money, all he or she would have to do would be to start bottling and selling any version of the dressing—and anyone could claim they were using the original. One wouldn't necessarily sell any better than the other one, since there was no way to prove it. And outside the geographical region of northern New York State, I was willing to bet nobody cared.

A large figure appeared in my peripheral vision. I turned.

"Hi, Sheldon."

The genealogist took up a lot of space. He gave me a big smile. "Georgie. Lovely to see you again. Can I buy you lunch? A cup of coffee or dessert?"

Generous. The expenses on Melanie's bill were mounting with a series of almost audible clicks. "Uh, no, but thanks. Any progress on the genealogy?" There was no one around, but I kept my voice low anyway.

"Yes," he said. "Let's go into the business center, where there's a table we can spread out at." He led me down a short hallway in the opposite direction of the dining room. Angela still hadn't appeared. No wonder her hotel didn't seem to be doing well, with that kind of customer service.

The business center turned out to be a square room painted a dull peachy color. Chairs upholstered in faded sage green woven upholstery flanked a mismatched rectangular table. At one end of the room, a huge old-fashioned fax machine—the kind with an actual telephone receiver on a curly cord attached—sat next to a small printer-photocopier combination. A cup full of assorted pens and pencils and a stapler with pretend wood panels rounded out the accoutrements. This little office would have been state of the art—about twenty years ago.

Sheldon sat down on one side of the table and began to spread out some papers. "I have to say, yours has been one of the more interesting families I've worked on."

Interesting? I supposed to an outsider, it would be. But "interesting" wasn't the word I would have used. Everything had changed—some things for the better, some decidedly for the worse—since I started learning about my family. I wasn't sure I wanted to learn anymore.

"You got the attorney's records I sent you? Did they help?"

"Not really. They know less than I do." His expression was the slightest bit smug.

Sheldon was making me work for it. Of course, he was getting paid by the hour, so it was to his advantage to drag things out. "Which is what?"

He sat back in his chair, which gave an ominous creak under his weight. "I've accounted for all the descendants from *both* of Elihu Bloodworth's wives. You, your daughter, your mother, and Liza Grant are it. The only ones left."

I let out a breath I didn't know I'd been holding. Thank goodness. This damn trust, what was left of it, was going to dissolve in February, and then we could put this behind us. Or could we? I needed to call Kim Galbraith and see what she'd found out about the supposedly failed mutual funds. Liza and Melanie, the legal heirs to the trust, would probably want to pursue Jim MacNamara's estate to see if any of the money could be recovered. After all, it was theirs. But so many people had died, so many people had been hurt. It was tempting to tell them to just let it all go.

Another thought struck me. "Didn't you say something about a cousin, Percy, who disappeared? What happened to him?"

Sheldon leaned forward again and shuffled the papers around. He pulled out a photograph printed on a sheet of copy paper and handed it to me. "As I suspected, Percy died fighting overseas in World War Two. He never married. No known offspring. Here's a photo of his grave at Normandy." I studied the picture. A simple white cross in a sea of thousands of other white crosses. A lump rose in my throat as I looked at his name and the dates of his birth and death. "He was just a kid."

"Most of them were," Sheldon said. "And an awful lot of them didn't come back."

I took a deep breath to compose myself, then looked up at Sheldon. "So that's it? No more surprise twigs on the family tree?"

Sheldon chuckled. "I've traced every descendant of both wives. I've even scoured historical newspapers—many of them are digitized now, so it's relatively easy—as well as the library's and historical society's records for any mention of illegitimate children. Or I should say *more* illegitimate than those from his second wife, your great-great-great-grandmother. I hope my saying that doesn't offend you?"

I shook my head. "Doesn't bother me."

"And I found nothing. So I'm confident we have this buttoned up."

I wished I could be so confident. Great Gramps seemed to have had rather liberal views when it came to fidelity. But I believed Sheldon had done thorough work. If anyone else decided to come forward, they were going to have to produce some spit on a swab and pay for some genetic testing.

Sheldon gathered up the papers and stacked them, then patted one short and one long edge into a neat stack, which he secured with a big binder clip. He handed the whole packet to me. "This is for your mother," he said. "I could wait around until she comes back from that island, if you want me to tell her in person what I found."

More likely, Sheldon just wanted to see Melanie again. "I'll let her know. And thanks for all your help." I stuck out my hand, and Sheldon took it.

"My pleasure. I'll prepare the genealogical charts and send them to you so you'll have a nice record, but I can do that from my office. The weather report says there's some bad weather coming in, so I'll check out and head home now before it hits."

I tucked the packet of papers under my arm and rose. "Send your bill to Melanie."

He smiled broadly. "Oh, I will. Maybe I'll hand deliver it."

Go for it, I thought.

◈ EIGHTEEN ◈

I was just finishing up my lunch at the counter in the Bonaparte House kitchen, after talking to the visiting nurse, who assured me she had things under control on Valentine Island, when my cell phone rang. I put down my Raphaela Ridgeway novel—regretfully, as the story was at a suspenseful point—and answered.

"Hey, Georgie," Kim Galbraith said. "We've got 'em."

I sat up straighter. "We do? What did you find?" Maybe Liza and Melanie, and eventually my daughter, would get their money after all.

"Those mutual funds? I did a random sampling and checked the actual fund prices for the dates on the ledger. Of course, there were fluctuations in the value, but over the course of the last twenty years, they've all shown a decent return."

That dirty Jim MacNamara. "Do you think this is enough to take to the police?"

"I don't know enough about criminal law to give you an answer. But it should be enough for an ethics complaint with the New York State bar, at least."

"But Jim MacNamara is dead, so realistically what are they going to do?"

"My guess is that you'd need to hire a new lawyer, maybe file a civil lawsuit and let him or her subpoena all the documentation from Ben. Then you could decide together whether there was enough to file a criminal complaint. Although who you'd file it against, I don't know, since the perpetrator is dead."

Great. More lawyers. A formal complaint and discovery process would probably take months, maybe years. "Thanks, Kim. I'll talk with Melanie and Liza and see what they want to do."

"Anytime. I'll write up a summary of what I found and e-mail it to you. Let me know what you all decide. If you want to share, that is."

"After all your help, I'd say you deserve to know the outcome. Talk to you later." I rang off.

Of course I planned to talk to Melanie and Liza. But I planned to talk to Ben MacNamara first. He was almost young enough to be my son and I had pretty good truth-detecting skills. I needed to find out if he'd known about this all along, and was just playing innocent about the locked filing cabinet.

Fifteen minutes later, I entered the law offices of

MacNamara and MacNamara. Lydia was at her desk. She looked up in surprise when I came in. "Hi, Georgie," she said. "The office is officially closed. Jim's funeral was this morning." I'd been so preoccupied the last few days, I hadn't bothered to read the obituaries in the *Blurb*, or I would have known that myself.

"Sorry," I said. "I was just hoping to have a quick word with Ben about my divorce. How it's going." Melanie and Liza had given me an authorization to look at the Bloodworth Trust file. It had said nothing about authorizing me to talk to the law firm about it. Lydia was an experienced gatekeeper. No way would she let me in if she knew I wanted to talk to Junior about the trust.

Lydia frowned, just a little. "He's in there, but now's maybe not the best time. Jennifer Murdoch came to the funeral and made a big scene in the Episcopal Church Fellowship Hall after the service. Can this wait?"

"I just need to know for my own peace of mind that Jim's death isn't going to slow the progress. I'm anxious to put my marriage behind me and move ahead." I knew I was being insensitive, and that I was pressing some buttons for Lydia. Her own divorce had been bitter, from what I'd heard.

She looked at my face, then nodded. "I understand," she said. "Let me see if he'll talk to you. Wait here." She rose from her desk, crossed the room, and opened a metal filing cabinet. After thumbing through the file tabs, she pulled one out and headed for the door to the interior office. She rapped softly on the surface, then opened the door. She disappeared inside.

While I waited, I looked around. Lydia's desk was enviably neat. No stray sticky notes or loose pens. A file lay on the blotter. The tab read, "Tripler Enterprises." The door to the office opened again, so I quickly glanced away, my gaze landing on an innocent coat hanging on the rack. I hoped I looked innocent too. It would be bad to be caught snooping in a law office, where confidentiality was king. Or queen.

"You can go on in," Lydia said. "And cut him some slack. It's been a tough day, and it's going to get tougher. His mother's in town. That's why he's hiding out here."

"Thanks." I made my way into the office and shut the door.

Ben was seated behind a broad mahogany desk. He looked up when I sat down in the visitor's chair across from him.

"You want to know about your divorce?" he said, opening the file. "I'm sorry I haven't really had a chance to get up to speed on all my father's files. He was working on this one himself."

"Yeah. When can I expect the decree?" He quickly reviewed the first few pages in the file. His hands shook slightly as he turned the pages. The guy was keyed up, though it was impossible to say why.

"It looks like we're just waiting for the time to run out. We should be able to apply for the final dissolution within a couple of weeks." I already knew this, but it was nice to hear it confirmed.

"Great. I hate to press you at a time like this, but I want to move forward as soon as possible."

"Okay," he said. "This will be one of the easier things I have to do now." He closed the file, picked up a pen, and began tapping on the manila cover. Junior was definitely agitated.

"Oh," I said casually. "While I'm here, thanks for that file on the Bloodworth Trust. My mother and Liza Grant appreciated it."

The tapping got faster. "You're welcome," he said.

"There's not as much money in there as we expected." I tried to keep my voice neutral while I watched his reaction.

His jaw stiffened. Junior knew something, but how much? "Oh?" he said. "I'd never seen that file until a couple of days ago, so I have no idea how much is, or is supposed to be, in there. You'd have to talk to my father about that. And that's not possible." He rose. "If you don't mind, my family is waiting for me."

Dismissed. I also rose. "Of course. How rude of me to keep you, today of all days. My condolences to you and your mother."

"Yeah, my mother needs condolences. Her alimony has just been cut off. Now she's probably going to sue Dad's estate. She'll figure out some way to squeeze money out of the old man, even now he's dead."

He followed me into the front of the office and

shrugged into the topcoat that had been hanging on the rack. I zipped up my coat and nodded to Lydia. *Thanks*, I mouthed. She nodded.

Junior and I left together, though we separated when we got outside. Once I was half a block away, I turned. He was headed in the direction of the Camelot. That was probably where his mother was staying, though I hadn't seen her when I'd been there. Ben lived in a condo owned by his father down by the marina. Jim had lived in one of the smaller Victorians—which were still huge, by today's standards—on Wellesley Island. Perhaps Junior hadn't invited her to stay with him, or perhaps bachelor pad living didn't suit her. The crime scene tape might still have been up at Jim's house. I hadn't been by, so I didn't know.

The back vent of the dark wool topcoat Ben wore flapped open as he walked away. The sight jogged something in my memory. The cold wind blew it away. I couldn't stand here all day staring after Ben. I turned back toward the Bonaparte House and started walking.

What was it Brenda had said about Jim? The day of the murder, she'd seen him walking down Theresa Street. Quite probably, he had taken the very same route I was taking now. She said he was wearing an overcoat and carrying a briefcase.

But when I found the body, there'd been no coat. No briefcase.

Which meant the killer must have taken those fairly bulky items when he left.

The Bonaparte House kitchen was warm and dry when I entered. The rest of the house, being two hundred years old, was drafty, but the kitchen was an addition and had some insulation. It was my favorite room anyway. I hung up my coat on a peg by the back door, then pressed a number into my cell.

"Brenda?" I said when she picked up. I wasn't sure why I made it a question. Who else would answer her phone?

"Yo."

"The day Jim MacNamara died, you saw him headed here, right?"

"Yup." She was monosyllabic today, but her words got the job done.

"And he was wearing a topcoat and carrying a brief-case, right?"

"Uh-huh."

"Where were you when you saw him?"

"Checking the trash can in front of the Chamber of Commerce. He went around back of your restaurant."

"The police must have asked you this, but did you see anyone come out, either from the back parking lot, or maybe the side or front door?" I hadn't thought to ask her that when we were talking just after the murder.

"Yup, the cops asked me that. I'd moved farther away, down by the jewelry shop. But I did see someone coming from that direction, maybe twenty minutes after I first saw the lawyer."

The suspense was killing me. "Was it Russ?" I hated to ask, because at one time Brenda had had a bit of a crush on my former dishwasher.

"The cops asked me that too. Naw. It wasn't him." She paused dramatically. "It was the lawyer again, Jim MacNamara."

◈ NINETEEN ◈

Huh? That made no sense. "You mean you saw him go in, and go out again? How could that be? He was dead."

"That's what the cops said. They didn't believe me. That's what comes of drinking for so many years. You lose credibility. But I know what I saw."

My thoughts raced. "I believe you," I said. I didn't know what it meant, but I thought she was telling the truth. Or the truth as she knew it. Which might not be the same thing.

"Of course, he was pretty far away at that point and I couldn't see his face. He had a hat on pulled down low. But there aren't many men that wear topcoats and carry briefcases in Bonaparte Bay."

She was right about that. The bank manager, the

funeral director, and the two lawyers in town were about it.

Which meant, unless Jim had arrived at the Bonaparte House, left, and returned, only to get himself killed, someone had worn his topcoat and carried his briefcase from the murder scene. If it wasn't Russ, who had it been?

"Thanks Brenda. I was just curious."

"Yeah, I'm curious a lot too. Gotta go."

I made myself a cup of coffee and sat down at the counter in front of Gladys's recipes. My phone sat on the counter and I stared at it.

I'd taken pictures of the restrooms, both before and after the demolition. It was possible they'd show something and I kicked myself for not thinking of it before. I opened up my photo gallery and began to scroll through.

There were a number of "before" pictures, showing the pink and black tile and the chipped porcelain sinks and scarred stall walls, both in the men's and ladies' rooms. Nothing stood out, other than general ugliness. Nor did I expect it to.

I scrutinized the "after" picture of the men's room. The sinks and toilets had been removed and were stacked up awaiting disposal. The entire room was covered in a white powder. Nothing stuck out at me other than a few footprints.

I moved on to the ladies' room. It had the same dismantled fixtures and stalls as the men's, the same white dust obscuring the surfaces. A lump rose in my throat.

Susannah Hardy

I'd stopped taking pictures when I saw Jim's body, thank God. I didn't need a photograph because that picture was seared into my brain. I examined the last photo again. More footprints in the dust.

A lot of footprints.

I sent that picture to my laptop, waited impatiently for it to load, then brought it up on the larger screen. The resolution wasn't all that good, but I could make out several distinct shapes. Several large ones had rounded toes and heels—workboots? That would make sense on a construction site. Another set had pointed toes and a horseshoe-shaped heel and led toward the body, which was just out of the view of the camera. An identical set led away. And there was a smaller pointed toe. No heel mark was visible. These all suggested dress shoes, which would make sense. Jim would have been wearing these. Russ would not.

But the footprints did back up Brenda's story that Jim had left again, after he'd arrived.

I e-mailed the photos to my scary friend Lieutenant Hawthorne. I didn't know what they meant. But maybe he would.

By now my coffee was cold. I put the mug into the microwave. While I waited for it to ding, I thought about what I knew about this murder. So far, it was just a whole lot of disjointed facts that didn't form any kind of pattern, didn't make any kind of sense. The only thing for sure was that Jim MacNamara was dead, and someone had seen fit to take his life in my home and business.

I set my again-steaming mug down on the counter and began to play with Gladys's recipes, shuffling the piles around, looking at the papers but not actually reading them. I was just about to pull one randomly and start cooking—anything to take my mind off it all, even if it was a cream soup casserole—when my cell phone buzzed. It was a good thing I'd bought a plan with unlimited minutes, because this thing was getting a workout.

"Georgie?" a woman said when I answered. "It's Marielle Riccardi. I wanted to thank you for taking care of things at the Casa."

"Hi, Marielle." Even over the phone, the woman made me feel guilty about my less than healthy eating habits and lack of exercise. "How's your dad?"

"Better. Maybe. I think. The concussion has messed with his head, you know? He keeps saying something about a waiter. 'The waiter has the slip.' Before this happened, I know he was thinking about firing that new woman he hired."

I thought back to Piper's uninspiring performance as a server. "She . . . had some things to learn." I'd feel bad if someone lost a job because of something I'd said, even if she clearly wasn't cut out for restaurant work.

"That's putting it kindly. She waited on me once and couldn't even remember to bring me a glass of water when I asked for it. I had to go to the kitchen myself."

"Sounds like your dad is confused. Maybe he means he wants to give the waitress her pink slip? Fire her?"

"I thought the same thing. Anyway, if you happen to

see her around town, would you give her my number so I can update her on when the restaurant's going to reopen? I can't find it anywhere, and she probably wouldn't know to contact me at the exercise studio. I'm not going to fire her right away, not till I know that's what Dad wants."

"Will do. She came into the Casa while I was there and I let her know it would be at least two weeks."

"Oh, then the urgency's off. That's good. Still, if you see her, have her call me." She rang off.

I looked at the pile of recipes. My laptop was right in front of me. I looked at the clock on the wall behind the grill. I had hours in front of me before bed. This was as good a time as any to start typing.

I opened up a fresh document and got to work.

Gladys had said that some of these recipes dated back to her mother, and I believed her. More than a few called for lard—a thing I wasn't even sure it was possible to get anymore, and I was in the restaurant business. I decided to type in the ones I wanted, as written. Later, if I decided they warranted a test, I'd probably substitute vegetable shortening or even butter. I'd already tried the Maple Walnut Sandies, and they'd been a winner, so I started with that one.

I wasn't the world's best typist, not like my daughter, whose fingers flew. I had learned the old method of touch typing—the one that had actually been developed a hundred years ago to slow down typists so they wouldn't make so many mistakes that were harder to fix back then. Today's kids seemed to have each developed their own system.

But I needed to concentrate to get the words and measurements on the screen. The effort it took was a welcome respite from the craziness of the last few days. So much had happened, so many people in my life were sick or hurt, one was even dead, and no answers were forthcoming about any of it. It was a relief to think about something other than that damn trust.

I was just entering the baking instructions for a yummy-looking lemon shortbread cookie when a thought popped into my head. One of those thoughts I'd been trying to keep out.

Franco's words echoed around. *The waiter has the slip. The waiter.* Right now, Franco had only one server on staff right now. Piper Preston. He didn't have a waiter.

Or did he?

More than twenty years ago, when I was just out of high school, I'd lived for a summer in an apartment over the Casa di Pizza. Four girls crammed into two bedrooms, with a tiny kitchenette that we rarely used, a living room, and one outdated bathroom that made getting ready for work a crowded proposition.

Outside our apartment, in the hallway, was a rectangular door about two feet by three feet, set in the center of the wall if I recalled correctly. Inside that panel was a shaft containing a platform that could be raised and lowered between floors.

A dumbwaiter.

We didn't know if whoever had assaulted Franco and searched the restaurant had found the original Thousand

Island dressing recipe he thought Franco had. Or whether that's what the attacker was looking for at all. Franco had been hit in the head, and was disoriented after the blow. Was still disoriented, according to his daughter. If the attacker, or attackers, did find the recipe, they weren't broadcasting it.

Franco might have been telling Marielle where he'd hidden the document.

Maybe this was all a bit of a stretch, but somehow I didn't think so.

Franco's keys were still in my coat pocket. And I wouldn't be able to sleep tonight unless I used them to check out the Casa.

If I left right now, this whole mission would take no more than twenty minutes. In the door, examine the dumbwaiter, out the door. It pained me to have to inconvenience a friend—again—to come with me, but if the events of the last few months had taught me anything, it was not to take stupid chances. Or at least to take as few as humanly possible.

So I dialed Brenda Jones. Her voice mail picked up. I left her a message telling her where I was going and to meet me there in the next few minutes if she could. I tried Kim Galbraith, and left a similar message. Before I lost my nerve, I put on my jacket, slipped into my boots, and headed back out into the cold toward the Casa.

The sun was starting to dip on the horizon, but there was still enough daylight for me to get this done more or less safely. Or so I told myself.

A Killer Kebab

The streets of Bonaparte Bay were empty, which was to be expected this time of year and this time of day. Up ahead, there was one open shop, and its light shone like a beacon in a sea of dark windows. The Express-o Bean. I'd get this done and out of my head, then treat myself to a hot specialty coffee, which would be way better than the one I'd left, cooling again, on the counter. Maybe I'd get a muffin too, if they had any left.

Buoyed by the thought, I walked around the corner and let myself in the kitchen door of the Casa di Pizza.

I debated. Should I lock it behind me, or leave it open for Brenda or Kim if they got my message in time and decided to come over? Locking seemed the better choice. After all, it wasn't like the thief/attacker knew that I was on my way here and had somehow gotten himself inside the building to wait for me. If that was true, I had way bigger problems than I was anticipating now. Still, it paid to be cautious. I locked the back door, checked the front door to make sure it was also locked, and grabbed a kitchen knife from the magnetic rack on the cabinet over the prep counter.

Whether I could ever bring myself to use it was a question I hoped I'd never have to answer.

I didn't actually know where the dumbwaiter came out on this floor. But I did know where it was above. So I took the back stairs, which hadn't changed much that I could tell in the last twenty years, and came out on the second floor.

This space had also not changed much, if at all, since

I'd been here last, what seemed like a lifetime ago. The walls were the same institutional pale green, though some of the plaster underneath was now spiderwebbed, or even missing in spots. The hallway was lit with the same unshaded single lightbulb, although Franco had switched to the more energy-efficient fluorescent style.

The knife, the same type of chef's knife I'd held pretty much every day of my life for a couple of decades, felt heavy in my hand as I approached the panel in the wall, which was right where I remembered it. My roommates and I had never actually used it, though we'd speculated it would be useful for transporting laundry and beer between floors. The ropes hadn't looked all that sturdy back then.

They looked less sturdy now when I opened the panel and peered up at them.

A flashlight would have been a lot more useful than the knife. Franco probably had one in the kitchen somewhere, but I didn't want to spend any more time than I had to hunting for one. I pushed the panel open as far as it would go to let in the maximum amount of fluorescent light.

Two ropes held the platform in place. Presumably, they were connected by some type of pulley system. I was no engineer, but I more or less understood this simple machine. The ropes were frayed and brittle looking. They wouldn't be lifting or lowering anything, ever again, probably.

I felt along the ropes as far up as I could go, then

around the inside perimeter of the opening. My cell phone beeped. On my way, Brenda texted.

That wasn't much of a relief. Even if she got here, she couldn't get in. But I'd be out of here momentarily, probably even before she arrived. So far my palpations of the cavity had only yielded a splinter in my right index finger. Fortunately, it pulled out cleanly, but it had been deep enough to hurt.

Next I examined the platform itself. It was made of four planks of darkly varnished wood, joined together. I ran my hand over the surface, my injured finger throbbing as I did so. I tried lifting up each plank in the hopes that there might be a hidden cavity, but none budged. Reaching in as far as my arm would stretch, I felt along each edge of the platform. The dank air assaulted my nose and I sneezed.

My last hope was to look at the underside. I wasn't going to the third floor to look at the ropes or panel up there, so this was it. If the recipe wasn't here, we'd either have to wait for Franco's brain to heal so he could retrieve it himself, of we'd have to mourn its loss and hope he could remember the ingredients and proportions.

Needing two hands to work the ropes, I set the knife near my feet and began to pull.

Whether because some part of the system was broken, or because the old ropes didn't roll through the pulley wheels correctly, or just because all that thick wood was darned heavy, it took all my upper body strength to move the platform a couple of inches. That still wasn't enough to get my arm underneath, so I heaved the ropes again. The apparatus gave a teeth-jarring screech, but barely moved.

I paused a moment to catch my breath, then gave another yank. Whatever had been holding up the progress broke free, because the platform suddenly rose up a good foot, throwing me slightly off balance. Once I regained my footing, I reached way underneath the boards, then gently felt the surface in a grid pattern. If something was hidden under there, it wouldn't do to send it dropping into the abyss below.

After a minute or two, my hands landed on something sticky. Not wet and nasty sticky. Dry sticky, and crinkly. I felt around until I located the edge of whatever it was and pulled it free. When I brought it out into the light, I could see it was a good-sized piece of clear packing tape. It wasn't yellowed, or brittle, or peeling up at the edges. In fact, it wasn't even dusty. This tape was fresh and a small corner of torn plastic bag adhered to it.

I stuck my hand back under the platform again in the approximate location I'd found the tape, gingerly patting to see if the rest of the bag was still attached.

Nothing.

Damn. It looked like Franco had moved it, or it had never been here in the first place. Or, what I thought was more likely, Franco's assailant had gotten here first. Which was good news and bad news. The good news was that if whoever wanted the recipe had secured it, had what he wanted, there wouldn't seem to be any further danger to Franco. Or to me, for that matter. The bad news was, a theft had occurred, and Franco wouldn't be able to go through with his plans to make the recipe available, free, to everyone.

I reached up and pulled the ropes again in the opposite direction, this time to return the dumbwaiter to its original position.

A blow struck me from behind, and I felt myself being lifted and pushed. Hard.

◆ TWENTY ◆

My face struck the back wall of the dumbwaiter shaft and everything went dark for a moment, then my vision burst into stars that weren't really there. I heard a snap, and suddenly I was weightless, falling, falling—

Until I hit bottom. The impact went through my entire body, but was immediately replaced by pain. My lungs could not take in air, and I felt a surge of panic. *Easy, Georgie. You've had the wind knocked out of you.* Finally, after several agonizing moments, I was able to draw a ragged breath of the air, which was thick with dust and rotting hundred-year-old wood.

I couldn't see a thing. Whoever had pushed me had closed up the panel so that no light penetrated the space. Had I fallen one story, or two, down to the basement level?

There was no way to know. More important, how was I going to get out?

Every movement brought a fresh wave of pain. My neck was already stiffening up, and my cheek throbbed from where I'd hit the wall. I reached up, thinking to grab the rope to help pull myself to a standing position. The rope, however, lay slack against the platform. It had either broken under my weight, or been cut. I thought of the razor-sharp chef's knife I'd left in the hallway. *Weapons only work*, I chastised myself, *if you actually have them in your possession.*

There had to be a way out of here. Brenda must be waiting outside. She would bring help when I didn't answer the door, unless my assailant had hurt her too. But somehow, I doubted that. The person must have already been inside the building. I'd been here for less than ten minutes when I was attacked. So whoever it was had a key. And my guess was that he was long gone by now.

Bracing myself against the walls of the shaft, I brought myself to a standing position. I hurt. A lot. Everywhere.

Since I couldn't see a thing, I reached out in one direction, then turned ninety degrees and reached out again. This time I touched something solid. A wall, but was it the wall with the door in it, or the other, solid one? I couldn't find the opening, so I spun and felt the opposite surface. This time, I could feel the framing around the little door. I breathed a small sigh of relief, then began running my hands around the perimeter. There had to be a catch or a latch or a knob.

But there wasn't. Oh, there was one on the other side, I was sure of it. But the designers and constructors of this building had clearly not anticipated a person being trapped inside a dumbwaiter. I did my best to suppress the rising tide of panic. What if Brenda didn't go for help?

Putting both hands flat on the panel, I pushed, then pushed harder. It wouldn't budge. Steeling myself, I rammed a shoulder against the door. Pain stabbed through my entire arm. Brilliant. Not only was I still in the dark, I'd just added one more body part to the growing list of ones that hurt like heck.

I sat back down. My phone was still in my pocket, so I pulled it out. No signal, which shouldn't have surprised me. But the light from the screen gave me a little hope. I shone it in a semicircle, then around the perimeter of the panel, which confirmed that there was no inside latch. I was in some sort of shaft. And I couldn't go down, up, or to the sides. All I could do was wait.

And kick myself for being stupid.

And wonder who had done this, and why, and how he had known I'd be coming here today.

Finally, after what was only a few minutes but seemed much longer, I thought I heard something.

I put my ear to the frame. Voices! I listened harder. One of them was Brenda, I was sure of it. I pounded on the panel and called out, "Over here!" It was a matter of moments before the door opened and light flooded the chamber. I blinked rapidly until my eyes adjusted. Deputy Tim Arquette offered me a hand and helped me climb out into a space behind one of the movable cabinets in Franco's kitchen. Based on how I felt right now, I was going to be hurting far worse tomorrow.

"What happened?" Brenda demanded. "You called me to come then locked me out. We had to break a pane of glass to reach the lock and open the door."

I explained my reasoning. Brenda didn't look convinced. Neither did Tim.

"I figured I'd be safe, locked inside, and I'd hear you when you knocked on the door. The question is, how did someone know I'd be here, when I didn't know myself until less than an hour ago?" There was only one answer, really. Someone was watching me. Or watching the Casa.

"Do you need an ambulance?" Tim asked.

Nothing appeared to be broken, or anything that over-the-counter painkillers wouldn't address. Probably. And I'd seen enough of the Bonaparte Bay Volunteer Fire Department Emergency Medical Services personnel in the last few days to last me a lifetime. "No. I'll be fine. I'll get myself checked out in the morning."

Tim looked at me skeptically again.

"Promise," I said. I had to take Dolly to see Dr. Phelps anyway. I'd ask him to take a look at me while I was there. "But I will ask you to come back and check out the Bonaparte House again, if you're still on duty tonight." I was so, so tired of not feeling safe in my own home. In my own town. Anywhere.

"I will, and I am," he said. "Just let me know when you're in for the night and I'll come by, then you can arm your alarm. In the meantime, I'll check out this place and get somebody to board up the window. Could you tell if anything had been taken?"

I debated how much to say. Would he believe that someone would attack another person over a salad dressing recipe? It sounded ridiculous, even to me. And I actually had no proof, only an idea, based on the ramblings of a concussed man, that the tape I'd found under the dumbwaiter platform had once secured the recipe. Who knew what else Franco had hidden away here in these three floors and a basement that someone could have been looking for? "No," I answered truthfully. "I don't know if anything was taken. And let me take care of getting this boarded up. I'm helping Franco until he's back on his feet." I felt a little bit responsible for the break-in, even though it—probably—wasn't my fault.

Brenda looked at her watch. "The hardware store will be closing in just a few minutes, otherwise I'd go get a piece of plywood and we could do this ourselves." "Ourselves" was stretching it. Personally, I wasn't very handy like that. But Brenda probably was.

"Thanks," I said, "but I'll call Dolly's beau, Harold. He'll have something in the barn." I needed to check on Dolly anyway.

"Then I'll park the patrol car out here till you get back with him," Tim said. "It's close enough to my dinner break that I can take it now." Tim went to his car and got in.

Brenda walked back to the Bonaparte House with me and made herself at home in the kitchen while I spoke to

Harold. Dolly had made significant improvement, and was on the mend, according to him. At least something was going right, something—someone—I didn't have to worry about so much. Harold agreed to meet me at the Casa in half an hour.

I called Marielle to let her know what had happened, downplaying my injuries. She had enough on her plate without wondering if I was going to sue her father.

"What the heck is going on?" she said. "What's in that place that people are getting hurt over? Dad doesn't keep anything valuable there. How come no one else is getting broken into?" Clearly her father hadn't told her yet about his discovery. Or she didn't believe a piece of paper with a hundred-year-old recipe could possibly be the cause of all these crimes. Franco could tell her himself once he recovered. It didn't seem like my place.

"I don't know." And I didn't, really. "But if you have an alarm system, maybe you want to use it?"

"You're telling me to be careful."

"Marielle, right now everyone in Bonaparte Bay needs to be careful."

She agreed and rang off.

I reached into a drawer next to the point of sale computer and pulled out a bottle of painkillers. My muscles and tendons and ligaments and whatever else had gotten damaged in my short freefall were making their presence known. I took the maximum dose and downed the pills with a glass of water.

Brenda was keeping herself occupied by looking at

the recipes on the counter. "Wow," she said. "I don't think I've ever seen so many different kinds of gelatin molds. I'm pretty sure my grandmother made this stuff—the green kind, with the cottage cheese mixed in."

Probably everyone's grandmother had made that salad—though there was nothing remotely salad-like about it, at least by today's standards. Not that I'd had a grandmother I ever knew. "Yeah, I'm thinking those may be recipes whose time is never going to come again and they're just going to go back in the box. You ready to go? I appreciate you hanging out with me."

Brenda shrugged. "That's what friends do." She put her jacket back on and jammed her bright red toque over her bright red hair. "Besides, there's not much to do this time of year. Not that I have to tell you that."

I bundled up again. "Let's take my car and blast up the heater. The cold isn't going to make these muscles feel any better."

"Cold doesn't bother me, but sure."

We locked up and got into the car. I switched on the ignition and turned on the heater. It would take a few minutes to warm up. In the meantime, my teeth chattered and my muscles tensed painfully, just as I'd predicted. It was time to break down and get one of those remote car starters.

The drive to the Casa parking lot took only a couple of minutes. Tim's cruiser was still there, and through the side window I could see him throwing back a cola, as though he were in a commercial. I pulled up a respectful distance away. He got out of the cruiser and came over to talk to us through the window.

"Report's done, and so's dinner. Harold's on his way?" I nodded.

"Then I'll wait till he gets here. You've been through a lot today, but we'll need you to come down to the station tomorrow and give a statement. I didn't ask you this before, because I figured if you'd known you would have told me. But you don't know who stuffed you into the wall?"

Such a nice way to put it. "No. I'd say it was a man, but that's all I can say. He came up from behind me, and it happened so fast."

"We really have nothing to go on. Could be anybody, a local or an out-of-towner."

"It's somebody from Bonaparte Bay," Brenda said decisively. "Why would somebody from out of town come back and hit the same place again?"

She had a point. I was also inclined to think it was a local. Particularly if my theory that this was about Franco's recipe was correct, though again I had to wonder why anyone would go to such lengths.

A car pulled into the parking lot, lights blazing, and rolled to a stop just in front of the back door. Harold had brought Dolly's metallic green Ford LTD instead of his own pickup truck. He left the lights on and the car running. The trunk lid swung open slowly, even dramatically. Which only made sense. It was a dramatic car. Harold exited, then pulled a full-sized sheet of plywood out of the trunk. I would have said it was impossible, but there it was. He could probably transport a couple of horses to the state fair back there if he wanted.

Brenda and I got out of the car and, together with Tim Arquette, walked over to Harold. Tim offered to help hold the plywood while Harold nailed it down. It was a two-person job, so Brenda and I just stood back, shivering, out of the way. From where we stood, I could see the converted house where MacNamara and MacNamara had their office. The outside light was on, which wasn't unusual. Lots of people left their porch lights on all night. There were also lights on inside the building. I glanced at my watch. It was after six. Junior must be working late.

On the day of his father's funeral? When his mother is in town?

Or maybe that was the point, to get away from his mother, whom I'd never met but had heard was a controlling woman.

A silhouette was framed in the window. Male. And was shortly joined by another silhouette. Female, with hair in a long braid that swung out as she moved. A tryst? Maybe, but they didn't appear to touch each other.

A thought emerged. If I could see into the law offices of MacNamara and MacNamara from here . . .

Someone at the law offices could see the Casa parking lot from their vantage point.

But that was making assumptions where they weren't necessarily warranted. From where I stood, I could also see the house across the street from the MacNamaras' and another next to that. I supposed I could check the addresses of those other buildings. See who lived there.

The *tap, tap, tap* of Harold's hammer continued. From wherever he was watching, the MacNamara law office or one of the other buildings, someone could have been watching the Casa without even braving the cold.

One figure left the window at the law offices. A few minutes later, a car engine started up from that direction.

I thought about following. Should I do it? I had only a moment to decide before the other car was warmed up and too far gone to catch up with. The last time I'd done this, with Kim Galbraith, we'd ended up at the River Rock. If I left now, Brenda with me perhaps, would it just be a repeat of the other night, with nothing to show for it? My guess was this was Jennifer Murdoch, maybe trying to extort money out of Junior, or still attempting to get the videotape back. Even if I could prove it was her, it proved nothing.

But my nature got the better of me. "Brenda, you wanna ride shotgun with me?"

"Yup."

❖ TWENTY-ONE ❖

I called my thanks to Harold and Tim, then we jumped into the car, which I'd left running. I drove to the edge of the parking lot, then waited until I could see the taillights of the other vehicle. Pulling out onto the street, I waited another few beats, then followed.

Was it the same car from the other night? I couldn't tell.

"Who are we following?" Brenda asked. "Not that it matters. As it happens, I don't have anything better to do."

"Honestly, I don't know. Just being nosy, I guess." Though it was more than that. The Law Offices of Mac-Namara and MacNamara were mixed up in some ugliness, ugliness that resulted in a man's death, as well as affected my family. So it was personal to me. Sure, I could have left it all to the professionals. But so far they had arrested Russ Riley, on whom they had some moderately good evidence. So they wouldn't be much inclined to look any further for the murderer of Jim MacNamara.

And what did I know? Russ might very well have done it. But I hoped, for his mother's sake, that he hadn't.

The car made a right turn by the public park that flanked the river and drove along it for a couple of blocks, before taking another right. Toward the River Rock. But instead of pulling in, the car kept going.

"I'm going to pull a little closer. There's a small notebook and pad of paper in the glove compartment. See if you can get the license plate."

What I'd do with the license plate, even if I had it, I didn't know. I was pretty sure you needed a subpoena, or to be in law enforcement, to access DMV records. But it gave Brenda something to do.

"Got it," she said.

I dropped back again, continuing to follow the tail-lights. The car took another right turn, which put it back out onto the main drag of Bonaparte Bay. I pulled over until I saw her clear the lone traffic light at the end of Theresa Street, then pulled out again. She took a left, then drove under the "Welcome to Bonaparte Bay" arch and out onto Route 12.

If this was Jennifer Murdoch, she wasn't going home. She was going out of town.

"Should we go any farther?" I asked Brenda.

"We don't know who we're following. Okay. But do we know why?"

"Er, no. Well, maybe. That woman has met with Ben

MacNamara twice that I know of since his father died. After hours." I guess I *had* decided to follow her a little longer, because we were still going in her direction.

"So are we just being nosy? Which I don't have a problem with. You'd be amazed the kinds of personal stuff people throw away. Believe me, I know. She's driving an older Ford Escort, silver or white." She rattled off the plate number.

"Have you ever seen that car while you're making your rounds?" We were passing the Can-Am Bridge, which was beautifully lit up now that night had fallen. I wasn't going to go too much longer, not without a clear objective. But the drive had been worth it just to see the bridge lights against the starless sky.

Brenda paused. "I don't think so," she said. "Though that's not a car that sticks out in your mind, like a jacked-up truck or a Corvette."

The car put its blinker on, signaling right. It was turning into a small community of riverfront condominiums that rented for a pretty penny during the summer. But this time of year, the rents might have gone down, letting her live in a nicer place than she could afford during the winter. But that was just speculation based on the age and style of car she drove.

"Should I pull in?" I caught my lower lip between my teeth. Suddenly, this didn't seem like such a great idea.

"We've come this far. Might as well see it through," Brenda said, ever practical.

I put on my own blinker and pulled in. The car was

maybe a hundred yards ahead now. "Watch where it pulls in," I said. "I'm going to hang back a little."

I counted slowly to ten, then started driving again.

"It's coming up on the right," Brenda said. "No garage. I can see the car parked in the driveway. She's putting her key in the lock of the house."

Because her back was turned toward me, I risked a look at the woman. I could see the long braid, but not much else due to the long puffer coat and thick hat she wore. She was about the same height as Jennifer Murdoch, but Jennifer Murdoch would never drive a car that old. Unless she was trying to hide something.

So who was Ben MacNamara's mystery woman? I had no idea. I kept driving, past the rest of the condos, then back out onto Route 12 and back toward Bonaparte Bay.

Brenda made a note of the house number on the mailbox.

This little jaunt had raised more questions than it answered. I realized a couple of other things too. I wasn't quite ready to go back home. And I hadn't had dinner.

"You hungry?" I asked.

"Jo-Jo's Family Diner is the only place open, and we're headed that way." Which was answer enough for me.

There were only a few cars in the Jo-Jo's parking lot, which was to be expected this time of night. Patty, the waitress who always seemed to be on duty no matter when I came in, looked a little disappointed when she saw me with Brenda. I couldn't blame her. I usually came here with Jack, and she flirted up a storm with him. It was all in good fun and Jack never crossed any lines. Somebody was occupying our usual booth, which was just as well. I was missing him powerfully, and sitting there would just make me sad. So we took a booth in the back and ordered. A couple of colas, a bowl of chicken tortilla soup for me, and a beef stew for Brenda. She liked her red meat.

While we waited for the food to arrive, Brenda pulled out her phone. It was one of those very large ones, somewhere in size between a normal phone and a small tablet. She put on a pair of reading glasses that looked very cute on her—the frames were a dark cherry red that made her blue eyes pop—then pulled out a slip of paper.

She pressed some numbers into the search bar. "No hits on the license plate. I didn't expect any, but it was worth a try."

Patty brought over our drinks and set them down. Her long pointy nails, polished to a high metallic purple shine, clicked on the Formica tabletop as she set down our paper-wrapped straws. She stared at the bruises on my face but didn't ask and I felt a stab of self-consciousness. But apparently Patty wasn't in the mood for chitchat, because she went back to her post behind the counter. Yeah, I missed Jack too.

Brenda looked down at the paper through her glasses, then pressed the phone again. "This is more like it," she said. "Here it is—1416 Sunset Boulevard. A two-bedroom, two-bathroom home built five years ago. It's assessed at a quarter million. And it's owned by someone, no, something, called Tripler Enterprises."

"Tripler?" I'd seen that name before, but where? Then I remembered. On a file on Lydia Ames's desk. "Google that name, will you?" I leaned forward.

Brenda did as I asked. She frowned, then swiped her thumb toward the top of the screen. And repeated the maneuver. She looked up at me over the tops of her glasses. "A bunch of things come up, but they look like companies in other states, and there's a bunch of things that look like get-rich-quick schemes. I don't see anything that looks like it's based in the North Country. They must not have a website."

Hmmm. Maybe the woman with the long braid was the principal of Tripler, whatever that was. That would explain why she was meeting with Junior. But why after hours? Maybe—

Maybe, just maybe, I was reading too much into it.

But when it came to anything MacNamara, I was pretty sure I wasn't.

Our dinners arrived. I sprinkled some crispy tortilla strips, some shredded cheddar, and some chopped scallions on top and tucked in. Delicious. Just a tiny bit of pleasant heat on the back of the tongue, but nothing to make me run screaming for a glass of milk. Brenda took a big spoonful containing a hearty hunk of beef covered in dark brown gravy and lifted it to her lips.

We ate in companionable silence, until Brenda picked up her baking powder biscuit and slathered some butter on it. "You gonna get Tim Arquette to check out your house tonight?"

The tender piece of chicken I'd just swallowed stuck in my throat. Asking Harold to put up the plywood on the Casa, playing Mata Hari by following the mystery woman, eating a late dinner here at Jo-Jo's, all these things were avoidance techniques. Truth was, I did not want to go home. No matter how good the alarm system—and it was a good one—or how thoroughly a BBPD deputy checked out the house, I'd been assaulted today.

"No. I think I'll stay at the Camelot again tonight. They're going to put my name on a suite someday soon." Plus I was going to need a long, hot soak in a Jacuzzi tub to combat the aches and pains that had already settled in. And the Bonaparte House plumbing just wasn't up to the job.

Brenda nodded. "That's smart. Then I won't worry about you." She didn't look up from her bowl as she said those kind words. I felt a warm fuzzy.

"Thanks," was all I said. Anything more would embarrass her. Or me.

❖ TWENTY-TWO ❖

The next morning, I slept late. The beds were comfortable at the Camelot, and I felt warm and dry and safe. Unfortunately, I also felt achy and *un*comfortable from my injuries from yesterday, every time I moved. My neck was stiff, and overnight I had grown a crop of blue-purple bruises splotched over my entire body. I'd left my bottle of painkillers in the bathroom, so I had to make a choice: stay in bed and lie perfectly still, or brave the pain, get up and take more pills. The pills won out.

I looked at myself in the mirror as I ran the water cold. Gorgeous. My left cheekbone was the color of a Stanley plum. Even if I'd had makeup with me, which I didn't, I doubted anything could cover that up. I filled a cup, then swallowed three pills, and went back to bed. I didn't have anywhere to be for a while.

When I woke up again a couple hours later, the edges of the pain had softened to a dull throb. My phone showed a text from the visiting nurse taking care of Melanie, Liza, and Caitlyn: All are stable. Conditions about the same. Will keep you informed.

I was still worried about them, but they were getting professional care, better than I could provide myself. And first things first: today I needed to take Dolly to see Dr. Phelps. I could get the details from him about the patients at Castle Grant then and find out when they could be moved.

It was an effort, but I threw off the covers. A half hour later, I was re-dressed in yesterday's dusty clothes and putting my key in the lock at the Bonaparte House.

Somehow, in the light of day, I wasn't afraid to go into my own house, as I had been last night. Sleep had given me a better perspective. I could think of no reason I, personally, would be a target for someone. I'd simply been in the wrong place at the wrong time yesterday. In someone's way.

And whoever it was behind the attack on me, I was pretty sure they already had what they'd been looking for. Something had been taped under the platform on that dumbwaiter, and it was gone. So there was no reason to think I was still a target. That's what common sense said anyway.

I checked the alarm system. It was still operational. I would be fine.

I went upstairs and took a shower, then changed into

fresh clothes. What color sweater looked best with bruises? In the end, I just picked whatever was on top of the pile in my drawer.

Moderately refreshed, I went back downstairs and made myself an egg on toast and a cup of coffee.

There were a few minutes before it was time to leave to get Dolly, so I went back to work on Gladys's recipes.

The pile of molded gelatin salad recipes Brenda had been looking at went back into the shoe box. I couldn't see a time, ever, when I'd make or serve one, so typing any up would be a waste of time. I reached for the cookie recipes and started inputting a molasses gingersnap that looked tasty.

When I'd finished that one, I placed the card at the bottom of the pile. I rose to refill my coffee, and as I did so, I knocked some of the cards and slips of paper to the floor. I blew out a sigh. Bending down was going to hurt.

I leaned forward from the waist, but that required me to put my neck at an odd angle that was too painful to sustain. So I went to my knees and began to gather everything up. Putting the papers into one hand, I used the other to grab onto the edge of the counter and pull myself to a standing position, then deposited the errant documents back on the surface in front of me.

After that effort, head pounding dully, I deserved that second cup of coffee more than ever and went to make it.

When I returned to the project, I began sorting again. It was only "Wild Game" and "Miscellaneous" that had fallen, and those hadn't been large piles, so it was quick work. When I got to the envelope, the one marked "Formica Cleaner," I realized that the recipe must have fallen out, because the envelope was empty, and there had been something inside when I first looked at it a few days ago. Brenda had asked for a copy of that one for her own counters. I set the envelope aside until the contents turned up.

But they didn't. I'd finished sorting everything into its proper pile.

Which meant I must have missed a fallen paper.

Which meant I was going to have to get down on my hands and knees again.

Honestly, if it had been mine, not Gladys's, I might have just let it go, to be found at some later date when the floor was cleaned. But it wasn't mine. So down to the floor I went. It hurt just as much this time as it had the first.

I finally located the paper, sticking partly out from under a movable stainless steel cart. Good thing it hadn't gone any farther underneath. It might have taken me a long time to find it.

Recipe in hand, I straightened. A fresh jolt of pain shot through me, from my neck out through my shoulders. Taking a few deep breaths helped somewhat. I went back to my seat and laid the recipe on the counter.

After all that trouble, I was curious. What was in Formica cleaner anyway? I wondered what kind of cleaners were commercially available in the fifties and sixties. Maybe everybody made their own, or just used soap and water.

The paper was yellowed, folded into a more or less

symmetrical square. The edges were soft, not quite frayed, but clearly worn. I undid the first fold. If the paper turned out to be too brittle, I would just put it back and have to remain curious. I wouldn't want to damage it.

But I managed to keep it intact as I undid the second fold and set the document down.

I was expecting the first ingredient to be water, or a soap of some kind. What I wasn't expecting was to see the word "mayonnaise" followed by the word "ketchup." Mayonnaise, well, maybe. That stuff was used for lots of nonfood things, including hair conditioner, though I'd never tried it. But ketchup for countertops? No way.

I scanned through the rest of the ingredients, then read the title, which I hadn't done before.

This was not a recipe for a cleaner.

This was a recipe for Thousand Island dressing. It couldn't be anything else. And it was called *Sophias Sauce*, no apostrophe, just like Franco had told me. There was a second sheet of paper, folded behind the first.

August 3, 1907

Dearest Phoebe,

Here is the recipe I told you about, the one I received from Mrs. Sophia LaLonde. I hope you will enjoy it.

Fondly,
May Irwin

May Irwin. I knew that name, though I couldn't have said how. I opened an Internet browser and looked her up.

May had been a vaudeville actress, famous for singing songs that would not be considered appropriate today. She was also a composer, and engaged in the first kiss ever filmed, an affair that apparently went on for several minutes at the behest of Thomas Edison.

And May had been a resident of the Thousand Islands, having built a large summer house on Club Island, and later having bought a farm on the mainland near the village of Clayton.

I looked at the date of the letter: 1907. That was the date that Franco had said was on his recipe.

I was willing to bet that May Irwin had written his recipe as well, though to whom we'd never know. The distinctive missing apostrophe, as well as the list of ingredients that I know I'd tasted that night at Franco's, including the lemon juice and the Worcestershire sauce, made me certain this was the same recipe.

I drew a deep breath. Now what? There was a piece of culinary history here in my hot little hand. The question was, what to do with it? It was worth something to somebody, that was for sure. And no one knew about it. Because if they did, it would already be gone.

I pulled out my cell phone. "Kim? Sorry to call you so early." The paper vibrated. My hand was shaking a little.

Kim laughed. "Georgie, we keep accountant hours here, not restaurant hours. What's up?"

"Do you have a safe? I have something I need to keep, well, *safe*, for a day or two."

"Bring it in," she said. "Of course we have a safe. And it's wired into the alarm system."

"I'll be there within half an hour. And thanks." I clicked off.

I had a couple more phone calls to make, but those would have to wait until later. It was time to go pick up Dolly.

❖ TWENTY-THREE ❖

I dropped off the recipe and watched Kim lock it into the safe. She didn't ask any questions, which I appreciated. It wasn't my secret to tell, not yet.

When I got to Dolly's, I left the car running, with the window cracked open and the emergency brake engaged, while I knocked on the door. She must have been ready to go, because only a few seconds later she came outside, fully bundled up, with a big gauzy scarf over her teased-up hair. I took her arm to walk her to the car.

"I'm moving under my own steam again," she said. "But thanks." She made it all the way to the front passenger side seat of my car before breaking into that rattly cough, which nevertheless sounded much less wet and intense than it had before. "Let's get this over with."

My fearless Dolly was back. I was grateful. When

Dolly was brave, it was easy for me to be brave too. "Shall we get some breakfast after the appointment?" I said. "Maybe at Jo-Jo's?"

"Let's see what the doc says," she said, her voice matter-of-fact. "I might not have any appetite once he tells me what the tests showed."

My stomach did a cannonball into the deep end. No. I wouldn't think about this until it was forced on me. Not all former smokers developed cancer. "Okay," I said, and left it at that.

"How's Russ? Is he doing okay?" The question had to be asked, for the sake of politeness, even though Dolly and I never stood on ceremony. And I didn't care all that much, honestly.

She *tsk*ed. "The usual. He's his own worst enemy. Still mouthing off to the guards. Watch out." She pointed ahead.

A big black-and-white cow stood in the road. "That'd be one of the neighbor's cows. Just pull in here." She indicated a driveway on our right. "I'll go let 'em know the cow's out." There was a small barn behind the house. Seemed big enough for only a few animals, so this cow probably represented most of the herd.

"You want me to do it?" I wanted to keep Dolly warm and dry.

"Naw. I want to thank her for bringing me a casserole anyway. I'll be right back."

While Dolly was inside, I decided to make one of my phone calls. Gladys Mongomery seemed delighted when I told her what I'd found.

"Well, how wonderful! Makes me want to jump on a plane from Florida right now to come and see it. But I'm hosting a dinner party tonight, then we're all going dancing."

Gladys was an inspiration. I hoped when I was a senior I would be having half as much fun as she seemed to be. "How do you think that recipe got in the box?" I asked.

"My grandmother was a friend of May Irwin," Gladys said decisively. "Grandma used to talk about May's parties, and how the men loved her because of that incredible curvy figure of hers. And how the women loved her because she was so funny and full of life. So it stands to reason May probably gave my grandmother the recipe. How it ended up in an envelope marked 'Formica Cleaner'? Not a clue. I'm sure I never looked in that envelope. But there are lots of other recipes in there I never looked at either."

I outlined my plan for Gladys. Technically, it was her recipe, so I needed her permission.

"What a lovely idea! Yes, of course. Handle it however you think best, dear. And say hello to my honorary nephew, Jack Conway, when next you see him."

Her words brought a little pang to my chest. It had been days since I heard from Jack. I didn't know what he was doing, or where he was. Nor could I know. My guess was that he was working some kind of undercover operations—I couldn't think what other kind of job would prevent him from at least talking to me. If he couldn't be with me.

Gladys must have realized she'd hit a nerve. "Oh, Georgie, I'm so sorry. He'll be back soon, I'm sure."

I shook it off. Dolly was stepping off the front porch. "It's okay, Gladys." It didn't actually feel okay. "I'll let you know when it's done. And thanks. This is the right thing to do."

"Of course it is. Bye-bye, dear." She disconnected.

Dolly opened the door and got in. Her breathing was slightly labored, slightly quicker than it should be. She sat down and buckled herself in. A woman came out of the house, someone I'd never seen before, but I didn't know *everyone* in Bonaparte Bay, especially those who lived on the outskirts of town. The cow was heading this way along the side of the road. The woman walked toward it.

"Should we give her a ride?" I wasn't sure what cow-human protocol was.

"Naw, the car might spook the cow off into the wrong field. Just head back toward my house and we'll take the long way around." She leaned back in her seat.

I did as instructed. This direction would take us back toward Silver Lake, then there was a road to the left that would take us back into Bonaparte Bay. Fortunately, we'd left early. I was still hoping for breakfast somewhere.

We passed Old Lady Turnbull's house. "Any news on Silver Lake?" I asked.

"Deal with the lawyer's dead, obviously. I heard the son might be interested. Then there's Murdoch, the builder, still in the running."

So Ben MacNamara wanted to take over his father's project? My gut feeling told me he didn't have the experience or organizational skills required to pull off a job that big. And the other question was whether he had the resources to get it rolling. Presumably his father had—he had all that money from the Bloodworth Trust squirreled away somewhere. And Ben knew something about that, though how much I wasn't sure. What if he knew about it, but couldn't access it?

And then there was Steve Murdoch. He could do this project in his sleep, and he stood to make even more money than the MacNamaras did, because he owned a construction company. He'd have to pay Mrs. Turnbull for the land, of course, but he'd only have to pay the cost of materials and his workers, with no upcharge for the design and build. It would be such a shame to mar that beautiful piece of pristine waterfront. But Steve was in the building business. It wasn't like anyone could tell him not to do his job.

Dolly grew quiet. When I glanced over, I saw that she'd closed her eyes. That was good. She needed all the rest she could get.

Fifteen minutes later, we arrived at the medical offices. When the car stopped, she woke up.

"We're here. You ready?" I asked.

"Let's get this over with."

◆ TWENTY-FOUR ◆

We let the nurse at the window know Dolly was here, then sat down in the waiting room chairs. I picked up a magazine but wasn't interested in any of the articles so I set it back down. Dolly watched the fish tank. I guess the movement and the colorful fish were supposed to keep us calm. I was nervous for Dolly. I couldn't imagine how she herself must be feeling.

Finally, a nurse with a clipboard in her hand appeared at the inner door. "Mrs. Riley? The doctor is ready for you."

We made our way through the door and down an interior hallway to an examining room. "You staying?" the nurse asked me.

I looked at Dolly. She nodded.

"Yes," I said. I rubbed Dolly's upper arm, hoping to give her moral support.

"Strip from the waist up," she said to Dolly, "and put on the johnny. We'll be back in a couple of minutes." She shut the door, and I could hear the clipboard being slid into place in its holder outside.

I turned away while Dolly undressed. She got herself covered up with the johnny, and I helped her climb up onto the paper-covered examining table, then folded her clothes neatly and set them on one of the chairs.

Dr. Phelps came in, reading Dolly's chart. He looked at me oddly. Maybe it was strange for someone who wasn't a relative to attend a patient's examination. But I didn't care. Dolly was family.

"How are you feeling, Dolly?" he asked.

"Better," she said. "Less coughing. More energy."

"Good, good. Let's have a listen." He placed his stethoscope on her chest, just inside the thin cotton garment. "Deep breath. Or deep as you can." He moved the stethoscope to a new position on her chest and repeated the order, then moved to her back. He closed his eyes, listening.

"Very good. You're not clear yet, but you're definitely on the mend. We'll get you another chest x-ray to completely rule out pneumonia before you leave." He wrote something on the clipboard.

Dolly looked at me. Her brave front had crumbled, just a little. *Ask him*, she mouthed to me.

I nodded. There weren't a whole lot of people I would

do this for, but Dolly was one of them. "Uh, Doctor? Did the prior x-ray show . . . anything else?"

He looked at us, then reviewed his chart. He must have already known the answer, but I was grateful that he was double-checking.

The doctor gave Dolly a smile. "No. Your lungs aren't perfect, but as long as you're asymptomatic, we'll just monitor you. I'll expect you in here for a physical every year for the duration."

Dr. Phelps's duration was probably quite a bit shorter than Dolly's. But I was so relieved, I could have kissed him.

"Your blood pressure and cholesterol are a little high. We'll talk about that when you come in next week for your final recheck."

Dolly's face creased into a huge smile that showed all her dentures to perfection. "Okay, Doc," she said.

Dr. Phelps wrote something else on his clipboard, then turned to me. "Mrs. Nik—"

"Nikolopatos. And yes?" I still hadn't decided if I was keeping my married name when I was no longer married, or going back to my maiden name, Bartlett. I hadn't been Georgiana Gertrude Bartlett in a lot of years. And I was pretty sure I wasn't that person anymore. Nor was I Georgiana Nikolopatos, except on paper.

"Let's leave Mrs. Riley to get dressed. I'd like to talk to you."

I looked at Dolly, who said, "Go on. I'll meet you in the waiting room."

Dr. Phelps led me to his office and asked me to sit. My heart was in my throat. Why would he want to speak to me privately?

"First of all, what happened to you? That's quite a bruise you have on your cheek."

"I, uh, took a tumble. It looks worse than it is." I wasn't sure if I should reveal anything, now that there was an active police investigation. He looked at me pointedly, no doubt assessing whether I needed some kind of battered woman intervention. And I was sure he knew that I'd found Jim MacNamara's body, and that Franco Riccardi had been sent to the ER from my restaurant. So whatever suspicions he had, well, there was probably a grain—or more—of truth to them.

"I'll advise you to get yourself checked out. Now, for the second thing. You know I went out to Castle Grant to examine your mother, her assistant, and Liza Grant?"

"Yes, and I want to thank you for that, and for arranging for the nurse. It's a load off my mind knowing they're being cared for."

The wrinkles on the doctor's face got deeper, if that were possible. "You also know I'm bound by patient confidentiality. However, when your mother was here a few weeks ago with her gunshot wound, she signed a release authorizing you to receive any and all information about her health care."

She had? I was her next of kin, of course, but I might have expected that honor to go to Caitlyn Black. "Okay," I said, waiting for whatever he was about to tell me.

"So you understand that I'm only speaking about your mother, and not about either of the other two ladies, right?" His eyes bored into mine.

A finger of dread poked around in my gut. "Okay," I repeated.

"When I examined your mother, my initial diagnosis was food poisoning."

"That's what I understood." *Initial diagnosis?* Was there another one?

"I sent out some samples for testing. I was going to call you with the results, but you've saved me the trouble. The preliminary results are in."

The lump in my throat was the size of a grapefruit. I looked him in the eye. "And?" It came out as barely a whisper.

He held my gaze. "Your mother has been poisoned."

"Right. Food poisoning." Why the need for the dramatic statement? We knew that.

"Not food poisoning. Poison was put into her food, systematically over a course of days. It's a good thing Ms. Grant called when she did."

I was gobsmacked. "You mean, poison as in Lucretia Borgia and old-fashioned crime novels, and *Arsenic and Old Lace*? Are you certain?"

He nodded. "Unfortunately, yes. We're still determining the exact chemical makeup of the poison. There are traces of a sedative in her samples as well."

Poison. The doctor could only talk to me about Melanie. But it was clear Caitlyn and Liza were suffering from the same thing. "The nurse I sent has been instructed to keep them on clear liquids from sealed bottles. She understands the situation."

"Did you call the police? Are they going to be all right?"

Dr. Phelps's face was neutral. He'd had fifty or so years of practice calming patients and families. "I do have a call in to the state police. And as long as your mother doesn't ingest any more of the toxin, I believe she'll be all right."

"I need to get them off that island. Bring them back where I can look after them. Can I move them?"

Dr. Phelps looked grim. "Normally, I'd say yes, though your mother will likely get even more nauseous from the boat ride. But have you seen the weather forecast? There's a storm coming in this afternoon. You know how the river gets in late fall and winter. I wouldn't risk it."

"But someone's doing this to them—her. I'm sure your nurse is very good, but she's not law enforcement." *And she's not me.*

"My suggestion is to call the police. Tell them you need help and see what they offer. Maybe they can get an emergency boat out there. Or call the Coast Guard."

His words were like a punch to the gut. Where was Jack when I needed him? But I knew I wasn't being fair. He was doing his job, and our relationship was very new.

"I still think leaving them where they are, at least until the storm passes, is your best bet."

"Thanks, Doctor. I should go now. Dolly's waiting."

Dr. Phelps was right. Until the weather was better, I shouldn't try to move them. If we got into any kind of trouble, if the waves were bad or the boat took on water, they would be too weak to help themselves. But that didn't mean I couldn't go to them. Make sure that they weren't administered anything else. Try to figure out who was behind this. And that was what I meant to do. But first I had some wheels to set in motion.

◈ TWENTY-FIVE ◈

While Dolly used the restroom at the doctor's office, I went out into the hall and used the time to make another phone call. Fortunately Marielle Riccardi was between classes, so she was able to speak immediately. Marielle had known about her father's recipe, but had not considered it as a cause for his attack, or the attack on me. She didn't know where the recipe was, but she agreed with my idea on her father's behalf. My asking was merely a courtesy. Franco had told me what his intention was with regard to the recipe days ago, and I could not imagine him going back on that. This was the quickest way I knew to bring at least this part of the problems in Bonaparte Bay to a head.

I called Kim Galbraith and asked her to call Alice Getz, the new reporter for the *Bay Blurb*. If all went according to plan, Alice would immediately start posting teasers on the *Blurb*'s social media pages.

When Dolly finally came out, I helped her into her coat and took her home. I quickly made sure she had lunch and didn't need me to do anything else for her. And then I peeled out and raced back to town.

The promised storm had not yet hit, but appeared to be imminent, based on the dull metal gray of the sky and the darker gray of the clouds. This would be lake effect snow, and chances were good there'd be a lot of it. When storm winds blew across Lake Ontario, they picked up water, which would then crystallize and fall as snow when the air hit land. Bonaparte Bay got its share of snow over the long North Country winters. But just a few miles south, snowfall amounts increased a lot. By January, it was nothing for snowfall amounts to reach three feet or more, and surface air temperatures to reach into the minus twenties, even lower.

But the forecast for today was for high winds and only a few inches of snow. To get me to Valentine Island and Castle Grant, I needed a boat and someone who knew what she was doing. I dialed Brenda Jones.

Brenda, bless her, didn't ask any questions. I was in luck, because she hadn't yet pulled her boat from the water. This would be the last excursion she would make, she said, until spring, and she'd need to pull the boat immediately after. We agreed to meet at the docks in an hour. "Dress warm," she said, and rang off.

As anxious as I was to get to the castle, I forced myself

to slow down and think. I let myself into the Bonaparte House, locked the door behind me, then set about gathering my winter gear. I didn't participate in any winter sports—unless you counted Staying Warm, Deciding Whether to Drink Wine or Eat Chocolate, and Reading Historical Romance Novels, all of which would make excellent Winter Olympics events, in my opinion. But I did have all the basic gear—waterproof boots, parka, hat, and gloves. And Cal, who was a skier, had some bibs in her closet. They would probably be too small, but I only needed to stay dry for a few minutes as we crossed the water.

I set about gathering up what I needed. I had my phone and a charger in case it decided to croak on me, as well as a little pistol that Sophie's cousin Marina had given me. I'd never fired it, and it wasn't even loaded—I'd had Dolly check it for me one day. But I could bluff or scare someone with it. Maybe.

It took most of the half hour, but I finally had all my stuff assembled. I thought about calling to let Liza or the nurse know I was coming, but my gut told me it would be better to surprise them. If, by some chance, the poisoner was still on the island—and there were plenty of places someone could hide—why take a chance on tipping him off?

I suited up. The bibs were too small, as I'd anticipated, but by not zipping the front and by sitting gently so as not to rip out the seat, I thought they'd be all right. Certainly better than nothing. I put on the boots, then layered on the parka and the rest. I was already too warm. And I probably looked like the puffy guy in those tire commercials. But I was no fashion plate, never had been, and wasn't about to start now.

Before I left for the dock, there was one more thing I had to do. I pulled up the *Bay Blurb*'s social media page on my phone and felt like cheering. The accountant and the reporter had come through. Pinned to the top of the page was the following post:

TI Mystery Solved. First Clue: 1 Cup Mayonnaise. Stay tuned.

Every hour for the next five hours, Alice would release another ingredient until all six had been revealed. And in two days' time, a feature story would appear on the front page of the *Blurb*, giving the mixing instructions as well as the history of the recipe and a scan of the original in May Irwin's handwriting, which Alice would try to verify if she was able to find another sample.

There were already some comments. None of them correct. But once the next clue, *1/2 Cup Ketchup*, came out, people would begin to understand. Then there would be no stopping it. The recipe would belong to the people of the Thousand Islands, which was as it should be. I hoped Sophia LaLonde and May Irwin would approve.

I zipped up, just as my phone rang. The display read *MacNamara and MacNamara*. I connected the call.

"Georgie? It's Lydia at the law office. Ben wants to see you. Can you drop by now for a couple of minutes? He says it's urgent." Her tone said she didn't quite believe him.

"I've got twenty minutes before I need to be somewhere. I'm on my way."

Had Ben heard about the *Blurb* social media page already? It was entirely possible, though the one clue posted so far was fairly obscure. Just how valuable was this licensing or trademarking thing anyway?

When I reached the office, I took off and hung up my parka, but left the bibs and boots on. They were too hard to get into and out of. Lydia said, under her breath, "Sorry. I don't know what's going on with him today."

I shrugged. I was pretty sure I'd forced his hand, and now I wanted to see what cards he had on the table. Lydia pressed a button on her phone and told Junior I was here.

"Send her in now," I heard him say.

Since his father died, Ben had moved into his father's larger, swankier office. "Sit," he commanded. I chose the chair in front of the desk. I remembered what Lydia had said. Even bundled up as I was, there was no way I was sitting on that couch.

"What is it?" I said. "I have to be somewhere in fifteen minutes, so can we make this quick?" I knew I was needling him and didn't care. Lydia was right outside the door. If she was anything like me, she'd be listening in.

"We can make it very quick," he said. "If you just give me the copy of the recipe you have and tell me who else you gave it to. I know you've got something." His face was tinged with red. "The recipe. The one you almost found yesterday, until I got there before you did. I saw that post on the *Blurb* page. You're releasing it in pieces."

"Where's yours? And how do you even know I've got the right one? Of course, in about four hours, you'll know for sure. But then it will be too late. It'll already be out there."

"I've got mine. I want to know where you got yours."

"What are you planning to do with it anyway? There's a rumor going around town that you're working on some trademarking deal for Angela Wainwright. The version she uses isn't the same as the Sophia LaLonde recipe, you know."

"Client. Confidentiality," he ground out.

"You got some kind of trademarking, or licensing deal? Who's it with, that it's worth this much potential grief? Because I know it was you who shoved me into a dumbwaiter and cut the rope. I could have been paralyzed. Even died." No reaction from the Boy Wonder. I had started out bluffing, but the more I thought about it, the more I thought I was right. "How'd you know I was at the Casa anyway?"

"Shut. Up. You are not calling the shots, you understand?" His face got redder. If he hadn't been so young, I would have been afraid his blood pressure was out of control.

"If you say so. What were you, watching the parking lot to see who went in? Did you leave some evidence there you didn't want the cops, or anyone else to find from when you beat up poor Franco?" I had no idea if he'd done the beating himself, or if he'd hired someone to do it. He was just as guilty either way.

"You're ruining everything!" he said.

That was a bold statement. *Everything?* I felt almost proud of myself, as though I were some supervillain in a comic book.

"Yeah, well, sorry. Getting beat up has that effect on me. How'd you get into the locked building anyway?"

He said nothing. Then I remembered. Franco had said, what seemed like eons ago, that Ben had worked for him at the Casa. "There must be another way in. Maybe through one of the adjoining buildings?" I'd lived over the restaurant too and hadn't known about any other entrance, but that didn't mean it wasn't true.

I stood.

Ben came around the desk, lightning fast, and grabbed me by the suspenders of the bib overalls. I nearly went down, but managed to stay upright by spinning around hard. I gave a shove to his chest and Ben fell. I started to run for the office door, but he grabbed my ankles and pulled me to the ground with him. I fell on my face. The side without the bruise. So now I'd have a matched set. The rest of my body was fairly well padded by all the winter clothing.

"Let me go, Ben." I kicked my feet against his hands, but it was no use. He had the advantage.

"I need that money to finance another project. Now call off the newspaper and give me your recipe." He squeezed tighter on my ankles, but he couldn't get a good hold with the slick fabric. One of his hands slipped off, and I used the opportunity to kick at his arm with my free boot.

"What's going on in here?" Lydia stood framed in the door. "Ben, are you insane? You're going to get disbarred!" She came toward me and took my arm gently, helping me to my feet, all the while glaring at Ben. "Georgie, are you okay?"

"Not really," I said. I pointed to my face. "This is his handiwork. By the way—" I turned toward Ben. "Consider yourself fired. I'll find a new lawyer to finish my divorce. I'll need my retainer back by tomorrow."

And I was going to press charges. This little jerk. Who did he think he was? Under normal circumstances I might have cut him some slack, with his father just dying. But he'd attacked me, not once, but twice.

I wondered what the other deal was he needed to finance.

"Oh, and I want to know what happened to the money in the Bloodworth Trust and I want it returned." His face went white. "I know all about it," I warned. "So start liquidating all those accounts. When that trust vests in February, I want the money available and paid out to my mother and my cousin."

Lydia's jaw dropped. "What are you saying?" she whispered.

"Ask him. I've got to go." I grabbed my parka from the coat rack so violently, another coat fell from its hook. I bent to pick it up. It was a dark charcoal gray wool topcoat. The letters "JBMSr" were embroidered inside.

"Sr"? This was Jim MacNamara's topcoat. Why was it hanging here? I turned back to Ben MacNamara.

Suddenly, I wondered if this was about more than a salad dressing recipe. More than some other deal he had cooking.

Had he killed his own father? Somebody had taken this coat from the crime scene. But how stupid—or arrogant—was he, to hang it up like a flag that screamed *I Did It*? Suddenly I felt sick. I had to get out of there. And my mother and my cousin and Caitlyn needed me.

◈ TWENTY-SIX ◈

I stopped off at the Bonaparte House before going to the docks, taking a few minutes to compose myself. When I went back down to the docks, the wind whipping around in icy gusts, Brenda was there waiting for me. She had her hat jammed down over her ears. Her little boat with the open cockpit was tied up, rocking away in the waves, which appeared to be picking up. If I'd felt nauseous in MacNamara's office, I actually needed a bucket now. It would be suicide to try to cross the water in that thing.

Brenda looked at me. "Yeah, I don't think we should try it either. But we need to get over there."

I looked out over the St. Lawrence again. Off in the distance, there was a lone boat headed in the direction we would be going. It seemed to be making progress.

Great sprays of white flew up from either side as it bobbed up and down.

Brenda was right. I *did* have to get over there. To see for myself that they were getting better. To take care of them. I could call the police or the fire department and ask them for a ride. But if I called, they'd tell me to stay home and let them handle it. Good advice, smart advice, until it was people you loved who were sick and in trouble.

Steve Murdoch's boat *Witch of November* was tied up at the dock. Brenda and I looked at each other. This was not the first time I'd borrowed a boat, but this one was bigger. And by the looks of that leaden sky and choppy water, we needed a bigger boat. This time, the weather was worse and the stakes were higher.

"See if you can find the keys. You better drive," I said.

Brenda nodded. She had far more experience than I, and frankly, my hands were shaking, so I trusted myself even less. We boarded, and we snooped until we found some keys, hidden under a seat cushion in the bridge.

Brenda switched on the twin engines, which rumbled to life.

The wind blew stinging mini icicles against my face and whipped the water around us into whitecaps that sloshed up against the side of the boat. Brenda steered away from the dock and pointed the bow out across the water. The boat rocked sickeningly. Fingers numb, I pulled out my cell phone and dialed the nurse. She didn't answer. Neither did Melanie or Caitlyn or Liza. Damn. What was going on over there?

I cupped one hand over my ear to try to drown out the noise of the boat and the wind and dialed 911.

When the operator, who wasn't Cindy Dumont, thank goodness, picked up, I shouted into the phone and asked her to call the police and the volunteer fire department EMTs. That I thought someone was having a medical emergency on Valentine Island, and possibly another kind of emergency. The operator promised to send help.

Brenda picked up speed, expertly aiming the boat straight into each small wave, which broke with a small thump and sprayed up in a cold mist along either side of us. Over and over. I closed my eyes, hoping to ward off motion sickness.

But it wasn't just the rolling of the boat that was making me nauseous. Why had I waited so long to go and get them? The fact that Dr. Phelps had said that Melanie, Caitlyn, and Liza were stable and should stay put did not make me feel any better. But I couldn't blame him. He'd gone above and beyond by making the trip to Valentine Island, examining them, and taking samples for testing. He had no reason to suspect poisoning until the results came back, nor had any of us. We were lucky that the tests he'd done hadn't taken much time.

Because time might be running out.

My mind raced along with the engines. Ben MacNamara was guilty of some things, but had he gone so far as to kill his own father? Over money? Surely if he needed cash, he could have simply asked his father—who, thanks to my family's trust fund, was almost certainly flush unless he'd spent it all. But Jim MacNamara had never displayed the trappings of the very rich. He wore nice clothes, drove a nice car, belonged to a nice country club, and sent his son to a nice school. But he wasn't Thurston Howell III tossing bricks of cash around as though they were candy bars.

As we neared Valentine Island, which wasn't that far from the mainland, the turrets and spires of Castle Grant were visible in the distance through a hazy filter of stormy air. They grew larger as we approached, though not nearly at the speed I would have liked. Brenda could only go so fast under these conditions, but that didn't mean I had to like it.

Finally, after what seemed like hours but was really only a few minutes, we pulled up at the Valentine Island dock, the side of the boat bumping up against the platform. I scrambled out and Brenda tossed me a line, which I tied off loosely.

"Go on," she said. "I'll tie us up and wait for the EMTs. Unless you want me to come with you."

"I guess you should wait here. And thank you." Brenda and I had been friendly in the past. But after the events of the last few weeks, I now considered her a friend.

She tossed me a can of pepper spray. "Give me your cell phone," she ordered. I complied, and she punched in a number. "Keep the screen open here so all you have to do is hit the redial button if you run into trouble. I'll be on my way. And be careful," she said.

I thanked her and race-walked onto the shore and up

the sidewalk, as fast as I dared go. Not for the first time in the last few days, I reminded myself I'd be no use to anyone if I fell. It was faster going on the frozen turf next to the stone walkway, so that was the path I took. Dry brown grass coated in ice and snow crunched under my boots. I gripped the can of pepper spray inside my jacket pocket.

The castle doors were unlocked when I reached them. I slipped inside, grateful for the sudden warmth but with my gut in a knot. "Liza?" I called. My voice echoed around the grand foyer and was met with silence.

It occurred to me now that I hadn't really thought this through. Should I look for Liza, or go straight to my mother?

It only took a moment to decide. I headed for the staircase, barreled up the winding steps, and only stopped when I stood, panting, in front of the door to my mother's room.

The hallway was empty. And silent. I threw open the door.

Sheets, duvet, and pillows lay askew on the bed and onto the floor. I surveyed the room. Melanie wasn't there. "Melanie?" I called. "Mom?" I checked the adjoining sitting area and the en suite. No one.

My heart rate ticked up. Where was she? This place was enormous. But she was weak. How far could she have gone under her own power? *If she's not already dead.* I silenced the thought.

Or perhaps the nurse had moved her, setting up some sort of makeshift hospital ward. If Melanie hadn't gone under her own power, but had been moved, either by the nurse or by someone else, she could be anywhere in this castle. Or anywhere in any of the outbuildings. She might even be off-island by now.

I opened the door to Caitlyn's room. Also empty.

Willing my breath to slow, I did my best to think logically. The next place to look would be Liza's private apartment. She was sick too, but not as sick as Melanie and Caitlyn, so she might have brought everyone to her rooms. I tried to orient myself. Liza's office and sitting room were on the first floor, and her bedroom was connected to them by a stairway. Not the ostentatious stairs I'd taken to get here, but a smaller, less obtrusive set. I didn't know the castle layout well enough to know if I could get there from here.

My gut told me that it would be useless to search the other rooms in this wing. It didn't make sense that Melanie and Caitlyn would have moved from one bedroom to another. And if somebody else had forcibly moved them, there'd be no point in taking them only a few feet.

So I ran for the stairs and trailed my hand along the ornate banister for support on the way down.

The foyer was still empty when I returned. What was taking the cops, or the firefighters, or whoever was coming so long? Melanie, Caitlyn, and Liza had not poisoned themselves, which meant someone was doing it to them. And that person could be here now. Probably was, unless he'd administered the fatal dose and fled, which was entirely possible, especially if whoever had done it didn't want to be stuck on this island all night. There were any number of places a boat could have been tied up around the island, and any number of places someone could have gone—north, south, or even to one of the Canadian ports. I was no sailor and even I could see that it was only going to get more dangerous to be out on the water.

I walked as fast as I could across the black-and-white marble floor of the foyer toward Liza's rooms, my boots making a wet sucking sound every step I took.

It would have been smarter to wait for help, or at least bring Brenda in with me. I knew that.

But I didn't care. My family was sick, maybe dying, and God help whoever had done this to them.

I knew who was behind it all. That snot-nosed little preppy Ben MacNamara. He was the only one who made sense. He'd made a good show of pretending not to know anything about the Bloodworth Trust. He was young and certainly had the skills to fake the trust documents. I was willing to bet he'd had his father's briefcase and keys to the locked filing cabinet all along, because he had his father's topcoat, which he must have taken from Jim Mac-Namara's body on my ladies' room floor. He could have lured his father to the Bonaparte House, killed him, then taken his briefcase and topcoat and worn it back to the office, which was why Brenda thought she saw him walking at a time when he was actually dead.

I had no doubt Jim MacNamara had been in this up to his eyeballs too. He'd been skimming from the trust for years before Ben was old enough to join the firm. Had he confided in his son? Offered to bring him into the family side business of stealing from clients? What if Junior wanted more than his father had been offering?

This was going to end now. Before Brenda and I left, and before I'd called the Bay PD and the fire department, I'd called Lieutenant Hawthorne and told him my suspicions about Ben, that patricidal brat. And my friendly neighborhood state trooper had told me, whether he should have or not, that he'd been watching Ben, and knew where he was right now. So yes, it paid to be cautious, but according to the lieutenant, Ben wasn't on this island. But Ben might have had an accomplice.

I needed to find Melanie, Caitlyn, and Liza. I pulled out my cell phone to dial Brenda and see if help had arrived.

Suddenly, everything went dark. My arms flailed as I tried to pull something off my face and shoulders—a sack of some kind? My phone went flying and I heard it skate across the floor as my arms were grabbed and bound. I kicked out, but felt only air.

◈ TWENTY-SEVEN ◈

Something hit my gut as I felt myself being lifted and thrown over a shoulder. I bucked and squirmed to try to throw my captor off balance, but it was no use. This was a strong guy. At least I assumed it was a guy. I wasn't light and whoever had me was moving us forward without too much difficulty. "Put me down!" My voice was muffled through the bag. I bucked again, but it was no use.

I was set down violently in a chair with my arms looped painfully over the back. I heard the unmistakable zip of a plastic tie as my hands were secured to the chair. The air inside the bag was wet and heavy with my own breath, which was coming fast and hard. It was dark inside, but I closed my eyes anyway, fighting off a wave of nausea. I'd be no good to anyone if I passed out.

"Who are you?" I said. "The cops are on their way, you know. They might already be here." I hoped my tone was defiant. "Where are the other women?" If this jerk had hurt them, any more than they already were, I'd . . . Well, there wasn't much I could do at the moment.

"Damn," he said. "I'm not gettin' paid enough for this." Footsteps ran across the floor and out the door.

I wracked my brain. He'd said only a few words, and I didn't recognize the voice. It wasn't Ben MacNamara, or Steve Murdoch, or anybody else I could identify. But something about it was familiar. Or not familiar. There was an accent. Not strong, but definitely not North Country. Where had I heard it before?

Then I knew. That guy who had been on Steve Murdoch's crew with Russ Riley, who came to do the initial demo at the Bonaparte House before the murder. What was his name? Zach something.

How was he mixed up in this? Had he killed Jim MacNamara, for reasons of his own or because he was working for someone? He'd certainly had access to the cabinet where I stored the gyro spit that had been used to skewer my lawyer. He could have even been the one to set up Russ to take the fall, by telling the police that he overheard Russ and MacNamara arguing.

I heard a faint noise. A soft moan coming from somewhere to my left. The sound of slightly labored breathing. There was someone else in this room.

Zach—if it was Zach—had not secured my feet, only my arms. I shook my head. The bag was loose. I might be able to work it off and then at least I'd be able to breathe. And see who was here with me.

I rolled my shoulders and neck until the cloth came free, then whipped my head back and forth so hard I almost tipped myself and the chair. The bag finally dropped to the floor.

After the dizziness passed, I opened my eyes. I was in a room in the castle I'd never seen before, but there were lots of those. I could be anywhere. My eyes went in the direction of the sound I'd heard.

Liza lay on the bed. Her skin was pale and her normally perfect blond hair lay in a tangled mess on the white linen. She was sick. Or injured. Or both.

I gritted my teeth. Damn! Now I could see, but I still couldn't *do* anything without the use of my hands. I tried standing up, and the chair came with me, but the front edge of the seat was pressed against the backs of my knees and it was impossible to move more than a few inches at a time. As I'd suspected, this was a lot harder than it looked on television cop shows. Liza was breathing. That had to be a good sign, didn't it? But if Liza was here, where were Melanie and Caitlyn?

I wiggled my fingers, but my wrists were secured to the chair. No way was I getting free without help.

"Liza," I called softly but urgently. "Can you hear me?" She was incapacitated, but not restrained, as far as I could tell. I glanced around the room. We were in a bedroom, rather sparsely furnished, unlike the more elaborate rooms in the other wing. I wondered if this had been a servant's room back in the day. There was a nightstand topped by a lamp next to the bed on which Liza lay, but nothing else. No desk that might have contained scissors or a knife.

"Liza, you have to focus." Her head came slowly around and her glassy eyes landed on my face. A glimmer of recognition passed across her features.

"I'm sure somebody will be coming back any minute," I whispered. "Look in that nightstand and see if there's anything in there—anything at all—that can cut these zip ties. You have to help me so I can help you. Do you understand?"

She picked up her head from the pillow and nodded weakly.

I glanced from her to the door. We still had time, but who knew how much?

Liza reached for the knob and, clearly using all her strength, yanked open the nightstand drawer. It clattered to the floor.

Damn! If that didn't bring back Zach, nothing would.

"Sorry," she whispered.

"Is there anything in there?" I craned my neck, but the angle was wrong for me to see.

Liza pushed herself up into a sitting position, braced herself on the bed, then stood. She started to sway. *Don't fall*, I willed her. She sank to the floor and reached into the drawer.

"Pen," she said, breathing heavily. "Book. Paper clip."

Nothing useful. There had to be something we could use, somewhere.

"I'll. Try." She came toward me on her hands and knees, but she was having trouble coordinating her movements.

I didn't think there was much she could do. She was barely moving under her own steam, and without a tool, there was no way she could break the zip tie.

"Who did this?" I said. "Do you know? Where are Melanie and Caitlyn? Where's the nurse?"

Liza opened her mouth to speak, but before the words could come out, there was movement at the door. Both our heads turned.

A woman stood there, hands on hips, lips pursed. "Well, isn't this touching?" she said.

My jaw dropped.

It was Lydia Ames. Legal assistant to Jim and Ben MacNamara. Her arm was extended, her leather-gloved hand holding a pistol.

"Lydia, thank God you're here," I said, playing dumb. Because I was pretty sure she wasn't here to save us. And I was pretty sure I knew who'd been driving that boat Brenda and I had seen off in the distance, before we started.

She rolled her eyes. "Seriously. You are the biggest pain in the ass I've ever met."

It almost sounded like a compliment. "What are you doing, Lydia? Why am I tied up?" Where were the cops? They could have swum here from the mainland by now.

"Do you know how many times you've messed up my plans? I've been working on this for years. *Years*. And then you came along and had to start sticking your nose in. People didn't really have to die, you know."

Keep her talking. Stall. It was my only hope. "What have you been working on?"

She rolled her eyes again. "The Bloodworth Trust, you idiot."

"But you said you'd never seen it before Jim MacNamara . . . died."

"Puh-leez." She gestured with the gun. "Do you actually think I could work in an office for that long without knowing every file and how to access it? A locked drawer is nothing when your boss leaves his keys on the desk when he goes out for a walk."

Liza sat up and leaned against the bed. Silently, I begged her not to try anything. She wasn't restrained, but she was weak. And we just had to stall long enough for help to arrive.

"So you killed Jim? How'd you manage it? Pretty clever, setting up Russ Riley to take the fall." Flattery, though it made my stomach roll, was worth a try.

It didn't work.

"Spare me," Lydia said. "Yeah, I did it. While he was working there, I had Zach Brundage find me a weapon in your kitchen, then get Russ to touch it. When Jim went out for coffee, I called him and told him you asked him to stop by the restaurant. Zach had already let me know that the construction crew was done for the day. There was plenty of time while you were at the accountant and the hair salon. I put on the topcoat and wore it back to the office."

"Where you hung it up, conveniently obvious, so it would look like Ben had done it? But why?" I dreaded the answer to my next question, but it had to be asked. "Are you another heir of Elihu Bloodworth? My cousin?"

She gave a little snort. "That trust is my inheritance. But sorry, no. We're not related, and this"—she swung the gun in an arc from me to Liza, who was still conscious and upright, but barely—"is not some family reunion. It's my inheritance from Jim MacNamara and his bratty kid."

"I don't understand." My jaw was tight and I could feel the kernel of a migraine forming behind my eyes.

"I don't suppose you would. But I put up with those two for a lot of years. The pats on the head and 'I couldn't appreciate you more' and 'If my wife calls, tell her I'm in court,' with fifty-cent-an-hour yearly raises and no retirement?"

"But you had a settlement from your divorce." The headache was beginning to grow. My face and bound hands felt clammy. I was still in my coat and boots and I was sweating.

"I knew that wouldn't last forever. So I created my own business. I think of myself as an investment company. An investment in me. Funded with the Bloodworth Trust money, which I figure I have just as much right to as your mother and your cousin. Maybe not a legal right, but they'd never done anything to deserve it either. I saw an opportunity and I took it."

"You said, 'People didn't have to die.' So who else have you killed?" Her next words confirmed what I'd been thinking.

Her face hardened. "I didn't kill anyone," she said. "Other people knew about the trust—or thought they knew about it. Whatever they did, it's not on me. But it is on *you*. You're the one who keeps picking at the scab. Well, now you're going to bleed." She waved the gun again.

The dull ache in my shoulders from the odd angle my arms were positioned throbbed in time with my accelerating pulse. *Keep her talking.* "Is Ben MacNamara in on this? Are you working together?"

Lydia rolled her eyes. "You're kidding, right? No, young James Benjamin is about to get himself disbarred for various other fraudulent activities. Just as soon as I finish you all off—and make it look like your friend Liza here did it in an attempt to keep all the Bloodworth Trust money for herself—an anonymous letter will be going to the grievance committee in Albany detailing his transgressions. I almost—*almost* feel sorry for him. He's way out of his league."

"But what about Jim MacNamara? He must have known what you were doing."

"Where do you think I got the idea? *Jim* and I worked together, not Ben and I. For years. We were going to split the money we . . . reinvested. But then I found out Jim was cheating me—had been cheating me—because he was paying Jennifer Murdoch to keep their escapades quiet."

I opened my mouth to say something, anything, to keep her engaged. But she was apparently done with the confession, because she came toward me. Lydia placed the pistol close to my temple. The smell of oil, intensified by my own sharpened senses, stung my nose. My heart rate increased again. *Please let help arrive. Like now.*

Lydia pulled the gun away, backed up a step, and smiled. "I'm going to regret not finishing you off myself. But it's better this way." She made a sudden move toward Liza, who'd managed to keep herself sitting up during this exchange, and grabbed her by the arm. Lydia yanked her to her feet and marched her over to me. My friend's face had a sickly cast but she looked me in the eye. *Not going down without a fight*, she seemed to say.

Lydia placed the gun in Liza's limp hand, then wrapped her own gloved hands around Liza's. I saw what was happening. Lydia was going to make it look like Liza killed me. "Where are Melanie and Caitlyn?" I said. "Are they already . . . dead?"

Lydia repositioned Liza's arm. The gun was now being swung slowly toward me. "Maybe," she said. "If they're not, it won't be long now. As soon as Liza finishes you off, she'll administer the final doses of poison to all four of them, that nurse included."

Four? For someone so focused on money, Lydia apparently couldn't count. Movement in the doorway caught my eye. Brenda! I held still, kept my gaze trained on Lydia.

Liza, apparently marshaling whatever strength she had left, began to struggle against Lydia to keep her from seeing Brenda. Lydia held Liza in an awkward position and was trying to keep the gun in Liza's hand. But Liza's arms were longer than Lydia's and she used the additional leverage to keep Lydia off balance.

Brenda took advantage of the struggle and raced into the room, our redheaded cavalry. She had something in her hand and made a sudden movement. Lydia cried out, stiffened, and fell to the floor, the gun dropping harmlessly from her hand. Liza staggered away, then dropped onto the bed, breath ragged, her strength spent.

Brenda kicked the gun away from Lydia and leaned over her prostrate form. "Glad to see this thing works." She held up a Taser and grinned.

◈ TWENTY-EIGHT ◈

"Me too," I said. "How long will she be out?" Brenda glanced at Liza, who nodded toward me. Brenda whipped out a bright red pocket knife and cut the plastic securing me to the chair. I brought my arms back into their natural position, which was painful enough—I was no yogi—but my wrists hurt more. The grooves in my skin were deep and raw. But I couldn't think about that now.

"Don't know," Brenda said. "Depends on things like weight and body chemistry. Let's not take any chances."

"Where are the cops? The EMTs?" I stood, then went to Liza and put my arm around her to help her to her feet.

"Tim Arquette is down at the docks. He caught a guy acting suspicious and trying to leave. They ended up getting into it, but Tim's got him in cuffs right now. The EMTs are tending to them, then they'll be right up." She put her Taser into her pocket and picked up the gun. "Go find your mom. I'll deal with this one till the cops come."

I turned to Liza. "Do you want to stay here or come with me? Any idea where Melanie and Caitlyn are?"

Liza leaned against me. "Brenda's got this under control. I'll . . . be no help to her. I'll come with you." We made our way to the door.

The hallway stretched in both directions, with a half-dozen doors on each side. "Should we just start opening doors?"

Liza nodded. "This is the servants' wing, where my seasonal help stays, at least in the summer." She coughed, then took a deep breath as she opened the first door.

"Melanie and Caitlyn first got sick, what, like a week ago? So who's had access to your food during that time?" The first room was empty. We moved on to the next.

"Since it was just a few of us, I've been doing all the cooking. I blame myself." She stumbled and I caught her.

"Stop that right now," I said. "You're not to blame. And I'm pretty sure you haven't been monitoring your kitchen twenty-four/seven. So who's been working around here?" I hated the next thought that popped into my head but I said it anyway. "Steve Murdoch?"

Liza's expression was horrified. "No. It can't be."

Unfortunately, it could. The pieces fit. Lydia Ames must have had at least one more accomplice. Steve had reasons to hate Jim MacNamara, both personally and professionally. Could he be working with Lydia? Had she played him, knowing he was vulnerable over his wife's infidelity? Helping Lydia would be a way to stick it to both Jim and Jennifer. Steve had access to every building on this island. It would have been nothing for him to open the refrigerator door and add the poison to whatever drinks, or soup, or even salad dressings he found there, day after day.

And I knew what Liza was thinking, without her having to say a word. She was kicking herself. She'd been taken in before by a pretty face and a tool belt, and people had paid with their lives.

"No." Liza shook her head. "It's not Steve. I won't believe it."

We went to the next room. "We have to consider the possibility," I said as gently as I could. "Who else has been here?" Honestly, I didn't want it to be Steve either. I liked him.

"I've only got two people on the payroll right now. They don't stay over. They come from the mainland every day and go home before it gets dark." The next room was also empty.

"Who are they?" I pressed. Why weren't we finding Melanie? She and Caitlyn could be anywhere in this place. My heart rate, which had slowed to somewhere approaching normal when we left Lydia in Brenda's capable hands, was ticking up again. This was taking too long. Lydia had said that the fatal doses had not been administered. But just like a Taser, poison must affect different people in different ways. My mother and her assistant might already be dead.

"Brandy Gates cleans for me."

Dolly's daughter. Russ Riley's sister. Oh no. This would kill Dolly. It would kill me. I trusted Brandy. We opened another door.

"And the only other one is Pru. Prudence Patton. This was her first summer with me. I kept her on to help with closing up."

Another empty room. *Prudence Patton.* The name jogged something in my memory, though I was fairly certain I'd never heard it before. Liza was clearly exhausted, moving slower and slower, and leaning on me more and more as we approached the last door on this side of the hall.

"What does Prudence look like?"

"Can we stop, for just a second?" We paused. "Mid-twenties. Tall. Slim. Long blond hair. Not a native, but she's living near Bonaparte Bay somewhere now."

I used Liza's resting time to paint a mental picture of the woman and pair it with the name. Prudence Patton. I knew a woman who looked like just like that. Except she called herself Piper Preston.

"What do you know about her?" I asked. "Can you go on?"

By way of answer to my second question, she put her hand on the doorknob. "Not much. But she gave Angela Wainwright as a reference."

Angela Wainwright. The door swung open and we entered. This room was a little larger than the ones we'd been in, containing three oak dressers and three narrow beds.

In each of the beds lay a figure. None of them were moving.

I went to Melanie first. Her platinum blond hair was unmistakable against the white linen of the pillow. "Melanie? Melanie, it's me. Can you hear me?" I grabbed her wrist. She had a pulse. I held my hand a couple of inches from her mouth. She was breathing. Her bare face was still, though. Even though she was only just short of sixty, without her customary heavy makeup, she looked . . . old. Small. Fragile. She'd lost weight she didn't need to lose and was now painfully thin. My heart swelled. In spite of everything she'd put me through, abandoning me when I was just out of high school, and generally annoying me every day since she'd been back in my life, she was still my mother. And always would be. I raised her bony hand to my lips and gave it a soft kiss before laying it back under the covers. "Help's on the way," I said. She gave a tiny nod.

Caitlyn Black, my mother's joined-at-the-hip assistant, lay in the center bed. Liza looked at me over Caitlyn's head. "She's alive," Liza said.

Caitlyn shifted. "Where's my phone?" she said thickly. "I need my phone." I hated to tell her, so I didn't, that she and Melanie would be putting their business and social engagements on hold until they recovered, so her phone wouldn't do her any good. But that was Caitlyn. Ever efficient, even though she was barely conscious.

Liza and I looked at each other. There was a third bed in the room, and it was occupied. Lydia must have drugged and/or poisoned the nurse as well. But Lydia had said she was going to finish off four people after she made it look like Liza had killed me. There were only three here.

I stared at the figure in the third bed.

No. No, no, no, no. It couldn't be. She wasn't even home from Greece yet. I raced toward her. Liza must have been right behind me, because she appeared at my side.

The figure in the bed had her back to me. But I'd recognize that dark head anywhere, anytime. I'd given birth to it, in a smaller version. Tears spilled out of my eyes as I sat on the edge of the mattress and put my hand on the shoulder, giving it a little caress. "Callista," I whispered. "Honey, I'm here."

She rolled toward me. "Mommy," she said groggily. "Surprise."

❖ TWENTY-NINE ❖

It took another ten minutes for the EMTs to reach the room in the servants' hall. Liza insisted on going to find them, despite the fact that she was also quite ill, because she knew the castle better than anyone and was unlikely to get lost.

Sure enough, when Bill Belanger from the Bonaparte Bay Volunteer Fire Department finally came through the door, he was all apologies. "We didn't know where to find you," he explained. "This place is huge."

Liza dropped into a chair. She was clearly spent. "The police are here, with reinforcements," she said then tipped her head back and waited her turn.

Bill started barking orders to the two other members of his team and they set to work. I held Cal's clammy hand. My daughter was here. She was safe. And I thought she was going to be okay.

Relief lifted the fog from my mind as the EMTs worked. *Angela Wainwright. Piper Preston, or Prudence Patton, or whatever her real name was.* Piper had worked for both Angela Wainwright and Franco Riccardi. And now it was clear she had also been working for Lydia Ames and probably Ben MacNamara too. Piper was the link, the unlikely connection between the Bloodworth Trust and the oldest known Thousand Island dressing recipe. Whether she knew that or not was anyone's guess.

Though it pained me to do so, I pulled out my cell phone, set it on my knee so I wouldn't have to drop Cal's hand, and dialed one-handed.

"Hawthorne," a brusque voice said.

"This is Georgie Nikolopatos. You need to go pick up Zach Brundage and Piper Preston. She also calls herself Prudence Patton. Tim Arquette from the BBPD has Lydia Ames here. She killed Jim MacNamara. And you might want to bring in Angela Wainwright. I'm not sure how deeply she's involved, but Ben MacNamara was behind the attacks on Franco Riccardi and me, at the very least."

There was a silence on the other end of the line. "You must have been completing your detective training on the down low," he finally said. "Sorry we don't have any openings on the force right now."

Man, he was annoying. I should have called, well, anybody but him.

"But I'll look into it. Thanks for the tips." He rang off.

A Killer Kebab

* * *

Two days later, I plunked myself into an orange pleather chair in the family lounge at Bonaparte Bay's small hospital. Liza and Melanie, who were being discharged today, sat across from me as we waited for the final paperwork to process. Cal and Caitlyn, being younger and generally more resilient, were back at the Bonaparte House already, having been let go yesterday.

The nurse had been found in a separate room, groggy but alive, zip-tied to a chair as I had been. Dr. Phelps promised that none of the five women would have any lasting effects from their poisonings or their ordeal.

"So what happened?" Melanie demanded. "I'm getting very tired of this hospital. And there wasn't even enough time to get another camera crew on-site to make it worthwhile." Last time she'd been here, after she'd been shot, her daytime drama had written a special storyline for her and filmed on location. She was probably up for a Daytime Emmy for her performance. She'd never won yet, but maybe this was her year.

I pulled a couple of bottled waters from my shoulder bag and set one in front of each woman. "Drink," I ordered. "You're off your IVs now and you need to keep hydrated."

Liza complied. Melanie gave a huff *and* an eye roll. She must be feeling generous with her scorn today. Normally, I liked to do these debriefings with a glass of wine and some kind of delicious snack, but the hospital vending machine seemed to be fresh out of both.

"From what I've been able to piece together, Lydia Ames, who's now in the county lockup, engineered everything. As you know, she worked for Jim MacNamara for years. When she found out he was skimming from the Bloodworth Trust, she demanded to be let in on the action. According to our new lawyer, who I went into St. Lawrence County to get—"

"Good idea," Liza interrupted. "Better to have someone a little farther removed from all this."

"That's what I thought too. Anyway, according to the new lawyer, Lydia was the one who came up with the idea of altering the trust documents to hide the missing money. It'll take months before all the various bank accounts can be traced. Lydia had her own, Jim MacNamara had his own, plus most of the money is probably in offshore accounts under assumed names, or buried inside shell corporations or something."

Melanie gave another eye roll. "Do we even know if there's any money left?"

"The lawyer's just getting started. We won't know that for a while."

"I guess," Melanie said dramatically, "my summer stock theater at our old family farm will have to wait. Unless I can charm some investors . . ." Her gaze went toward the windows overlooking the St. Lawrence River, no doubt thinking who in her acquaintance might be charmable. I certainly wasn't.

"Maybe we can talk about that later," Liza said, her voice thoughtful.

"Back to the story—" I gave Melanie what I hoped was a pointed stare. Which she ignored. "When Jim Mac-Namara took up with Jennifer Murdoch, Lydia thought Jim was going to try to cut her out of the deal. Jennifer was demanding, and pushy, and she had Jim wrapped around her little finger. It wasn't too big a leap to think that Jim might start trying to pressure Lydia into giving up some of her share of the money. Maybe Jim had something on her, something that hasn't come to light yet."

Liza said, "Let me guess. The trust was almost empty at that point, because between Jim and Lydia, over the years, they'd diverted nearly all the money. And since the trust was about to vest in February, and it was quite possible that one of us was going to question what had happened to the millions that were supposed to be there, Lydia decided to make a preemptive strike. She killed Jim, using Zach Brundage to set up Russ Riley."

I nodded. "Right. And because Jim MacNamara had been Russ's lawyer the last time he'd been in trouble, Lydia knew that Russ was the perfect fall guy. He had an ax to grind against my family, and she knew about the argument Russ had had with Jim. It was simple for her to have Zach go to the police saying he'd overheard the argument."

"And then," Liza said, "she set about getting rid of the rest of the heirs to the trust. Some, like our cousins Big Dom and Doreen, were already gone, killed by people with their own interest in the trust." She swallowed, no doubt remembering who had killed Doreen and why. She went on, "And she hired Piper Preston to poison our food, either to weaken us, or to kill us outright. If there were no heirs, there would be no one to question what happened to the money. Or at least no one who would care all that much."

"And Lydia was good at altering documents," I said. "She could have directed the authorities to Jim's skimmed investments, after she covered her own tracks, of course. Jim was dead, and so, in her scenario, were all the heirs. Lydia was banking on the fact, pun intended, that Jim would take the whole blame and no one would look closely at her, a mere assistant."

Melanie was still looking out over the water. I had a feeling she was probably wondering if she could pull off Blanche DuBois and how much it would cost to put on *Streetcar.* But she surprised me by pulling herself back into the conversation. "What about that little brat, the son?"

"Ben's up to his eyeballs too," I said. "In salad dressing. He was working with a company called Tripler Enterprises to put together some kind of licensing deal with one of the big home shopping channels."

"Tripler. Triple R," Liza said. "River Rock Resort? Angela Wainwright?" I was pleased to see her take another sip out of the bottle of water.

"Right. Angela needs money to fix up the River Rock and pay the mortgage on her condo. So she, or Ben, or both of them together, came up with this idea to trademark Thousand Island dressing. To make it stand out, they needed an original, proprietary recipe—or at least one they could say was an original recipe—until they could get the stuff through the trademark process and into production."

"Seems like a dumb idea," Melanie said matter-of-factly. "Stuff's been around for a hundred years. How much could it be worth?" She examined the nails on her right hand and frowned. She'd be wanting a manicure when she got out of here.

"Yes and no," I said. "If she could get the name trademarked, she could hold every restaurant owner along the river hostage. According to the new lawyer, if she owned the trademark, she could try to prevent all of us from offering Thousand Island dressing on the menu. Of course, we could call it something else, but it's a tradition here. One of the things that makes us who we are. She might even be able to take on some of the national salad dressing brands, make them pay her to use the name. There was potential for some money, even if it wasn't guaranteed."

"Angela's not the type to physically hurt anyone. So who beat up Franco and ransacked his restaurant?" Liza asked.

"The new lawyer says that Ben MacNamara confessed to doing it, that Angela wasn't involved. Once his father was killed, Ben got desperate. He'd been working on the salad dressing deal, but now he needed it to go through immediately because he couldn't figure out how to access the Bloodworth Trust money his father and Lydia had skimmed. He used Piper as a go-between with Angela, because he wanted to keep the potential trademark and licensing quiet until the paperwork was filed and didn't want anyone guessing what they were doing."

Liza nodded. "He probably didn't know where his next paycheck was coming from."

"Right. He needed that money even more after his father died, because he wanted to try to take over the Silver Lake development project. If he could have managed it, he would have set himself up for life."

"So what happens to all the clients of that law firm?" Melanie said. "Including us. Are we just out of luck?" She had moved on to examining the nails of her other hand.

"Our new lawyer says that since Jim is dead, and Ben is likely to go to jail for assault and battery—maybe even attempted murder—the state bar counsel will have to appoint another attorney to come in and contact every client the MacNamaras had, inform them of what happened, and help them find new representation."

Liza leaned forward and patted my arm. "I can't really miss what I never had, so it won't be too hard for me to wait to see if any Bloodworth Trust money ever shows up."

"Speak for yourself," Melanie said.

Liza ignored her. "Not that it wouldn't come in handy, with my repair bills coming up. But I'm more concerned about you, Georgie. How much longer will you have to wait for your divorce?"

The same thought had crossed my mind. I shrugged. "I don't know. But I'm pretty sure freedom is in my sights."

EPILOGUE

"Whew." I blew out a breath, raised my forearm, and wiped my brow, which was damp with perspiration, while I surveyed myself in the mirror of the Bonaparte House's brand-new ladies' room. Face flushed, I pressed a damp paper towel to my cheeks and combed my hair, then repositioned a bright orange gerbera daisy in the creamy vase on the counter. I gave the dish of potpourri a little stir to release its spicy fragrance. The walls seemed to glow with a pale yellow light when the afternoon sun hit them, just as I'd imagined they'd look when I chose the color what seemed like a lifetime ago.

Steve and his new crew, minus Russ and Zach, had finished the renovations on schedule. All traces of the murder of James MacNamara were gone, replaced with brand-new tile and new fixtures. I closed my eyes. No, I couldn't feel him here, so I had to assume he was at that great country club in the sky, sitting at the celestial nineteenth hole with a scotch and soda in front of him and deciding whose wife he was going after next. I washed up and stuck my hands into the new high-speed dryer, which had the approximate power of a jet engine, then headed back out to the dining rooms.

The Bonaparte House was full on Thanksgiving Day for the first time ever and it appeared the experiment was a success. Cal, Inky, Spiro, and I had set up the tables for larger than normal parties, and Dolly and I had prepared a buffet turkey dinner with all the trimmings—including a few nontraditional ones like Greek salad and dolmades (brined grape leaves stuffed with rice and lamb), which turned out to be a nice foil for the heavy American fare. We'd gone through a dozen assorted pies, and it looked like we'd calculated just about right, as my guests seemed to be winding down with coffee, tea, and conversation and there were only a few desserts on the serving table.

Ten dollars from every dinner was being split between the food pantry and the school PTOs. My mother-in-law, Sophie, would have a fit if she knew, since she wasn't terribly civic-minded—okay, not at all civic-minded—but I'd sworn my family to secrecy. And speaking of my family, they were all here except for Sophie and her cousin Marina, who were enjoying the Aegean sunshine on the other side of the world. Melanie and Liza sat together at a table up front with Inky and Spiro. Melanie was sticking her fork into her pumpkin pie and twisting it around, deliberately not taking a bite, while the others seemed to be enjoying their desserts with gusto. Melanie and Caitlyn were staying at the Camelot now that Liza's spa had closed up for the winter, and she'd be heading back to California right after Christmas to begin taping her show again. We'd settled into a tentative relationship, even though she'd refused my offer again to stay with me while she recovered. We'd never have a conventional mother-daughter relationship—largely because Melanie had a hard time admitting she had a daughter who was approaching middle age—but it was good enough for now.

Steve Murdoch sat on the other side of Liza. The two of them appeared to be deep in conversation. I smiled. Steve had some things to work out, now that Jennifer had left town, but I couldn't help wondering if something— someone—better might be on the horizon for him. He'd decided to go ahead and purchase the Silver Lake property. Old Lady Turnbull's granddaughter was going to get to go to medical school after all. But Steve had changed his mind about developing the lakefront. Instead, he was selling the land to a forever wild trust at a very small profit. Not that anyone asked my opinion, but I approved. It made me happy to think that that beautiful shoreline would be preserved.

Russ Riley sat with Dolly—whom I'd insisted needed to sit down and take a break—his stepfather, Harold, and his sister, Brandy. Russ had been released from prison quickly once the real murderer had been caught. And he'd gotten what he wanted. His hunting land had been protected by Steve's purchase. But Russ's probation officer and the court had come down hard on him when they learned he'd violated his probation and left the state for Florida just before returning to the North Country, and just before he'd been arrested on suspicion of murder. He could now walk the woods to his heart's content, but carrying a firearm was out of the question. There'd be no legal hunting for him for years. He claimed he had no intention of going back to jail by violating his probation again, so if he was telling the truth, the Silver Lake deer were safe for now.

Brandy had agreed to trap and take the big orange cat home to live in her barn, which was a bit of a relief for me. She said she'd let me know whether the cat would be called Hortense or Horace.

Franco and Marielle had stopped in to say hello on their way to a family Thanksgiving of their own.

An arm snaked around my shoulders. I turned to see Cal's smiling face. "Great job here, Mom."

I smiled back. "I couldn't have done it without you and Dad and Inky and Dolly." My heart swelled with love for my baby girl turned young woman and I reached up and tucked a lock of her shiny dark hair behind her ear, making the dangly silver earrings she wore dance in the dim light from the candles on the tables. Now I'd have to go wash my hands again before I touched anything food-related, but I didn't care. She'd be leaving me again after Christmas to go back to Greece and back to school, and I'd have to let her go.

"Say, Mom?" She caught her lower lip between her

teeth and wrinkled her nose, the way she'd done since she was a child when she had something to tell me and wasn't sure how I'd react.

"Yes, sweetie?" *Please don't let her say she's leaving early.* Though of course I'd let her go if she asked.

"Um, I know it's Thanksgiving night and all, but do you think once the dishes are done and the food's packed up . . . would you mind . . ."

"Spit it out, Cal."

"Well, Ewan Murdoch asked me to go the movies in Watertown tonight." Her eyes searched my face. "I won't go if you're going to be alone, though."

My heart gave a little squeeze. Out of the corner of my eye, I could see Ewan sitting next to his father, his mother conspicuously absent. He cut his eyes in our direction, obviously trying not to be obvious. He was a good-looking guy like his father, with curly chestnut brown hair and brown eyes, and dressed in a tweed sports jacket he'd probably borrowed from Steve since it seemed a little big in the shoulders. The poor kid was going through a tough time, with his parents having just announced their breakup. He could probably use a night out with a pretty girl. I knew as well as anyone that Callista Nikolopatos was good company.

"Oh, go on," I said, giving her a gentle shove. "I'll get Dad and Inky to help me wrap things up here, then I'll invite them to stay over and we can watch old Cary Grant movies and eat the raspberry pie and vanilla ice cream I have hidden in the walk-in."

Her face split into a broad grin that was worth every penny we'd paid for expert orthodontic work when she was younger. She gave me a hug. "Thanks, Mom. I love you."

"I love you too. Now go ask Ewan and Steve if they need a refill on their coffee." She headed off to do my bidding.

I had no idea if Inky and Spiro would want to stay. Probably not, though Dolly's pie was a pretty good incentive. They had their own lives to lead now, and I didn't need anybody feeling sorry for lonely old me. A lump formed in my throat. I could feel plenty sorry for myself all on my own. And I had pie to keep me company.

My cell phone buzzed in my pocket. The dining room seemed under control, so I headed out into the hallway and toward my office to take the call. I frowned as I reached for the doorknob. It wouldn't turn. The phone continued to buzz. A look at the screen told me I'd missed a call from Jack and my heart sank. I tried the doorknob again and felt resistance. This wasn't funny. I knew I hadn't locked the door, and the key was right where it belonged—in the top drawer of my desk inside the office.

Well, heck. Now I'd have to see if Inky with his illegal but useful skills could either pick the lock or go in through the window that faced the employee parking lot and open the door from the inside. Blowing out a sigh, I spun on my heel to go find him.

A gentle breath of air kissed the back of my neck and the hinges of the big oak door creaked behind me. The muscles of my back stiffened. I turned around, slowly.

A Killer Kebab

Jack Conway stood in the door frame, grinning his movie star smile and looking better than any raspberry pie ever could. He reached out his long arms and drew me close, pulled me into my office, and shut the door. I pressed my cheek against the soft wool of his dark sweater as tears welled up into my eyes. I hoped I didn't ruin the sweater with my waterworks. His chin rested on my hair, which I knew probably smelled like the restaurant kitchen, but he didn't seem to mind.

Jack pulled back and looked into my eyes, his hands coming to rest on my waist. "Miss me?"

"You know I did," I sniffed. Darn it, I forbade myself to cry. Jack couldn't help that his job with the Coast Guard sometimes took him away for weeks at a time, or that he couldn't tell me exactly what he did or where he was going.

"I've just been out at Gladys's house, turning on the furnace to warm the place up. I don't suppose you'd like to come out there later to help me decorate for the holidays?" He ran his hands around to the small of my back, leaving a trail of warmth that spread pleasantly to . . . other places. I stepped forward into his embrace.

"Funny, you don't look like Martha Stewart," I said.

"You wound me. My scones are things of beauty."

I laughed. "I'll bet they are. Will there be a fire in the fireplace?"

"What kind of host-in-someone-else's-home would I be if I didn't make a fire?"

I wrapped my arms around him a little tighter, brazen

hussy that I was. Maybe this would be a good night for Cal to stay with her father after the movie. "Do you even know where Gladys keeps the decorations?"

He pulled one hand away from my back, and I was disappointed at the loss of contact. He reached into his front pocket and pulled out his closed fist, which he raised above his head. His fingers uncurled to reveal a sprig of dark green leaves attached to white, waxy berries. Mistletoe.

"I figure this might be all the decoration we need," he said. Jack leaned forward and pressed his lips to mine in a soft kiss.

Give me understated decorations anytime.

AUTHOR'S NOTE

According to a recent survey, Thousand Island is the sixth most ordered salad dressing in restaurants across the country. In Northern New York, and the Thousand Islands region in particular, the number is probably somewhat higher. There are many origin stories for the dressing.

The most popular is that it was created on a yacht owned by the manager of the Waldorf Astoria, George Boldt, by his famous hotel maître d' and sometimes chef, Oscar Tschirky, while Boldt was on a boating excursion in the St. Lawrence River somewhere around the turn of the twentieth century. Tour boat operators have been repeating this story for decades, because it dovetails nicely with the story of Boldt Castle, the most famous landmark in the Thousand Islands. However, there appears to be no evidence that Oscar ever visited the area, much less cooked personally for Boldt.

The Blackstone Hotel in Chicago claims that its chef, Theo Rooms, created the dressing for the 1910 opening of the hotel. Why a Chicago hotel would name a dressing after a geographical region nearly a thousand miles away has not been explained.

In the Thousand Islands area itself, the owner of a restaurant a few miles upriver from Bonaparte Bay says that he found the original recipe in a safe when he bought the building. He bottles and sells the dressing, but keeps his recipe secret. Various other restaurants claim to have, and serve, the original recipe.

Another version involves vaudeville actress May Irwin, who summered in the Thousand Islands in the early 1900s. May was served a dressing created by a woman named Sophia LaLonde, who was the wife of the captain of a charter fishing boat. Sophia created the sauce to go with the fried fish her husband served as a shore dinner to his customers. May, who was a collector of recipes, loved the dressing so much, that she allegedly gave it to George Boldt, Theo Rooms, or both, and suggested that the dressing be served in their hotels.

Evidence has come to light in the last few years in the form of a recipe, in May Irwin's handwriting, called "Sophias Sauce" (no apostrophe in the original document), which has been dated conclusively to 1907 based on a letter associated with it. One look at the ingredients and it's clear that this can be nothing other than Thousand Island dressing. Interestingly, May Irwin produced a cookbook in 1904 (*May Irwin's Home Cooking*), which did not contain a recipe for the dressing and lends credence to the idea that the dressing was created somewhere

Author's Note

between 1904 and 1907—or at least that May didn't know about it until after 1904.

Sophia's is the version of the story I like best and the one that makes the most sense, and it's certainly the one that has the best documentation, so Sophia gets the credit in *A Killer Kebab*. By the way, no one seems to know why the dressing became known as Thousand Island, rather than Thousand Islands. Let me know if you have any theories.

RECIPES

❖

Thousand Island Dressing, circa 1907

Makes about 16 servings.

1 c. mayonnaise
½ c. ketchup
2 T. Worcestershire sauce
2 T. lemon juice
¼ c. sweet pickle relish
1 hard-boiled egg, chopped fine

Mix all ingredients except egg in a bowl, using a fork or whisk. Refrigerate for at least 2 hours before serving (overnight is better). Just before serving, mix in chopped egg.*

Delicious served on a crisp wedge of iceberg lettuce, topped with cooked, crumbled bacon; as sauce for a burger; or as I believe it was originally intended, as a sauce for fried fish. Dressing will keep for about a week in the fridge without the egg.

Note: I found when I tested this recipe that the egg, if added and allowed to sit, overpowered the dressing. The early recipe does not differentiate between dill or sweet pickle relish, so I went with sweet, though I think dill would also be tasty. And don't expect this dressing to look or taste like the kind you can buy in the supermarket. The original has quite a tangy, pungent kick from the lemon and Worcestershire, so use judiciously.

❖

Tiropita (Greek Cheese Pie)

Makes about 24 rich, cheesy triangles.

¾ lb. feta cheese, drained and crumbled
8 oz. (1 c.) ricotta cheese
¼ c. grated romano or parmesan cheese
2 eggs, well beaten
1 t. ground white pepper
½ t. ground nutmeg (or 10 to 12 scrapes of a fresh
nutmeg on a tiny grater)
½ lb. phyllo dough
2 sticks (1 c.) unsalted butter, melted

Preheat oven to 350 degrees.

Prepare a baking sheet by covering with parchment paper.

Using a fork or spoon, mix cheeses together in a good-sized bowl, then add beaten eggs and spices and mix well.

Unroll phyllo and lay three sheets on a cutting board. Cover unused portion of dough with a barely damp kitchen towel (really squeeze the water out, or the phyllo will get too soggy). Using a pastry brush and a very delicate hand, liberally brush the top of the three-sheet stack with melted butter. With a sharp knife, cut the stack into three lengthwise strips.

About an inch from the end of each strip, place about a tablespoon of the cheese filling. Bring one corner of the phyllo over the filling to the opposite edge of the dough, forming a triangle. Gently flip the tiropita up and over, side to side, aligning the edges and encasing the filling, until you reach the end of the strip and have a triangle several layers thick. (The technique is just like folding an American flag. See the author's website for photos.) Brush the triangle with a bit more butter, and place on the parchment-lined baking sheet, leaving an inch of space around each savory pastry. Repeat with remaining phyllo (covering the unused portion with the barely damp towel) until filling is used up. Bake for about 20 minutes, or until flaky and golden brown. Serve warm or at room temperature, as an appetizer or light lunch or supper, with a salad of romaine, ripe tomato, onion, and cucumber, dressed with a vinaigrette. Also delicious with tomato soup.

Maple Walnut Sandies

North Country people love their maple syrup. These tasty cookies will melt in your mouth.

Makes about 3 dozen cookies.

2 sticks (1 c.) plus 2 T. butter
2¼ c. all-purpose flour
⅓ c. sugar
1 t. vanilla
1½ t. cinnamon
¼ c. plus 1 T. real maple syrup
1 c. finely chopped walnuts
1 c. powdered sugar

Preheat oven to 325 degrees.

Line a baking sheet with parchment.

Beat 1 c. butter with an electric mixer on medium speed for 1 minute, until light and fluffy. Add half the flour, sugar, vanilla, 1 t. cinnamon, and 1 T. maple syrup. Combine thoroughly, then add remaining flour and nuts. (You may need to do this last step with a wooden spoon and some muscle if you don't have a stand mixer.)

Roll into balls the size of a walnut and place on the parchment-lined baking sheet, leaving 2 inches of space around each cookie. Bake for about 15 minutes, or until the bottoms of the cookies are very lightly browned. Cool on a wire rack set over a rimmed baking sheet or a piece of foil with edges turned up.

When the cookies are cool, make the glaze: Melt 2 T. butter in a microwave-safe bowl. Whisk in ¼ c. maple syrup and ½ t. cinnamon, then powdered sugar, to make a medium-thick glaze. Drizzle over cookies and allow glaze to set before serving.

◈

All-Purpose Greek-Style Seasoning

2 t. salt
2 t. garlic powder
2 t. dried oregano
1 t. white pepper
1 t. dried dill
1 t. dried mint
1 t. dried basil
½ t. dried thyme
1 t. cinnamon
½ t. nutmeg
1 t. cornstarch

Mix all ingredients together and store in an airtight container in a cool, dark place (I use a cute glass jar with a tight-fitting lid). Shake or stir before using in recipes.

This delicious seasoning can be used in many ways:

—Mix 1 or 2 t. seasoning with olive oil and lemon juice for a delicious Greek vinaigrette to top a salad or steamed green beans or broccoli.

—Mix 2 t. seasoning with 2 T. olive oil and brush on chicken before baking until the juices run clear. For a deeper flavor, brush the mixture between the chicken skin and flesh, then bake.

—Cut 2 pita breads in half (to make 4 circles), then cut each circle into 6 triangles. Place on a foil- or parchment-lined baking sheet. Mix 2 t. seasoning with 2 T. olive oil and brush lightly on each triangle. Bake at 375 degrees for 7 to 10 minutes, or until crispy and lightly browned. Keep an eye on them, as they go from perfect to burned very quickly. Enjoy with *tzaziki* (see *Feta Attraction* or the author's website for the recipe).

For more recipes, visit the author's website at
www.susannahhardy.com.